A Truly Higher Life Form

BY

James I. McGovern

WingSpan Press

Copyright © 2014 by James I. McGovern

All rights reserved.

This book is a work of fiction. Names, characters, settings and incidents are either the product of the author's imagination or used fictitiously. Any resemblance to actual events, settings or persons, living or dead, is entirely coincidental.

No part of this book may be reproduced or transmitted in any form or by any means, electronic or mechanical, including photocopying, recording or by any information storage and retrieval system, without written permission from the author, except for the inclusion of brief quotations in reviews.

Published in the United States and the United Kingdom
by WingSpan Press, Livermore, CA

The WingSpan name, logo and colophon are the trademarks of WingSpan Publishing.

ISBN 978-1-59594-527-3

First edition 2014

Printed in the United States of America

www.wingspanpress.com

Library of Congress Control Number 2014938876

1 2 3 4 5 6 7 8 9 10

A Truly Higher Life Form

1.

In an affluent Chicago suburb, in the middle of the night, a man nearing 70 stood at his living room window. He was awaiting the arrival of a taxi, which would glide up the circular drive to whisk him to the airport. The man planned to never return in his present form.

He'd informed a close friend, a long-time business associate, of his decision. The friend would inform the man's wife. The couple had attended dinner-theater the night before and she was sleeping upstairs. She was content, as she'd been through most of their marriage, but the man was not and was reaching for more. He had the means and so he'd make the move. Adjustments could come later.

"Early plane tomorrow," he'd reminded her.
"Oh yes, L.A. Time to start delegating, don't you think?"
"Yes, a younger man. I'll be acting on it."
"That will be nice."
"I wholly agree. Another drink?"

He'd first heard of the process as most people had, through leakages to the media which they sensationalized. More careful study through his doctors and others had revealed a genuine resource. Life had been good for him and he was not about to let it disintegrate while there was this option. And he wasn't alone, others having gone before him, though he also understood the opposition.

Opposition, he thought, and strong. I'm a radical in the end. Except it isn't the end, that's the point of it all. He smiled.

The taxi arrived and he picked up his single suitcase. They'd advised him to travel light. Anyway, he assumed, his clothes wouldn't fit him afterward. He was soon moving away down the quiet, tree-lined street, another client for the retooled Progress Island.

* * *

In a country to the south, in an area of near-desert, the manager of a guarded compound stood within its closed gate. The man from Chicago would arrive here during the coming day, in keeping with company procedure. All new clients made a visit here before proceeding to Progress Island. It let them see some results of the service they'd receive, to back out if they wished. To date, however, no one had, most becoming even more enthused.

The manager, whose name was Andrew, felt like having a cigarette, but he didn't want to tempt the posted guard, who wasn't supposed to smoke on duty.

"I'll be walking," he told the guard, and moved off inside the fence, passing behind a large sign on its other side. Viewed from outside, the sign would read:

JenssenHoagle, LLC

Creation Revisited

Andrew lit a cigarette as he passed the administration building, which was also his residence and that of his assistant and the engineer. The night was chilly and the stars very bright, typical for this location, though the days were very hot. The buildings were all air-conditioned, with full climate control for the clients' cottages. All their needs had to be scrupulously met while they remained at the compound. Strong and vigilant security had to be maintained, enabling the clients to feel confident in their new lives. There were external threats, opposition to the company's program at many levels, but the company was strong and would succeed. Andrew reminded himself of this as he reached the corner of the fence behind the administration building. He could see down the road that fronted the compound, faint lights in the village two miles away.

Opposition at many levels, he thought, from the sullenness in some of the day workers to the legal vendettas in the clients' home countries. Before they could safely return, each of them had to be recognized as human and with the same identity he or she had before. Until then, this compound was home, courtesy of the company via payment to the host government. With time, as precedents were set, this oasis would become unnecessary. He might be out of work then, Andrew knew, but this should be an impressive line on his résumé.

He turned to keep walking along the side of the compound, still just inside the fence. He was in his late 30s, had been an assistant hospital administrator, had leapt at this chance to move up, establish himself professionally. He'd been engaged a couple of times but never married, relationships tending to disintegrate for him. His work thus became more important for him. Perhaps the recruiter had sensed this in him, understood he was someone who'd fully function in these bizarre circumstances.

Beyond the rear of the administration building, Andrew passed one end of the client cottage area. It stretched across the compound to the fence on the other side. There were three rows of six, all but two of the cottages occupied. If none were freed up soon, he'd have to place new clients in the medical building on the corner he was approaching. But it wouldn't come to that, Andrew thought. There were promising developments in their legal cases and he could work with Jens and Kurt to slow the influx of cases. They were the company's eponymous heads, the restorers of youth on Progress Island.

Andrew didn't like the clients, actually, especially the "finished products" awaiting citizenship. They had all been wealthy people, which allowed them the luxury of JenssenHoagle's services. They had essentially been returned to youthful bodies, mid-20's physically, and some to more attractive ones than their originals, while retaining all the memories of their elderly selves. This naturally caused exhilaration but, since they were economically upper-class, also gave rise to a confidence akin to arrogance. While Andrew took care to seem affable and supportive toward the people/products, he inwardly saw their elitism as the most plastic, puerile sort of human values imaginable.

He reached the medical building and paused inside a corner of the fence. A low range of mountains, or high hills, sprawled across the horizon in this direction. The work of eons, Andrew reflected, non-judgmental even in majesty. Unlike the acrimony of lesser beings, like some young men from the town who'd gathered out there one evening. Some clients had still been using the pool, in front of the medical building, and found the young men menacing, so a security jeep dispersed the gathering. Warning was given and the town constable notified. It wasn't over, though, Andrew feared, the incident no doubt just a symptom of some general attitude among the locals. He again recalled the growing sullenness in the day workers.

He walked along the back fence, alongside the medical building. It was well-equipped and could accommodate in-patients, though this was rarely needed. The reborn clients were thoroughly treated and tested before leaving Progress Island. The facility here was a safeguard, staffed with a full-time doctor, nurse, and technician. They also resided in the building, which made them readily available and gave them convenient access to the pool and the dining/recreation building beyond it, in the next corner of the compound. The medical staff thus had frequent informal contact with the clients, which allowed easy monitoring of clients' condition and behavior.

Coming to the kidney-shaped pool, Andrew sat in a deck chair facing the water and the central lane of the compound beyond. He could thus see all the way to the front, where the guard he'd left was now talking with a colleague, one of them smoking. The pool was roofed but some clients would sun themselves along the edge when it wasn't too hot. They delighted in being out here, displaying their new bodies for all to see and admire, anticipating more of it upon return to their home countries. Having long lost their original youth, which they'd taken for granted, they were ecstatic with this new youth, determined to make the most of it, flaunt it. They had the benefit of long life experiences, but those were the lives of rich people, given more to acquisition than to wisdom, with a penchant for excess, self-idolizing.

Andrew moved on. Leaving the pool, he walked along the fence side of the dining and recreation building. He'd delegated its operation to his assistant, Bobbette, but had a nagging suspicion it should have a separate manager. The largest number of town people worked here during the day, so security might call for closer supervision. Bobbette was his colleague and consultant on many aspects of management, and they'd grown personally close as well, so he could use another boss for watching the locals. At heart, of course, it was mostly his fondness for Bobbette that made him want her with him, and perhaps his fears. This job was increasingly coming to seem something other than a career step, perhaps an interlude of danger. Where you have enough resentment, you have an ongoing threat.

He reached the corner but didn't stop, walked on behind the dining/recreation building. He looked out over the arid plain, toward the city a half hour drive away. He'd certainly have preferred a less isolated location. The company's options had been limited, however, and this was considered adequate with strong security in place. There were two guard contingents of ten men each, and they worked alternating weeks. Their residence/office was within the next corner of the fence, beyond the rows of client cottages that Andrew was again passing. The guard facility was thus to one side of the gate, opposite the administration building, with security and civilian vehicles parked in the space between.

Rather than continue to the corner, Andrew turned into a lane between the cottages and the guard facility. There were always lights at one end of the building, where the office and monitors were, and two or three guards lingering about. One would occasionally make the rounds as Andrew had done, or take a jeep out to check the surroundings. An animal or two might be startled then, but they hadn't yet had a real incident at night. It was disturbingly calm, Andrew felt, as if inviting disruption. Any new development, any addition to the tension, might tilt the balance and set off events he couldn't handle. The new client came to mind.

He crossed the parking area to the administration building. He'd join Bobbette for a few hours rest before dealing with the looming day.

* * *

In the Los Angeles airport, the man from the Chicago suburb awaited his connecting flight. His name was Kittridge and he was well-known in business circles. By traveling at this time, however, he'd likely avoid encounters and the need for explanations. He loitered watchfully as early morning vendors opened their stalls. The same old trappings of business travel, he mused, but soon it would all be over for him. Well, so be it.

Kittridge had mixed feelings about his destination. He'd have preferred to go directly to Progress Island, get right into things. But he cared enough about his goal, the eventual outcome, to do what the company required. He was accustomed to folderol, after all, and there'd be more of it afterward, the legal sort. But he was used to that too, toughened against it, and he'd be tougher than ever in his new, prefab body.

He recalled his original youth, his lithe form at evening parties, the pool, and especially the tennis court. He envisioned a game against an acquaintance of his wife, a peppery sort who got flustered whenever he lost a point.

"Hit a crack!" he yelled as the ball got by him.

"What?" Kittridge demanded.

"Hit a crack, right there," said the smaller man, gesturing with his racket.

Kittridge had smiled sarcastically, long hair tousled by a breeze, but he let it go. He wouldn't engage in pettiness with a lesser man, and he'd never have patience with people who made excuses for shortcomings, their own or other people's. He had no use for social workers, activists, gurus and the like.

Although, he reflected, he was taking a leap of faith himself now. He'd checked this thing out as much as possible, but it wasn't a proven commodity by any means. Of course, he could *afford* to gamble now, being well up in years and without much to lose. Only money, which lost its relative value as you aged, there being less and less you could buy to improve your happiness, certainly less that was new and worthwhile. Hopefully, with luck, this procedure would prove an exception.

2.

Outside a vegetable mart in northern California, Hedges pushed his loaded cart down a parking lot aisle. His wife of one year, Livia, had entrusted him with shopping for the Oceanic Cultural League, of which she was a prominent member. At 65 and comfortably retired, Hedges had plenty of time to accommodate her. And he was only too willing, Livia having filled a vacuum in his life since they'd met in her homeland a couple of years before. That had been an adventure, and dangerous, but now they were settled as a couple and content to enjoy the mundane comforts of mature people.

Reaching his vehicle and raising the hatch, Hedges hesitated. He reflected as he often did on an event from that other time. He'd undergone a medical process to extend his lifespan and it had made him appear ten years younger. This dovetailed nicely with his meeting Livia, two decades his junior, and they were quite happy for now. But there was a distant future that came to mind, a time when Livia would age past him, with questions as to what he could do about it. The process had been abandoned and he was almost unique in his predicament.

"Ah, what the heck," he said aloud, and forced his mind back to the present.

But as he cleared a space in the cargo area, preparing to load the groceries, there came a sound like a string of firecrackers exploding. Simultaneously, the grocery bags in his cart were torn to shreds, vegetables flying in every direction. Hedges dove away from the cart and lay on the pavement, stunned. He heard a squeal of tires and people's excited voices. He got up when he knew it was over, when a crowd started gathering. The police arrived minutes later.

"You have no idea who it was?" one of them asked.

"No. I have no real enemies."

"It might have been random. But it has the appearance of a warning, them just shooting the groceries."

"Maybe they mistook me for someone else."

"Yes, that's possible."

No one had gotten a good look at the attackers, and the car was only vaguely described. The police said they'd check store security tapes for leads. Hedges declined medical attention and returned home with police escort. Later, with Livia present, a detective came to the house with follow-up questions.

"It'll be on the news, Mr. Hedges. Wide coverage since you were a celebrity."

"But that's years ago," Livia objected. "It could've been anyone out there today. Not just Irv."

The detective regarded her. Livia's hair was still long and wavy, her complexion gold in the warm weather.

"You know they've started the place up again, don't you? Out in the South Pacific?"

"But that's completely different. It's not what Irv went through. It's–"

She broke off, looking to Hedges.

"It's not a chromosomal procedure," he said. "Nor is there much surgery, as far as I know. It's a whole different thing except the basic goal."

"Yes," the detective acknowledged, "but that's enough for people to lump you in with them. We're getting strong statements from high-profile people, not to mention the Internet rant. The weaker minds eat it up, become dangerous sometimes."

"What can we do?" asked Livia.

"Be careful as you can for a while. Maybe limit being in public, make sure everything's secure here. We can have someone watch a couple days, but you know we're a small department. So it's mostly up to you yourselves."

"Thank you, detective," said Hedges. "We appreciate your help."

As he got up to leave, the detective said he'd keep them informed on the investigation of the shooting. Hedges had a sense, however, that it had been a symptom of something larger. With their return to Progress Island, Jens and Kurt had stirred up moral outrage from years before. The outrage, in turn, might well be converting to indiscriminate violent force.

* * *

Kittridge was walking with Andrew through the compound, both in straw hats against intensifying sun. The resident clients, or clones as the world considered them, were not about. They were cooling in their cottages or using the dining/recreation building, perhaps the pool. The two men walking would soon be in sight of them.

"You could use some shade trees here," Kittridge commented.

"I agree," said Andrew, "but this climate does not, unfortunately. We're looking into an awning along the central lane."

They heard a woman's laugh up ahead, between the pool and the the dining/recreation building, on the terrace.

"Sitting outside," said Kittridge.

"Yes, we have it well shaded there. And there's plenty of cooling drinks."

They came to the pool and saw no one was in it, nor was anyone sunning. At the tables before the building, four people sat at one with a man and a woman bantering, while three others sat at a table some distance away. Drawing closer, Kittridge noticed not only how youthful the people were, but how perfectly proportioned and attractive. They had full physical maturity, beyond adolescence, but with no sign of decline or any defect. Although they were of various nationalities, the guiding principle had clearly been to return each to as perfect a state in life as possible. They greeted Andrew as he passed with his guest, while Kittridge was treated to some odd looks, perhaps of pity. Or else, he thought, it's disbelief that they once looked as crummy as me.

"We can have lunch out here if you'd like," Andrew offered.

"Inside is fine, thanks."

They entered the building and found Bobbette instructing a couple of townswomen. Her dark hair was in a ponytail that danced as she made a point. She was young, Kittridge knew, and nice-looking enough, but her appearance was a comedown from those demigods on the terrace. What a difference a few years and the hassles of work could make in a person! Andrew introduced them and Bobbette gave her practiced greeting.

"We also keep a kitchen in the front building," she said, "in case you don't want to come down here some time."

"Thanks. I'll probably take you up on that."

The two men ate in the dining room, which they had to themselves.

"She seems quite efficient," Kittridge said of Bobbette.

"She was happy to come here. She was managing on-board services for an airline. Lots of pressure and all."

"You must get that here, too."

"Nothing we can't handle so far. It's a great organization, really. Supportive."

Kittridge gazed out the window, obliquely viewing the terrace with its loungers. A sense of distance from them welled in him.

"So they're clones then, basically?"

Andrew stopped chewing.

"I mean, not really natural. Synthetic. Engineered."

Andrew took a sip.

"You've had the process explained, haven't you? Your cell implanted in host egg, guided acceleration of growth, the transfer of scanned memory? These are the same people who came to us like you did. They just have new bodies. Everything in their minds is the same as before. Identities, personalities–everything."

"Sure," Kittridge acknowledged, "I understand. I'm just thinking, with identity, there's this instinctive feeling about a body: this is me, I was born, grew up, my parents were, et cetera. With this clone body—*new* body—I'm going to know it's not really mine. I'll have that knowledge, just like *they* must out there."

"It might take some getting used to. But you can see from these other clients it's not especially difficult. The advantages dispel any afterthoughts. And we'll be around to assist you, follow through on our service."

"Hey, I'm not doubting you or the company. I'm just looking ahead, trying to be objective. Will I really believe, I'm thinking, that it's me with a new body? Or will I feel like the clone stole my mind, like I'm a prisoner inside him?"

Andrew hesitated, sat back in his chair.

"In your case, the replacement body—the clone—was an outgrowth from your own tissue, unlike some clients who choose a new form, from someone else's tissue. Any sense of "otherness" toward your new body should therefore be less than some of those people out by the pool. Of course, you can still withdraw if you wish. Part of the purpose of this visit—"

Kittridge waved in the air.

"No, no. I'm not backing out. When I commit to something, I follow through. And I'm sure as hell following through here. I just wanted to clear the air a bit, see my way better."

Andrew smiled reassuringly.

"Sorry, I misunderstood."

After lunch, Kittridge remained in the building while Andrew returned to the front of the compound. Bobbette showed the visitor around, Kittridge deciding to remain in the billiard room, kill time during the day's heat. After he'd knocked the balls around awhile, one of the clients he'd seen by the pool came in. It was a male, tallish, with olive complexion and full black hair, wavy and neatly trimmed. He wore a shiny aquamarine shirt, stood ramrod straight, and smiled as he chalked his cue.

"I hope you are ready for kick-ass game," he said.

Kittridge straightened and removed the cigar from his mouth. Readier than you, friend, he thought to himself.

"My name is Sergio," proffered the other man, hand extended.

Kittridge accepted and relaxed his thoughts. That was my old self responding, he decided. The self of his youth, both original and future, wouldn't give a damn about this Sergio or needing to prove his manhood. Because the self of his youth was already confident of his manhood, as seen in that tennis game he'd recalled. No, he needn't be concerned about challenges from the Sergios of the world. Not now. Not with Progress Island operating.

"Bill Kittridge," he said. "Care for a cigar?"

* * *

Hedges was inspecting the exterior of his house, security concerns in mind, when Livia called from a window that he had a call. He found it was Hugh Bernard, corporate attorney.

"Long time no hear," he spoke into the phone.

"That's often for the better," Bernard answered. "I was sorry to hear about your trouble today. Are you okay?"

"All right for now, though the police said to be careful, take precautions and all."

"That's good advice, maybe better than they realize. There's a swelling of interest in JenssenHoagle, my clients, and it's mostly negative. There's a violent crest to it–I'm talking hatred–which is what you got a taste of today."

"They'll target anyone they associate with them?"

"Even mistakenly, right. Fact is, you're not safe there, Irv. You need a haven for a while. You still own that cottage on Progress Island. With the location and our security there, it's definitely the safest place now for you and Livia."

"The cottage? Well, we were thinking of a vacation there, but–"

"We don't want anything to happen to you, Irv, either my firm or JenssenHoagle. Personally, of course, my loyalty continues from the other time. Give the okay and I'll have a team there tomorrow for a light-speed move."

3.

Viewed from the air, the island had the shape of a chubby deep-sea fish with its jaws open. The jaws, however, were actually a gentle cove lined with near-white sand. A retirement community had been planned here, but it was aborted when the company went bankrupt. Only three of 27 home sites had been built on. The firm coming later to the island, JenssenHoagle, completed the other 24 structures to use for its own purposes. The houses accommodated guests, clients, clones, and processed clients. The latter were former clones into which clients' minds had been transferred, awaiting shipment out. One of the houses, at the tip of the southern end of the cove, had a private absentee owner, Hedges.

Progress Island had autonomous status under a nearby island kingdom. The government of the Kingdom had recently seen a purge, triggered by the disastrous failure of other life extension work. A legal team representing investors had protected the island's status, there still being promise of profits. Jens Jenssen and Kurt Hoagle, lesser figures in the failed earlier project, had a compelling new approach that attracted support. Both engineers, they swiftly commenced operations in the familiar scientific compound. They were ably assisted by a microbiologist, Anna, who was promoted from her role in the earlier project.

"We're still meeting challenges," Kurt commented to Jens.

"They still want to give us grief." He smiled within his short blond beard, well trimmed.

"Right," said Jens, "but we'll handle them. Should be child's play."

They were in a conference room at the scientific compound, Kurt at the table and Jens fiddling with a monitor at one end. Both men were tall, Kurt a bit more so, but Jens was burly and more imposing.

"We've been with this colonel before, haven't we?" Kurt inquired.

"Yes, he seemed all right then. Probably heard the rumblings. We'll just put him right."

"Seal it with a little gift."

"Better than a kiss, hey?"

They laughed, Jens moving to a chair across the table from Kurt.

"Then," Kurt said thoughtfully, "we have the client, Kittridge."

"Yes, what's the problem? I thought we had him vetted."

"Maybe nothing. Andrew thought he waffled a bit over lunch."

"That's a great specimen he's getting. Hard to believe it's his natural."

Kurt nodded in agreement.

"Beats most of our hybrids, all right."

"Anna's bringing it over, then?"

"Yes. She'll keep it next door while we pacify the colonel."

"Good. Once Kittridge sees it he'll have no doubts."

"Especially after his next look in the mirror."

Jens only smiled, reluctant to laugh at a client.

"Yes, that always convinces."

"I think I hear Anna out there."

"Good, we're about to connect here."

"I'll just take a peek, then get back in the picture."

The screen on the monitor flickered and an image appeared from the holding compound across the ocean. Andrew was seated next to a smaller man in military uniform. The officer appeared tired and somewhat bemused by the format of the meeting. Greetings were exchanged and reception quality confirmed, Kurt returning to his chair on Progress Island.

"Col. Alfons has some concerns he'd like to share with us," said Andrew.

"They are *growing* concerns," the officer emphasized, "growing with the population of your place here."

"Population?" rejoined Jens. "We're still within capacity, Colonel. Things are totally under control, with state-of-the-art facilities, ample security–"

"There is clearly a lack of movement of the–these *individuals*. Rather than a rest stop, this seems to be a permanent settlement for them."

"Well, we've been having legal battles, of course. But things are definitely looking up on that front."

"Actually," Kurt jumped in, "we expect to send two clients home next week."

Col. Alfons was unimpressed.

"Perhaps you should have another of these places in another country. Perhaps you should have several. With only one, we have all the pressure put on us here. You know what I mean, I think, the moral opposition to your work. Just this morning, a client of your previous company was attacked with automatic weapons. Perhaps you heard."

"We understand your concerns, Colonel," said Jens. "We sympathize fully. But, unfortunately, the legal obstacles to another facility are even greater than those delaying the clients' returns. Of course, that makes us appreciate all the more your accommodation, and–"

"Have you considered using your island there?" Alfons interrupted.

A momentary pause, then Jens replied.

"It's a necessary part of our procedure, of the treatment, the service we provide, to move the restored client to a new, different environment as soon as possible. Away from the clinical surroundings, the client's old life and such."

The colonel sighed.

"Well, I can only repeat there is apparent danger. Not

just idle rumors but credible warnings. There are others I must account to, ones with growing anxiety about this."

"I assure you," Kurt intervened, "we'll make every effort to implement your suggestions. And, as always, we're ready to compensate for the latitude we've received. Andrew, do we have those refreshments ready for the colonel and his party after their long drive?"

"Yes, of course. All set."

Col. Alfons nodded.

"I advise you to move quickly on this, gentlemen."

"We definitely will," Jens stated.

When Alfons was out of the picture, Jens leaned toward Kurt confidentially.

"We'll get back to Bernard, tell him it's gloves off. Start holding feet to the fire."

Kurt winced.

"And maybe sweeten them, too? Spread the wealth a bit more?"

"Whatever it takes. We use all our resources to make this thing work."

Kurt smiled widely at the image on the screen.

"*Bonjour*, Bobbette!"

She gave a quick wave, preoccupied with getting Kittridge into position. She left once the client was settled, no doubt to attend to Col. Alfons. Kurt went to fetch Anna and the clone.

"Well, Mr. Kittridge!" said Jens. "Enjoying your stay? Everything to your liking?"

"Sure, fine," the client replied, but he looked a bit edgy.

"I've explained the preview to him," said Andrew. "He's prepared to see how others will see *him*, to be fully confident in the move he's making."

"Great!" said Jens.

The future body of Bill Kittridge was led in by Anna. She installed the clone where Kurt had been sitting, then took a position behind it. Kurt sat behind Jens. The clone had the form of a tall, rangy young man with piercing expression from deep-set eyes. There was the strong nose and jaw, longish light brown hair, and hint of controlled power that left no doubt for Kittridge that this was his own flesh.

"I don't know what to say," he muttered to Andrew at their venue. Then, turning to the screen, "Hello–uh–friend!"

The clone didn't reply.

"He doesn't understand," Jens explained. "He only responds to simple commands."

"It's a default mentality," said Kurt, leaning forward in the picture. "It'll be displaced by your complete scanned memories."

"He's like me in every detail–like I used to be, I mean."

"And will soon be again. He's awaiting your input, then he'll *be* you."

"And you, him," Jens added. "A unity. Bill Kittridge, recreated."

The client was mesmerized by the sight of his young self, unable to think beyond the image before him.

"Wow! I saw the others but this is different, way different. You folks are amazing!"

Objective apparently achieved, Andrew decided to lighten the moment.

"Mr. Kittridge played billiards with a returning client. Sergio."

"Well," said Jens, "you can look him up for a rematch when you're done here. Play on an even field as they say."

"Yeah, I'll do that. I will, definitely. I think I've seen enough here, Andrew. Think maybe I need a drink."

Andrew escorted him out, advising him to wait for Bobbette in the next room. Back on Progress Island, Anna led Kittridge's clone from the conference room. Jens and Kurt exchanged satisfied looks, Kurt indulging in a low chuckle.

"That takes care of that."

But Jens quickly sobered.

"There was our earlier guest, though. That does need attention."

Kurt agreed.

"There's also the return of Mr. Hedges," he said. "Maybe even tomorrow."

Jens raised his eyebrows, not sure what to make of it.

"Well, as you say, we're still meeting challenges."

Anna turned the clone over to an orderly who started walking it back to the cove. She watched the pair depart and cross the field toward the trees that divided the island. She was reminded of the walks she would take with apes and dogs on the previous project. She'd felt compassion toward them, as she did now toward these clones, but loyalty to the work let her leave them to their fates. She was an assistant then, in a limited, well defined role, but now she had some authority. Her role was open-ended.

She began walking toward the southern shore, behind the buildings of the compound. She passed her main facility, the developmental lab, formerly the synthesis lab where artificial chromosomes had been made. Anna smiled as she thought of Mr. Hedges returning soon with their chromosome in his system. The chromosome comes home, she thought. Her smile was modest, giving her a shy look amid the wavy brown hair she'd allowed to grow long. She was of sturdy but proportionate build and usually wore a lab coat.

She passed the gestation center that had once housed experimental animals. The hill overlooking the heliport came into view on her left, the line of trees before the cove on her right. She soon reached rough vegetation above the southern shore, which was rocky with boulders strewn through the water like a mini-archipelago. They would later cast long shadows in the salmon afterglow of sunset. Anna reflected on the continuing goal: substantial life extension, near immortality. The previous project was considered a disastrous failure, with nothing useful surviving for further work. But there was a certain vial that Anna had stored separate from the others, a second backup for the procedure on Hedges. It had seemed unwise to keep all the perfected chromosomes in one place. Now the vial was in the developmental lab, Anna's domain, available for use at her discretion.

Herself? Someone else? Who should benefit? She might use it to replicate, figure out the steps somehow. But the old data were useless, didn't work, and her predecessor had quit on it. Anna wasn't sure what to do with the vial, but for now kept it secret as her personal treasure. It was enough that she helped Jens and Kurt with their current strategy. That proved her commitment to the basic goal, the cause. But she was also entitled to something of her own. She deserved it, after all. She'd worked for it.

4.

In her room in the administration building, Bobbette lay awake with Andrew nestled against her. He'd been restless, sometimes muttering, clearly more bothered than usual. It would apparently continue through the night.

"I'm getting up for water, Andy. Dry throat."

She eased out of bed and found her light robe, exited to the hall. The night seemed even quieter than usual, no passing vehicles or shouts from the guards, and darker as well. The moonlight or lack of it made a great difference here. Bobbette passed the guest room, heard the deep snores of Kittridge inside. Beneath a door across the hall flickered bluish light. Their young engineer, Henrik, was in a late session on the Internet. He still browsed and played games to unwind from his duties here, and perhaps from loneliness. The systems in the compound were a heavy responsibility, especially for a recent graduate, but Jens and Kurt said he was a genius. Bobbette strongly hoped they were right, since she was Henrik's backup.

Within the guest room, Kittridge woke from the slaps of Bobbette's slippers. Though a deep enough sleeper, his innate alertness made him sensitive to unusual noises, especially in a place this isolated. He sat up in bed but heard nothing much at all. He got up and went to his door, opened it and saw the bluish light from Henrik's room. From down the hall came a kitchen sound, someone getting a drink. No big deal, he thought, better get back to bed and avoid looking worried. He'd stirred up enough concerns already.

As he lay back down, however, he couldn't escape the doubts and fears that he'd had since he viewed his clone. The sight of it there, staring out from the screen, was a surreal experience. His flesh and blood persona of forty years before, more vivid and accurate than any memory, any photograph. It was amazing, yes, as he'd told them, but it was also daunting. To have that vitality with all he now knew, his experience, not to mention his wealth. Could he honestly believe he was capable of controlling it–that *thing*, after all? Or would it run amok? His mature mentality, developed tastes, mellowed outlook, might well cave in to that powerhouse of passions and impulses. And my present self, Kittridge thought, my *real* body, will be gone. Disposed of like trash. Medical waste.

He shuddered. He wanted to sleep. He thought of his wife back home, calmly anticipating his return from a business trip. He envied her. Home, he thought, should I go back there? How do I get out of this? I can leave, yes, but how do I live with myself then, justify my committing and then backing out? That isn't me. That isn't Bill Kittridge. The others followed through, even that silly Sergio. Why can't I?

He lapsed into a whirlpool of questions, a loss of the most painful consciousness, an ability at last to snore.

In the kitchen, Bobbette sipped her water and gazed through a window over the dark, empty landscape. She was aware of Henrik, bent over his computer nearby, much as he was when he explained the compound's systems to her. She felt attraction to him then, to his youthfulness and intensity, his innocence.

"Could you explain that again?" she'd often ask, whether or not it was necessary, leaning close to him as he repeated himself.

But then there was Andrew, his importance for the place and for her. They were more or less a couple, she realized, and out of necessity here. They had to support and assist each other, strongly. The planning of the compound, outwardly efficient, had always been of secondary importance to the company,

Progress Island being where the action was. The potential stress here was unforeseen, so a beleaguered few now dealt with the world's hostility. Andrew was at the forefront, Bobbette behind him as lieutenant and lover. He mustn't fall, she felt, or she herself would become the prime target of irrational righteous hatred.

What was that? Out there, on the arid plain. Lights!

She watched as the distant spots moved within a small area. Flashlights maybe, or the headlamps on motorcycles. Perhaps the guards, she hoped, but they'd be in a jeep and she'd have heard something. Also the lights were moving away, more or less toward the town, not making a return to the compound. The town, with the day workers she supervised in the dining and recreation building. They'd been rather edgy the past day, in addition to their usual moodiness. What did they know?

Bobbette put her glass in the sink and moved off toward the bedrooms. The darkness around her felt alive somehow, and not just with the glimmer under Henrik's door. She was visited by an unwelcome memory of the forests in her part of the homeland. The shadows there, the hints of movements, the strange sounds, had suggested an ageless presence to her when she was very young. It seemed intrusive, unnecessary, and therefore wrong, a lurking evil. It was a form of life that spoiled an otherwise beautiful setting, haunted it. She ran from the evil at times, fearing it as a distinct, threatening entity. She now realized, of course, that it was not only out there, in the darkness, but in the hearts of people it had possessed, leading them into error, wrong courses, the ways to destruction of others and themselves.

Coming to the room where Andrew lay in bed, Bobbette peered in. That was her own room, she and Andrew alternating in sharing each other's beds. She should go in, she thought, but she also needed to sleep this night, to rest from this place, and Andrew would keep her awake. So she turned instead to Andrew's room across the hall, approached his vacant bed, sat on it in the darkness, but knew she couldn't stay. He would be understanding, of course, that was not a problem. But Bobbette saw she would rest no better here, and probably much worse.

Because however much Andrew moved against her, nestled and clutched her, it could never disturb her as much as facing these nights alone, these nights with their unseen terrors.

She got up and went to him, returned his fitful embraces.

Behind the flickering crack beneath his door, Henrik was bent over his laptop as Bobbette had pictured him. His thin face and short blond hair were deathly pale in the computer light. He should log off soon, he knew, and not only because it was late and he needed sleep. It was also because, in addition to games and surfing the Web, he couldn't resist participating in "chat rooms" on various sites, injecting his own comments as well as following the discussion. He tried not to be too specific–give away his location or the company he worked for–but the need to express himself, for others to understand, to support him morally, could be overpowering. It was a holdover from his student days, something to be grown out of and replaced with genuine relationships, but the need for it here was great and relationships not so available.

Eventually he would sleep, Henrik told himself. He had to. He was drowsy and didn't know what he was doing.

5.

It was a crisp, sunny morning, a time when Hedges would normally be relaxing after breakfast. Instead, however, there was a blue passenger van parked in front of his house, its driver waiting while two companions helped Hedges and Livia to pack. Hedges was ready first, his free valet carting a single suitcase out to the van. Livia delayed a bit, the female team member leaving her and joining Hedges in the living room. This was Marjorie, from Hugh Bernard's firm, smartly tailored with chestnut hair tied back. She apparently was in charge.

"Should I wear dark glasses?" Hedges asked.

"Not unless the sun bothers you. We'll get you through all right."

Hedges nodded and gazed out the window, reflecting again on how sudden all this was. One morning you're buying vegetables, the next you're being whisked across the world.

"I suppose they're armed," he said, gesturing toward the van.

"Yes. We take your safety very seriously." But then she lightened. "I envy you, actually. I was there once at Reverie Cove. Just a few days, but I know how beautiful it is."

Hedges smiled, foggy memories encroaching.

"Guess it's a lot different now," he said absently.

"Well, they built on the other lots, so it's a ring of homes around the cove now, but that's what they planned anyway, isn't it? The company that went bankrupt?"

"Yeah. Yeah, they did."

But his thoughts were of the whole island, what it had represented to him and many others, how that continued to affect his and Livia's lives. That meaning had given way to something lesser, not transcendent as the earlier process had seemed. While he well understood the shortfalls of that vision, Hedges nonetheless wished that Livia could share in its fruits as he had. Then she would not age past him and their life together would be extended substantially. The current strategy at Progress Island seemed crude by comparison, unacceptable, and his only other solution was a strategically timed suicide. Or he could live without a solution, as he did now, but this would become increasingly painful as Livia's aging intruded.

Marjorie had said something. He'd missed it.

"I'm sorry, what was that?"

"I said one of us should help your wife along. Time is getting short."

Hedges gave a slow nod.

"Yeah, I was just thinking that. Don't worry. I'll take care of it."

* * *

An unusual number of day staff were absent from work, so Henrik, the nurse, and a couple of guards were assigned to fill in. Bobbette was still hard-pressed, the clients/clones expecting their usual levels of service and quality. Though a seasoned professional, Bobbette felt a flicker of resentment at the blithe, presuming manner of these sleek, perfected organisms. Didn't they realize how much effort all this took, how much risk? Besides the work here, there were all the legal battles, the unseen threats, the pressure on poor Andrew trying to hold things together. Bobbette tried to keep moving and lose herself in the work. If she stopped, the lack of sleep would catch up with her. She might lose control.

Finishing breakfast in the dining/recreation facility,

Kittridge saw that Bobbette looked rather frayed. As he got up, he resolved to have lunch in the administration building, relieving Bobbette of one customer. He could well understand her disgust with the clones, as he saw it, since it mirrored his own feeling toward them. There was also a tinge of fear for him, a reaction from childhood to movie monsters. Their breezing about normally in such a bizarre situation betrayed a mentality that was other-worldly, maybe psychotic. He wanted nothing to do with them.

Outside, he stopped near the edge of the shaded pool to light a cigar. A lone swimmer, female, was doing laps with long, easy strokes. Kittridge thought about his home to the north, recalled instructing a friend to inform his wife about things. He needed to make a call to tell his friend to hold off. Then there was that medical exam today. Glancing over at the medical building, Kittridge decided he'd best keep the appointment, keep everything steady for now. Tomorrow, when he left for the city, the airport, was a better time to change course. He didn't want any more sessions with that clone they'd made from him.

As he gazed up the central lane, seeking shade for his walk to the front, a form approached from one side.

"Won't be long now, will it?"

The swimmer had pulled herself out and stood dripping before him. She had long blond hair, darkened by the water, and skin that was uniformly tan. Her smile revealed perfect teeth, her slightly hooded eyes were coy, playful, her nose and chin sculptured. She was somewhat tall with a slim but healthy build.

"Ah, no," Kittridge managed. "Not long at all."

"My name is Cece," and she held out her hand.

"Bill Kittridge."

"Nice to get to know you, Bill."

He held the wet, smooth, long-fingered hand longer than he should have, unable to break from the goddess-like gaze.

"It's really *great*. You won't be sorry, you know. Not ever."

He suddenly remembered what he was talking to.

"I'm sure," he responded, the words tight in his throat.

"Stick around," a gesture toward the tables, "keep me company while I dry. Tell me all about yourself."
"Can't. Andrew's waiting for me. Gotta go. Sorry."
The perfect smile was undaunted.
"Stop by my cottage later. Number 12. We'll plan for later, for when you're finished."
"Uh, sure. Thanks."
He left Cece gazing after him as he strode off beside the medical building, heading for the town-side fence. His conviction hardened against going to Progress Island, against the whole current strategy there. He felt deep aversion to the clones and wanted nothing more to do with them. And he had no qualms now regarding his commitment. Sure, he thought, it isn't like Bill Kittridge to back out, but it's even less like me to be one of *those* things! It's a lot better to be inconsistent than to be insane.

As he walked along the inside of the fence, Kittridge noticed two men at a distance out on the plain. One seemed to gesture toward him. Slackers, Kittridge thought, no-shows for work here today. Guess I can't blame them, considering what's here. Anyway it's not my problem. None of it is. I'm out of here tomorrow and good riddance!

* * *

It had been hectic, but Hedges and Livia could relax now as their plane crossed the ocean. He reclined with his eyes closed, unaccustomed of late to busy days, but she looked alertly about the cabin and out the window. She wasn't yet acclimated to things.
"This time tomorrow," Hedges intoned, "we'll be at Reverie Cove."
"I meant to ask you–" Livia began, but then hesitated.
"What?" he asked, one eye half open.
"I was thinking of staying back in the Kingdom a day or two, I'm not sure how long, to see my family, take care of some things. Could you go on without me?"

"I could just stay back, too."

"No, it might be a little awkward, and they're expecting you on the island. Don't worry, I'll follow as soon as I can."

Hedges hesitated, both eyes now half open.

"Sure, no problem," and he shifted to resume his doze.

But Livia had more to settle.

"I know it has a special meaning for you, the island. More than just for vacation."

"Well, it did *once*, but—"

"I mean it gave you something, rare and precious."

"It gave me you. At least the trip there did."

"It gave you your change."

Hedges hesitated, then: "I thought we stopped talking about that."

"But not thinking about it. You, I mean. I can see it in you sometimes."

Hedges was silent.

"I know there's nothing we can do about it, us by ourselves. But there's something doing on the island again, right? Different from before but not completely. Maybe you should scout around a little, see what's available to maybe balance our situation. You know some of the people, after all. They should be open with you."

Hedges became fully awake, frowned deeply.

"What they're doing there is—I don't know, crude. Dehumanizing. Not at all on the level of what I had. I could never subject you—"

"But maybe the people there know about other things. Other methods being tried, other places. It wouldn't hurt to ask around, Irv."

He looked at her, softened from the familiar emotion.

"You really want me to?" he teased.

"Yes!"

"Okay, Livia. I'll ask around."

* * *

Andrew sat in the outer office of the medical building, in the chair of an absent clerk-receptionist. Through windows in the front he watched several clients/clones using the pool. He almost envied their indifference toward other people's concerns, such as his own about the compound and now Kittridge. The client had slipped into a lack of enthusiasm toward his coming transformation. In the administration building, and in their walk down here for his check-up, he gave every indication of just going through the motions.

Dr. Shah came out from the examining rooms. He was rather short, with a round face and dark hair combed flat to one side. He approached Andrew with eyebrows raised.

"Physically he's okay, but you were right. He shows markedly low morale."

"Did he seem nervous to you?"

"No, not nervous."

"So what can it mean?"

The doctor shrugged.

"We seem to have a yellow flag, like it's not all-systems-go."

Andrew considered a moment.

"Maybe I should call the legal people, give them a heads-up. But we don't have anything solid, do we? Something to inform our actions."

Dr. Shah glanced out at the swimmers.

"Maybe someone can watch him at the airport, see which flight he gets on."

"Ah! If the wrong one, we know we're into damage control." A hesitation. "He doesn't seem like the talk-show type, but who knows?"

"Bernard and company will make sure."

The two men reflected a moment.

"We came a long way without this happening," the doctor said.

"It was inevitable, I suppose. Just so things don't slide overall."

"You have a sense of something else?"

"I'm not sure, but–"

Kittridge appeared from the back, cutting Andrew off.
"Upbeat now," said Dr. Shah, and he turned to the patient with a smile.

* * *

Hugh Bernard sat with Marjorie in an upscale cocktail lounge. He was about twice her size, tall and husky with high forehead and reddish hair. They were celebrating her successful airport maneuver. They had also reminisced about their visit to Progress Island, years past now. Bernard had grown somber, however, as he mulled present issues.
"I had a disturbing call from Andrew. A possible reneger."
"Want me to work on it?"
"No, stay with the Hedges couple. I'll have to help anyway since it's the first one."
"A setback, then. Too bad."
"More important is the backdrop, the larger picture. Andrew mentioned some unrest at the holding facility, this along with our conflicts world-wide."
"We're making progress in the courts, two or three repatriations coming up."
Bernard looked away from her, into the shadows of the lounge.
"If the whole operation can last that long," he said.
"You, uh, have some fears on that, sir?"
He gave her his hard courtroom stare.
"We're only lawyers, Marjorie, functioning in the rational, civilized world. There are darker forces out there that don't give a damn about us or rationality. Forces beyond our control when they get too widespread. Too impassioned. Frenzied."

6.

Despite the signs, despite misgivings, what happened next and its timing could not have been foreseen.

It had been a difficult day. As Andrew walked beneath reddening sky, there were still a few clients/clones about, one of them jogging the inside perimeter. The last of the day workers passed through the large gate, which the guards locked after them. Andrew entered the administration building to await Bobbette and some supper she was bringing. He found Kittridge at an office computer, perusing reports of the day's market activity.

"Things looking up?" Andrew ventured.

"Ah, same old same old. Win some, lose some. You know."

"Right. They're connected on Progress Island if you want to keep up. All world markets, secure transactions."

"Yeah? Great."

But Andrew noted a hollowness in his tone.

"Bobbette's bringing food from the dining hall. Better than our pantry here. She shouldn't be long."

Andrew went upstairs to their living quarters. He saw Henrik asleep in his room, exhausted after his strenuous work day. Andrew felt sorry for him, a young man caught up in something so abnormal, so far from home. Hopefully these things would straighten out but, despite his will to make things work, Andrew couldn't believe they would.

He went to the kitchen to wait for Bobbette, poured himself

a glass of chenin blanc. He sat idly at the table as the sunlight lost intensity. Bobbette arrived with fragrant packages that she set aside. Andrew poured her a glass of wine. They sat facing each other in the failing light, mindful of the compound around them, little needing to be said of their uncertainty, their shared sense of dread.

"I don't think he's going to the island," Andrew said, giving a head tilt toward the stairs.

"He's told you so?"

"No, but it's there in his attitude, his actions. All day he's been busy with other matters, except for the check-up. Even then he wasn't very interested."

"Hm. So what will it mean for us? A demerit or something?"

"It shouldn't. The man was free to change his mind. We did our best. If the heads don't like it, screw 'em."

"That's it, my leader. Stand your ground."

Andrew caught her eye as she sipped her wine. He felt himself smiling and wanted to respond, but they were suddenly interrupted by an unfamiliar sound.

A scream. In the direction of the cottages.

Bobbette's expression froze, seemed to ask him "What now?"

But Andrew had no answer. Because as they listened at the table, there quickly followed shouts, general noise, and–was that a gunshot?

They heard people running, a couple more shots. Continuing shouts, screams.

"Stay here," said Andrew, inspired to action, and he bolted for the stairs.

Kittridge was rushing up. They almost collided.

"Stay in your room, Mr. Kittridge. Lock the door!"

Andrew ran through the office, its accouterments now meaningless, and reached the exit. Throwing open the door, he faced the broad back of the sergeant of the guards, who stood with gun drawn. The sergeant whirled but, seeing Andrew, turned back to the scene outside.

"It is all right, sir," he shouted over his shoulder, "we have you protected!"

There were three more guards in the parking area, one taking random shots through the fence. Another was on the phone in their office beyond.

"You should please stay in the building," said the sergeant. "We will handle them."

"What about the others?"

"A jeep went to the clinic. Three officers. They will be okay."

Quickly figuring, Andrew saw that only two guards, at most, were left to protect the clients/clones.

"Can you stop them?" he pressed. "We heard screams, terrible noises."

"We will get them, sir. But do not worry. They are mostly after the freaks."

Andrew was stunned a moment. Freaks? This was the leader of their guard contingent talking, yet his message was that of their enemies. Involuntarily, Andrew stepped out toward the cottages, the shouts and screams and banging and occasional gunshots. It was quite dark now.

"Return inside, sir," said the sergeant. "I must insist."

His hand was on Andrew's chest, pressing him back. Andrew retreated uncertainly. The scene outside was soon eclipsed by the door closing firmly in front of him.

"What is it?" came a voice. "What's happening?"

Andrew turned to see Henrik standing near the stairs. The engineer was holding the small caliber pistol he'd brought with him for shooting snakes.

"Nothing we can do much about," Andrew found himself saying. He stared at Henrik's pistol, which mirrored for him the impotence of the entire plan here, and of JenssenHoagle, LLC. It was over, he thought, for himself and many others.

"Are we going to die?" Henrik asked.

"It's less likely if we go upstairs," said Andrew. "Less stray bullets."

So they ascended to Bobbette and Kittridge, a computer screen still flashing in the office behind them.

* * *

The reports were fragmentary at first, and clouded by rumor, speculation, and moralizing. As the major news services took charge, however, a coherent account emerged. On computer screens, television, radio, and later in print, the masses were fed the sordid details:

According to Col. Alfons of the national police, nine of the resident clones were killed and six injured. There were also two attackers killed and at least three injured, with an unknown number escaping into the desert. One guard was injured, but all other employees survived unscathed. An unidentified visitor to the compound was also unharmed.

The one clone surviving without injury had been practicing billiards in a room removed from the violence. This clone will be deported to Italy, Col. Alfons stated, while the injured clones will be dealt with as their medical conditions improve.

The attackers gained entry by rushing to a cut in the fence made by an inside accomplice. The accomplice was a daytime employee from a nearby town who hid in the compound at quitting time. . . .

The continuing reports were embellished with background on JenssenHoagle, Progress Island, and the procedure employed there. Attempts were made to identify clients, dig into their pasts, and elucidate their sources of wealth. Throughout it all ran a mood of shameless curiosity and righteous horror, as well as confidence in the beloved, now reconstructed, cosmos.

* * *

Jens stood at the edge of the heliport, on the path leading from the compound, and stared into the afternoon sky. He was still stunned by Andrew's call. While he'd reacted appropriately, informing Kurt and Anna and deciding to vacate, he couldn't get a handle on exactly what was happening, the facts and logic that comprised it. They'd been on the cusp of transcendence, all contingencies covered.

Now they were being swept away by the ubiquitous tide of banality that was common man. He couldn't understand it, couldn't accept it.

Kurt was loping up the path toward him, computer printouts in hand. Details were flowing in, Jens thought, and felt something in his stomach.

"All this doesn't change anything," he said when he'd seen the papers. "Andrew's call was enough."

"For what?"

"To know it's the end." He looked away but felt Kurt's stare. "A chopper will be here within the hour. It might be the last one."

"The last?"

"Just the water taxi after that, then through the Kingdom, the airport."

"Does Anna know?"

"Tell her for me, will you? She might have things to pack."

Kurt joined him in viewing the hill the chopper would circle.

"It's incredible," Kurt said. "We got up this morning with a work day ahead of us, busy but enjoyable because success was at hand. Now, even just the work–"

"I've been through this before," Jens interrupted. "The other project on this island. Others had the control but I went down with them. You were mostly an observer then."

But Kurt wouldn't be distracted.

"All the work, our vision. This great service we developed, its significance to mankind. Beyond all previous achievements!"

"Which doesn't mean a damn thing," Jens said bitterly, "if your funds dry up. And for us the faucet is shut, my friend. Believe me."

Kurt had no answer to this, or to the situation. All that was left was their work relationship, for which they were grateful to each other. But Jens felt isolated in the current failure, seeing it as *his* failure, and wanted to stew in private. He therefore suggested to Kurt that he go and check on Anna. Kurt walked off disconsolately.

He found Anna in the developmental lab, writing in a

notebook. She looked the same as she had on other days. She showed no sign of being affected by the news.

"I won't be going yet," she informed him.

"But it's the last helicopter–"

"It's okay, Kurt. Really. I'll be fine with the water taxi. You and Jens just go ahead."

"Things could be problematic, Anna. Workers leaving or getting angry, clones on their own, who knows who showing up on the island–"

"Don't worry," she smiled, "I know what I'm doing." A hesitation. "See, I want to have a gentler departure. I'm leaving, but I don't want to just jump off. The island has meant too much to me. Personally, I mean."

Kurt studied her, trying to comprehend.

"You'll be seen as the one in charge, you know. A person responsible."

"So be it." She offered her hand. "Go now, Kurt. Take care of yourself."

He left and Anna was alone. He'd been right, she knew, about the changes coming now, things to watch for and be careful of. But for her this meant it was time to move on her own little project. Little but big, once in fact the focus of this place.

She returned to her notebook, which she'd turned face down when Kurt entered.

Anna had recalled from memory the formula for an "elixir" they'd used in the earlier project. It was a mix of many nutrients, organic and inorganic, that was given to a subject preparatory to infusion with the artificial chromosome. It assured and maximized the success of the procedure. The formula was in her notebook now, the ingredients stored in the lab here, accumulated while she worked for Jens and Kurt. She'd take the elixir this evening, then in a day or two infuse the chromosome. And then she would live for centuries.

Outside, the workers and clones continued in their activities, oblivious to the collapse of JenssenHoagle. Evening would fall much as always, but on a project already abandoned.

7.

The water taxi was still approaching the island when Hedges sensed something amiss. He'd been the only passenger coming out but there were eight to ten people on the pier waiting to board. It was late morning, not the end of anyone's work day, and the clones here wouldn't be free to leave. As the craft eased in, Hedges noticed that the people wore work uniforms, including several security guards. The group seemed out of sorts, complaints and curses issuing forth. As Hedges debarked, however, one of the guards smiled broadly.

"Going the wrong way, uncle! Out of business!"

One or two others laughed, but most began aggressively boarding with their parcels. Hedges gave a mystified look, then turned to inspect the situation on his own. He crossed the landing, a tropic buzz replacing the voices at the pier, and continued down the path toward Reverie Cove. He soon passed the northern point of the cove, reached the beach and turned southward. The path here was a ridge of firmer footing above the sand, fronting the 27 houses that ringed the cove. His own cottage stood at the end of the path on the southern point.

Most of the houses he passed were in pastel shades of blue, coral, or dull yellow, with broad white trim. The only exceptions were his own and two others that had stood when he lived here. These older structures were in earth tones and seemed more solidly built. The overall impression was that of a public housing project engulfing a tropical paradise. Along the beach and before some of the houses Hedges met attractive young men and women with vapid expressions who did not respond to his greetings. They were markedly idle, appearing lost, and he realized that these were clones. In the shade before one house stood a man and a woman in white uniforms. They were apparently watching the clones but offering no direction or other involvement.

"Good morning!" Hedges called vigorously.

The man looked away with a frown. The woman smiled flatly and looked away less pointedly. Hedges continued along the crescent enclosing the cove.

Approaching his cottage, number 27, he noted the signs of its non-occupation. Despite the gentle climate, years of non-use had invited deterioration. A paint job was in order, along with new screens and a thorough cleaning, and the solar panels should be checked. Then there were the systems inside, he considered, and braced himself as he unlocked the door. Once within, he saw that a window was broken on the side away from the cove, facing out to sea. Sand and salt from blowing spray had fanned out over a wide area. Dead insects lay beneath the various windows. Trying the lights, he saw they were dim, thought again of the solar panels.

"Guess I'll have to hit Kurt for some generator fuel," he muttered.

But suddenly the scene at the pier came to mind, and then the wandering clones. With Kurt and especially Jens in charge, how could such laxness be occurring?

He shrugged it off and went through to the game room, which looked onto the patio and now another house. The pool table's green surface was muted by dust, the cues in their rack joined by cobwebs. Hedges stared into the network of lines and sensed the stillness around him. How in the world, he wondered, could a man ever come here to live by himself? Day after day, indefinitely. How could that man be me? Even after getting to know Livia, he'd persisted. It was she who'd finally acted on the situation.

He shook his head. He felt sick of the cottage, had to get out.

After taping a piece of cardboard over the long-broken window, Hedges locked up and headed down the southern coast of the island. The shore here was rocky and soon became entirely rocks where the sea met the coastline. He passed a male clone who'd apparently strayed back from one of the houses. The clone was gazing out to sea, only giving Hedges a dull glance. It was tall and strongly built, and would have had a piercing stare if it were capable of thought. Hedges continued on.

He came to the point where the sea intruded between the larger rocks, forming a mini-archipelago. He moved inward, avoiding the water line, toward the scrubby trees and undergrowth above. He kept hiking toward the eastern end of the island, the hill that helicopters circled. When he'd progressed to high ground, the buildings of the project were in view and, near the eastern edge of the island, the heliport. He saw no activity below. Curious and again sensing something ominous, Hedges descended toward the compound.

He found Anna in the project offices, seated before a computer.

"Is Kurt around? Or Jens?"

"No, they've both left."

Hedges looked at her, vaguely nodded.

"I saw just now the gate was open, no guard posted."

Anna seemed to sense his confusion.

"You've heard about the attack? The killings?"

"Attack? Which attack?"

Anna hesitated, then: "Sit down, Irv."

She related the news that he and Livia had been too busy to hear, and its consequences for JenssenHoagle. Hedges listened raptly. While it fit what he'd noticed since arriving, he was further confused as to how he and Livia would handle their future. Being linked to the island would someday fade–he could hasten it by ditching the cottage–but remaining were their out-of-sync lifespans. The people involved with the project here, their knowledge and connections, were where Livia had sensed an answer. He'd started to believe it himself, but now this promising resource was falling apart on them.

"Terrible," he said about the attacks. "Really terrible."

"Yes. We too were shocked."

"So they left right away, Jens and Kurt? Leaving you here?"

"I could have gone with them, but–" A hesitation. "I wasn't quite through here."

Hedges studied her, the small features below the tangle of brown hair. Despite the news he'd just heard, Livia's concerns were still paramount, and Anna was the only remaining hope here.

"I have to tell you about something," he said.

She was familiar with many of the details, so he mostly stressed concern about the future and the need for some direction to take. Anna listened patiently, her expression darkening a bit as he went on, her gaze drifting from his face to the middle distance. When Hedges stopped talking Anna looked down, thinking awhile, then looked up resolutely.

"I have something to tell *you* now," she said.

She disclosed the existence of her treasure, the vial containing the priceless chromosome. Again the listener was familiar with past details, so her focus quickly dwelt on current issues. Here was a resource, potent and irreplaceable, an anachronism but a thing of potentially wonderful value in a given situation.

"I want to give it to Livia," Anna said.

Hedges sat still a moment, processing what he'd heard, hoping it was real. A nascent burst of gratitude was growing within him. There was no way they would refuse this.

"But what about yourself?" he had to ask.

Anna stiffened a little.

"My priority has always been the work, not myself. Being here has helped me more than anything else could. Anyway, the chromosome was yours, *is* yours. It was a backup for your procedure so it should serve you now. Serve both of you, I mean, by helping Livia."

Hedges nodded, indulged in a smile.

"I admire your ideals, your integrity. I don't know how we can thank you."

Anna looked away as if embarrassed, idly fingered the computer keyboard.

"Maybe you can help me pack," she said.

Their lunch was prepared by a kitchen worker who hadn't left yet. Anna was letting her take some food supplies with her, so the woman had prepared an ice chest for this purpose. On seeing this, Anna asked Hedges to prepare one for the special cargo. While the vial would be in an insulated carrier, they could use some extra insurance against the heat.

"Do you need to go back to your cottage?" she asked him.

"No, I'm finished there."

Later, they stood on the pier awaiting the water taxi, the ice chest and Anna's suitcase beside them. Also there were the woman who'd fixed their lunch, an elderly janitor who'd imbibed Jens's liquor, and the couple who'd been watching the clones. When the boat arrived, Hedges had to carry both ice chests aboard, as well as half-carry the janitor. The couple from the cove loaded piles of towels and bed linens as their share of the booty. The boat pulled out under a pleasant sky of scattered white clouds, the water slightly choppy. Everyone looked back as the island receded, no one among them intending to return.

"What will happen to them?" Hedges wondered aloud.

"The clones?" Anna responded.

"Yeah."

"I'll have to notify the national police. I suppose they'll send a humane detachment."

"Humane? Like with animals?"

Anna nodded grimly.

"It's the best we can do, I'm afraid."

Hedges returned her nod. On Progress Island, humanoids wandered Reverie Cove, some approaching the scientific compound. From the air things might look unchanged. The change was too subtle, too recent, to detect from a distance, but it seemed to assure total ruin. This because it was the loss of something vital: human rationality, which now had failed twice on this intended island of progress.

8.

Two Years Earlier

On a rainy evening in an eastern American state, a dim light shone from a government building window. A computer screen was source, the man before it scrolling through an unwelcome assignment. He'd been appointed receiver for the eighth time during his service on the state corporation commission. He was starting to regret his legendary success, saving an old local company and the jobs it provided. Thanks to his resulting reputation, he was now saddled with garbage like this mess before him, and it came on top of his normal day-to-day duties. At 60, the everyday routine was plenty for him, but he had his retirement to think of, maintaining or increasing his pay and benefit levels. He had to elicit smiles from the faces of power around him.

Of course, as Fauss was well aware, there was also some vanity involved. Since childhood he'd relished the praise he received for giving answers and insights. He'd retained his general appearance since then: below average height, stocky though not fat, and owlish even without his glasses. He'd typically have his chin raised and lips slightly parted, as if eager to say what he knew. In high school he was often addressed as "brown," short for "brown nose." He was lightly regarded by the other top students, and by teachers as well, so he suspected some sort of elitism and resented it. Yet he wanted to be elite himself, so after his bachelor's degree he pursued a master's and then a doctorate, relaxing at last as an associate professor, enjoying adulation from students for his answers and insights.

Unfortunately for Fauss, his peers and superiors still didn't appreciate him. Or maybe they found his affectations presumptuous: the goatee, the pipe-smoking, the super-casual manner. It was a small, private college, they explained, and very few were given tenure, so perhaps he should move on. Embittered, Fauss relocated to a state university in another part of the country, accompanied by his former student who was now his wife. He'd become involved with her during the tenure struggle, desperate as he was for relief and comfort. Now he saw her as ordinary, unattractive, and more or less in the way. She was gone after the first academic year, appalled by Fauss's materialism. His professed commitment to his field, Renaissance literature, was just a vehicle for self-promotion; his commitment to her was nil.

Fauss's new colleagues seemed to sense this, too. His eagerness, his insistence on things, his need to be right and agreed with–all were met guardedly, sometimes with bemusement. He sensed that, secretly, they were seeing him like the long-ago classmates who called him "brown." He'd never pass the peer-review for tenure; he was a joke. He came to hate his field, finding it tedious and useless. So, using his free tuition benefit, he enrolled in the university's business college and breezed to an MBA, driven by his thirst for self-promotion and praise. His teaching of Renaissance literature became quite shabby, of course, and he did no research in the field. But Fauss couldn't care less; he was just hanging on for the pay until he could leave.

Assuming that private business wouldn't think much of his background, Fauss applied for a state position in financial regulation. Though already in his mid-thirties, his MBA gave him a boost up the ladder to an age-appropriate level. From there it was simply a matter of resorting to his old study and work habits. He gave the job his full energies with intense attention to detail, had plenty to say at meetings, elicited feedback on his progress and prospects. He shrugged off resentment by his coworkers, catered shamelessly to higher-ups. He submitted suggestions on the official form, volunteered for work details, handled official charity collections from employees. He stood out when there were openings for promotion, and the higher-ups trusted him. Eventually he was one of them, at a later age than some and a junior in the group, but to Fauss that didn't matter. He'd been appreciated, praised; he had succeeded.

Unfortunately, he now considered, being a commissioner brought with it these occasional receiverships. The first couple had been okay, especially the one in which he'd saved the old local company, the people's jobs. The positive press, kudos in the commission and in the capital–it had salved a lot of old wounds, that unjust abuse from morons in his past. But his success had set him up for additional assignments; he was a "man for the job." He felt pressured. There was nothing more for him to gain; he was simply maintaining what he'd achieved until he could exit in glory and comfort. He was therefore increasingly irritated as he scrolled through materials relating to this latest assignment, perhaps his messiest.

Deville had been steady enough at one time, he saw. They'd had modest success dealing in defunct or foreclosed farms and vacant, long-term investment land. Under new leadership they'd branched into housing development before the market collapsed, building on some of their vacant holdings. People bought at ballooning prices using sub-prime loans, most becoming "walkaways" once the rates adjusted against large negative equities. Upscale neighborhoods became rows of shabby houses with overgrown lawns, here and there one still inhabited, an oddity in the waste. But Deville had their profits and tried to parlay them into more, building eye-catching strip-malls along rural highways. They could offer cheap leases in those outlying areas and expected businesses to respond well, but it didn't work out. Few units were leased and it was clear they'd misjudged. Unable to sell the underused malls, they were short of capital and had to be creative, perhaps gamble, in a move to recover.

The island had been available for some time, but its remoteness had apparently made it uninteresting to developers.

A Truly Higher Life Form

The seller, a glorified bureaucrat in the nearby island kingdom, was also reluctant to lower the asking price. Deville, unable to raise sufficient capital, was directed by the official to another inquirer on the property and together they worked out a joint purchase. The resulting tenancy in common was immediately modified by an order of partition establishing the boundaries for Deville's development, as well as for the other establishment, Vasquibo Institute. The Kingdom's documents on all this were printed in ornate letters, causing Fauss to squint, and were festooned with ribbons and gold seals.

"Archaic *crap!*" Fauss muttered, reminded of his years in Renaissance literature.

He was answered from the screen by another fancy document, signed by token royalty, granting the island autonomy within the Kingdom. This was followed by a more mundane "memo of agreement" between Deville and Vasquibo. Each party was to provide its own desalinization for fresh water, but Vasquibo agreed to handle waste treatment and removal. Deville, in return, would maintain the docking facilities in the common area. Not a bad trade-off, Fauss reflected. They actually did something right.

His satisfaction was short-lived, however, as he viewed the status of Deville's development: only one property sold, an odd piece at the end with a small cottage, and another sale in legal limbo pending his involvement. The bad economy had put a kibosh on exotic retirement, apparently. Meanwhile the expenses mounted: tribute to the Kingdom for protection against invasion, maintenance of the large model home, interest on Deville's loans to co-purchase the island. The caretaker received a generous salary in addition to residence in the model, living expenses, and—what?—tuition reimbursement for his daughter?

Fauss felt his temperature rise. He had to control himself, he thought, stay calm. There was always one best course. Just find it.

Maybe he could get this pending couple, the Hoagles, to accept the model instead of the specifications in their contract. Let the caretaker live in a tent, home-school his daughter.

Or maybe this idiot in the cottage, Hedges, would sell back and the cove could be sold as a unit for resort construction. Or maybe Vasquibo would want it for expansion. Then again, why not work on someone in this silly kingdom to void the original sale?

Yes, clearly there were possibilities. Fauss felt better in the darkened room. He'd straighten this mess out as he had all the others. He'd let a deputy deal with the rural malls–routine work until Reverie Cove was resolved. He himself would focus on the island, travel there and give it his full energies. Understanding colleagues could cover his commissioner duties. In the end they'd be praising his competence again, or at least acknowledging it.

Leaning back in his chair, Fauss reflected on people's jealousy, not only of his accomplishments but of the person he was. They sensed what he knew: he was a higher order of being, a kind of mental superman surrounded by yapping humanoids trying to bring him down. Fighting them off had been his life. Soon he'd retire, and he wanted to do it in triumph.

9.

In the southern latitudes lay the island, nameless and unused through the ages, that had suddenly become the scene of enterprise. As in all human ventures, success would not necessarily follow. It was clearly delayed, at least, for one of the two companies, while the progress of the other was cloaked in mystery.

Viewed from the air, the island had the shape of a chubby fish with its jaws wide open. The jaws, however, were actually a gentle cove lined with near-white sand. The cove was being developed as retirement properties by Deville Associates. Most of the rest of the island belonged to Vasquibo Institute, a research firm. Along the northern coast, or dorsal fin of the fish, was a common area with docking facilities, while the southern coast was rocky and unusable.

At the tip of the southern end of the cove, the lower jaw of the fish, was a modern one-bedroom cottage with number 27 on the door. Its owner's address was thus "27 Reverie Cove," the cove having been named by the developers. This would be followed by "Progress Island," courtesy of the research firm, and the name of the island country about twenty miles distant. The only other house on the cove was number 1, across the water on the opposite tip, which was the model and had three bedrooms. In the semicircle between the two homes were 25 other properties, marked with little flags and waiting to be built upon.

The man who lived at number 27, Hedges, had been on the island about three months. When he'd wanted only one bedroom, the developer was disappointed, but Hedges had grown solitary and sought to hold down expenses. At 63, he was secure from the sale of his business but had no prospects for the future. He'd had to be financially conservative in ordering construction here. He was careful of other details as well, such as using the air conditioner sparingly. He didn't want to drain his solar cells and have to rely on the backup generator. He'd have dim lights and watery ice for a day or more.

Shooting pool one day in his game room, Hedges felt the day's heat rising. A breeze had been wafting from the living room in front, passing through the rear screens to the outside shore of the island. Considering the air conditioner, Hedges recalled that he hadn't visited Wang, the development's caretaker who lived in the model, for several days. It seemed a better alternative this day than starting up the air-con. Though solitary, Hedges recognized the need for occasional human contact to avoid slipping toward insanity.

He'd grown up in a small city, or large town, on America's west coast. He'd had an older sister and younger brother, both better students than he. He wasn't good at sports except for pool, where his tall, flexible frame served him well. He disliked crowded activities–dances, parties, concerts–but he also shunned outdoor pursuits like camping and hunting. Their complications were too much for him. He'd earned a bachelor's degree in accounting and went to work for his father, a distributor of copper pipe fittings. He'd sometimes be seeing a woman and had male friendships as well, but these things always petered out. The women eventually wanted more and the buddies moved on in some way. He never married, never served as best man. His father died and he inherited the business, doing well from the new trade agreements. His loneliness growing, he got into photography for a while and tried exotic travel. He enjoyed the trips but they had no lasting effect on his life. While not religious, he decided he was some sort of monk at heart, that he needed to get away and stay away from the useless course of his life.

Hedges looked up at the sound of a helicopter approaching. Exiting onto his shaded rear patio, he watched the chopper disappear behind the rise in the island, to the east. The heliport, property of the research firm, was on the opposite end of the island. It was little used until the past few weeks, with arrivals and departures now frequent and unpredictable. Hedges would never be a passenger, he knew, unless he was in critical medical condition. Residents of Reverie Cove were limited to the water taxi for most crossings to the Kingdom, but it was fairly dependable.

Gazing past the stony outer beach, over a jade slab of sea, Hedges reflected on his own crossings since coming here. Perhaps he should drop his phony reasons, simply admit to anyone interested that he was going to a special friend. It was natural, after all, for most people if not for him. And Livia was highly appealing–had to be in her job. Yes, he was too far along in life, too secure, to worry about people knowing. And they'd see through him anyway, eventually. How much business could he have, after all, when everything he needed or wanted could be delivered to the island? He had the technology for ordering, as well as for other business and leisure. And he'd hardly be crossing for the crowds and activities, having come to this island to escape them.

Hedges turned from the sea, returned to his game room, and racked his cue. He sensed again the rising heat, his brow moist beneath his salt-and-pepper locks. He'd have to get a haircut when he went to see Livia, he decided. She'd even mentioned it, suggested a barber. He'd oblige. She was a person of quality, of value to him, a promising balance to his life on the island. The balance might become necessary. He was fine so far, but he mustn't let the relationship die like the others had.

He moved up to the living room, toward the front of the cottage facing the cove. The same business and trade magazines littered the coffee table as when he was in America. He recalled Livia leafing through them on her lone visit to the island. She'd pretended to be interested and he was grateful, but she must have been bored those two days. Solitude wasn't for everyone, hardly anyone in fact. He'd take the magazines over to Wang today, he decided, stop the subscriptions by phone or email.

Out on the front porch, unscreened, he stood tall and gazed across the cove toward number 1, the model. Glancing to his right, he watched seabirds coast over undeveloped properties, past the fence of the research project. A project, he reflected: something new, progressive, a fresh focus for work, enthusiasm. Something that had always eluded him. He'd done what had fallen to him naturally, he'd been efficient, he'd avoided crises. He'd been happy enough until these older years, the encroaching sense of emptiness. His project of sorts had become escape, this island. But once here, he saw that it was a project without purpose, so not a real project at all. It was a reflection of himself, also without purpose.

He went back inside to get the magazines for Wang.

* * *

Hedges walked along the beach of the cove, magazines held with one hand and sandals in the other. There was a firm pathway at the top of the sand, fronting the properties, but he savored the powdery feel under his feet. It was a return on his investment, or rather, his indulgent purchase, making it a little more *like* an investment.

He always enjoyed his conversations with Wang. The caretaker was a family man, or had been until his divorce, and could therefore relate experiences that hadn't been possible for Hedges. Wang was partner in a mail-order pharmacy business in his homeland, but the operation had taken a downturn, so he felt pressured to take outside work. He had a teenage daughter whom he wanted to send to university. This would take extra money in addition to making up the business losses. Wang also had a son, failed as a student, who drifted from one shaky job to another. His fate was the core issue in Wang's broken marriage, so the father was especially grieved by it. He deeply needed to see his daughter succeed, to have past failures obscured by a bright future. He was grateful to the development company for

A Truly Higher Life Form

hiring him and paying well. He was loyal and hard-working, seeing Deville's success as vital for his own and his daughter's.

Usually, Hedges would find Wang busy with small tasks, keeping the model in mint condition to impress potential buyers. He might also be out on the unsold properties, inspecting the ground and flag markers, or over by the dock. Today, however, he was sitting on the front porch, a full veranda on this larger house, framed by hanging pots of flowers and smoking a cigarette. His expression was somber and he hardly glanced at Hedges as he approached, simply motioning to an empty chair beside him, woven wood with seat cushion, companion to his own. Hedges handed over the magazines as he took a seat.

"More freebies," he said.

Wang inspected the covers and then opened one, a catalog of pipe fittings with small color photos. He turned a few pages, distracted briefly from his cigarette.

"They look like jewels," he said.

"Well, I guess they are in a way. Valuable. Value from being needed. Then for me, of course, they were my business. All I ever did."

"Yes, your business. A very fine business to be in it so long. Now you are here."

He continued to turn the pages, drawing again on his cigarette.

"Would you like a beer?"

"No, thanks. Little early for me."

"Calimansi juice?"

"Maybe just some water."

Wang left to get it and Hedges looked out over the cove, the sea beyond. The great expanse, he thought, the emptiness between me and my previous life, all I knew and did, my business with the shiny new pipe fittings, the jewels. This emptiness: I float in it on this island, a powerless little kingdom nearby. There was something I heard about an emptiness—the great void—not really being empty, that it's really potentiality, containing everything somehow, all possibilities. Wang might know about that. But for me it's just nothing, a separation from my old life, what made me what I am. That's why I'm here. It's enough. It's what I needed though I'm not sure why.

Wang returned with the drinks, a pair of ice waters.

"Hotter than usual," he commented.

"Yeah, time to take a break from caretaking."

Wang grunted in response, gazing out over the sea. He lit another cigarette.

"Family okay?" Hedges ventured.

Wang shrugged.

"Tia is fine, still doing well. A good student. She's happy, gets along with people. She'll be okay. As for Bing, well, you know, it stays the same. He makes a move, changes jobs, meets someone new, and it's just a new worry for me. There's no quality, no step up."

"Is he still selling phone services?"

"No, it's a time-share operation, maybe a scam. They try to sell shares that people want to dump–there's many of them now. They charge big fees upfront, even advance commissions. They keep the money even when there's no sale, which must be often. The way times are, the bad economies, who wants an item like that?"

"Yeah, the economy. Maybe it's the main problem for Bing, him and other young people. The good jobs, ones with security and advancement, just aren't there."

Wang reflected on his cigarette.

"Anyway, Tia is okay. Things will change."

They were silent awhile, Hedges with no family news and Wang distracted in his thoughts. Hedges was about to mention Livia when Wang leaned toward him confidentially. This though no one else was in sight.

"Actually, it's hitting us here now. The company filed for bankruptcy."

Reflexively, Hedges looked to the boundary fence.

"No, not them. Us. Deville Associates."

Hedges took a moment to process this. The company from which he'd bought his cottage, Wang's employer, was dropping out of action with 25 empty properties between his place and the model. The future Reverie Cove loomed as a desolate place.

"Bankrupt? How can that be? They seemed like a solid company."

Wang shrugged.

"I don't know. I just got the call last night. The general collapse, I guess."

"What about your job? Do you get to stay awhile?"

Wang blew some smoke, ending with a dismissive flourish.

"They say I'm okay for now. Someone has to look after things. No promises, of course. Whoever takes charge will contact me. They don't know when."

Hedges looked toward the unsold properties.

"That's rough. But then, you might come through all right. Why should they bring in someone new when you know all the nuts and bolts?"

Wang gave a soft laugh, picked up the catalog of pipe fittings.

"Yes, and now pipes, too."

Hedges smiled at Wang's resiliency, admired his tenacity. The concern for family, staying connected with people, an eventual legacy: Hedges saw the value in these things, the intensity of living they implied, though he didn't wish this for himself. If that meant he was empty, perhaps his void was potentiality. Another Reverie Cove, personal and private, carried around within him.

10.

Night had settled on the capital, but a restaurant off the main streets had answered with its own golden aura. It was a quiet place chosen for easy conversation. At one of the few occupied tables, Livia sat opposite her client for the evening. She wore a gray evening gown, her long dark hair draped over her shoulders. She drew gracefully on a cigarette, glancing occasionally at a small box next to her companion's wine glass.

"Aren't you going to put it on?" she asked. "You've paid. You might as well get the benefits of membership."

"Later," he replied. "They know you here anyway, do they not?"

"Yes." She looked aside. "There aren't a lot of European places in the capital. More on the north coast, the resort area."

He said nothing, even looked at his watch. A cold fish, she thought, but an important catch. He was the head of a foreign research project on a small neighboring island. His check was in her purse. He surprised her now by lighting a cigarette and smiling through his smoke. His eyes relaxed behind his glasses.

"Will you stay in town tonight?" she asked. "The water taxi might be closed."

"I made special arrangements."

"Oh."

He glanced around the restaurant.

"I wonder, though, if we might stay in touch on a business

basis. Directly, I mean, not through the ministry or the club. Things sometimes arise–confidential, sensitive–in which a special contact can be of value."

Livia waited but he didn't elaborate.

"I'm always ready to help," was her default answer.

"Excellent. Of course, I might also be able to assist *you*. Contacts if you travel abroad, references, and perhaps–" He gestured toward her purse with his cigarette.

Livia hesitated, then returned his smile.

"It's always good to have friends."

"Especially when they can do things for you."

The candlelight glinted on the gray strands in his hair. He was in sync now, she thought, in his controlling mode. When he worked in science he was alone, or with taciturn assistants, so he was ill at ease in social matters. But feeling connected again to his position, back in charge, everything was fine with him.

"Shall we have more wine?" she suggested.

* * *

Freshly bathed and powdered, Livia fastened her dress before the mirror. She was alone in her apartment, stray sounds of daytime rising from the street below. The dress was white with a black floral pattern, flattering to her mature figure. Her wavy hair cascaded over her back, accenting skin quite fair for the islands. Even now some mistook her for a foreigner, those unfamiliar with her role in government. But the country was tiny and she'd always worked, been part of the social bustle, so Livia was familiar to most whom she met.

The dress fit more snugly, she noticed, than it had a few months ago. That was before she'd met Hedges. She hadn't been eating much for a while and people thought she might be ill, but she told them no and gave other reasons. The truth was she'd been bored and when she asked herself with what the answer was with everything: her situation in life and the people in it, her country and culture, herself. It had been building a long time without her even knowing it. She'd always assumed she was accomplished and happy as could be, having worked hard early on and made moves when she should, avoided pitfalls. She'd been a good student and attended the general college, become a teacher. Through a contact, a student's parent, she'd moved to government work, having seen that a life with children was not for her. She'd avoided marriage and useless, unpromising relationships, so available in her land. She consorted only with the upper echelon, people who could help her, and she'd moved up. But as she stayed in her current and highest position for an extended time, she saw that, although she was comfortable and secure, nothing more would change and something vital was missing.

Hedges had reminded her of a man from long before, a young New Zealander. There was the same gangling frame and deferential innocence, or maybe innocent deference. But Hedges also had the mature sense of time that she herself was developing. He saw his life with some perspective and, though maybe he'd run from it, he could offer it as a contrast, enhancement, framework for her own. She usually didn't care for Americans–the smugness, brusqueness–but Hedges held back in a way that gave you room to be close to him. There was nothing extraordinary about him, no adventurous or noble past or great achievement. But he himself seemed conscious of this and accepted it, so he also accepted her. While he'd left his other life–needing change, seeking more of something–he saw her as part of what he sought. For Livia, he was a dimension of relationship from beyond her life in the Kingdom, a life grown stale. She felt fresh with him.

As she took one of her hats from the pegs near the window, she glanced out at the street below. There was little midday activity in the upscale neighborhood. A scooter going by, a single peddler. She'd have to walk to the corner to flag down a tricycle. The motorized three-wheelers were the Kingdom's standard taxi service, cars being few.

Soon she was passing beneath flowers hanging on street lamps, feeling inspired despite the day's heat. She was on her way to see him again. The tedium of the evening before, of so many other such meetings, was dispelled by thoughts of Hedges at their restaurant table. The duties of her post had finally yielded a special, personal reward, something beyond pay and cocktail parties, praise from pretentious men. She'd approached him as she had the others, as special assistant to the deputy trade minister. She'd explained the reasons for the E List, short for Elite Citizens List: there were cultural projects to support, expenses of the royal family, national sports teams. There was an initiation fee, annual dues, once in a while a special collection, entirely voluntary. In return the member got a pin to wear, but it was more than a pin. It guaranteed "special service" when dealing with government agencies and major businesses in the Kingdom. The people in charge of things were on the E List themselves; cooperation among members was assumed.

She put a hand to her hat as the tricycle whisked along. She was in a double seat behind the driver, a canopy above her. They passed some vacant areas and shabbier neighborhoods, the ring of stores, hotels, and other businesses, then the banks and government buildings. They reentered the commercial ring where it coincided with the waterfront, eventually stopping at Poseidon's restaurant, where Hedges sat nursing an old-fashioned. They were meeting inside, rather than on the terrace, due to the day's heat.

"You look weathered," she said. "Have you been swimming a lot?"

"Some, but it's mostly from sitting around with Wang."

"Out in the wind and sun, the blowing salt?"

"It's good for reflecting, sharing great thoughts."

Livia ordered a whiskey sour.

"Well," she said, "I hope they bring you some neighbors soon. A caretaker and a secret project seem very limited company."

"Ah well, there's these visits."

They exchanged smiles as Livia brought out her cigarettes.

"Actually," Hedges continued, "there's a thing on that. According to Wang, the company's bankrupt. Something's going on in court. So, no new neighbors for a while."

"Sorry to hear that."

"Well, seclusion has its points."

"Yes, and you have these visits."

Hedges calmly studied her. Livia wondered what he saw, how fond he was of her. Was she right about this?

"Have you thought any more about the pin?" she asked.

"Ah, the pin."

"I do have to bring it up, you know. It's the official reason for our meeting."

"Oh, of course. I don't want to get you in trouble. Let's see, why don't we say that, believe it or not, I still need more time. I have special issues. After all, I came all this way to separate myself–from things, from people–so the idea of joining, being a member, is kind of–well, it's a tough row to hoe."

"What?"

"And anyway, once I buy the pin, I lose my official reason for seeing you."

"Oh, I'm sure we can arrange something."

"I don't know. I kind of like to play it safe."

Livia's drink arrived and they raised glasses. Cigarette smoke snaked between them.

"Mr. Ulib suggested that I ask you to a party," she said. "His place next week."

"Whoa!"

Ulib was her superior, the deputy trade minister.

"It wouldn't be bad, really. We could leave after a short time. But if you hate the idea, couldn't stand it–"

"No, no. It's okay. Like I say, I don't want your career to suffer."

"You're sure? I don't want you to suffer, either."

Hedges only smiled in reply. Good enough, she thought.

"We won't stay long. We'll laugh about it later. And you still won't have to buy the pin. He's not the pushy sort. Not personally, I mean. Not directly."

"Good, because *you* are my salesperson."

Livia gave him a fond look.

"I made a sale last night to your neighbor out there."

"Wang?"

"No, Dr. Numerian. From Vasquibo."

"The secret project."
"Yes. I didn't pry at secrets, though. I have to be diplomatic."
"Hey, I don't care about them, anyway."
"You don't? Come on, now. Everyone cares about secrets. They're interesting."
"Okay, you're right. But what about the guy himself? Was he a hard sell?"
"No, not at all. He's an agreeable little man. A little shy, uncomfortable, but eager to please, get along here."
"Not like me, huh?"
Livia winked as she smoked.
"Anyway, he stressed that he had to get back, like there was something he couldn't leave for long. I didn't get to know him much."
Hedges picked up a menu.
"Are we going to eat today?"
"No, we'll just survive on whiskey and cigarettes."
"And," he hesitated, "on love?"
"Oh! Do you see it on the menu here?"

11.

On a narrow bed in a plain, utilitarian room, an elderly man lay awake. The final check had been made for the night so he'd be undisturbed till dawn. There was another bed against the opposite wall, heavy duty and equipped with restraints, but it was unoccupied. The man could do what he wished and not be detected, satisfy the urge that had grown since his procedure.

He sat up in bed, slipped out from the sheet, sat with feet on the floor. He reflected on the bed opposite. His donor hadn't required it, being dead. He wondered how they'd disposed of the body, and of his own old organs. No matter, he decided, he was on the way up now, and stood to remove his silk pajamas.

He felt the scars on his chest, minimal evidence of the doctor's neat, expert work. They'd allowed for healing before infusing transgenes, the second stage of his rejuvenation. Though it was much more than that, he understood. It was decades of life he would otherwise not have, and with the vitality he now felt surging.

He pulled on his navy blue swim trunks, hesitated to don his robe. It was lighter in color, would make him more visible, and the night was still warm. He left it.

Sneaking away from the unit, from the compound, he kept low until he reached the tall weeds. He stayed on the path to the heliport, then continued past the hill to the shore. The beach was narrower on this end of the island, the water much choppier than at the cove. Nevertheless, he waded in, invigorated by the water and knowledge of his action.

He started swimming when he could no longer touch bottom. There was no real pain though he was conscious of physical anomalies. More important was the difference in his mental self, the readiness and will to live as a younger man, albeit with the fruits of his successful career and life. He'd present a new persona, putting the lie to ageist comments overheard. The image of a panhandler in Brisbane flashed in his mind.

"Thank you so very much, old fart," the man had said, dissatisfied with his handout.

A bit off there, mate, thought the swimmer. I'm back in my prime while you're a wreck in the gutter. No matter, all's forgiven.

He swam parallel to the shore at first but then struck further out. It occurred to him suddenly that he should save his strength, that he'd need as much of it for the swim back. He trod water for a while, admiring the stars, reflecting on how all was wonderful. The coast of the island began to look inviting, its solidity offering rest. He started to swim toward it with calm, even strokes but noticed he wasn't going quite where he intended. He was moving laterally against his will to where the coast was farther away. After a time his swimming slowed, he was making no progress, and then he was underwater.

* * *

Wang had felt sluggish getting up, sensing something oppressive in the dawn. The morning light was diffuse, yet opaque, reminding Wang of smog. He instinctively fumbled for a cigarette, not bothering to start the coffee first. As he stood now taking his first draws of the day, gazing absently through the blinds, he noticed a difference in the seabirds' flight. The circular tendency, replacing the usual quick, random passes, drew his gaze down to the shallows of the cove, where an object had washed up and lay waiting for inspection. Wang squinted out, analyzing the shape, the size. Unready though he was for more bad news, he couldn't escape the likelihood that it was a human body.

Close to midnight the night before, the phone had rung in the model home. Anxious at the thought of another misstep by his son, Wang had answered quickly. The voice on the line had babbled rapidly in English, identifying the caller as Frost or Fizz or something similar, perhaps Fuzz. Rather than concerning Wang's son, the call was about the future of Reverie Cove, the caller apparently being the official in charge. Frost/Fizz insisted the model be prepared for the couple whose house wasn't built yet, delayed as it was by the court filing. They were committed to a moving date and had to be accommodated. No mention was made of where he, Wang, was to go, and he was reluctant to pose questions under the influence of drink. The caller had sounded frantic, perhaps unstable, and Wang's confidence in the future took a hit.

He walked groggily down the beach to the point nearest the body, regretting that he hadn't started the coffee maker. He glanced toward Hedges's cabin at the far end, relieved that at least it couldn't be him in the water. The lone home owner was still in the Kingdom with his girl friend, due to return that afternoon and drop off cigarettes at the model.

Coming to the right spot, Wang waded in.

The water was uncustomarily chill at this early hour, and dark, adding to Wang's sense of oppression. Why, he wondered, was he in this situation? A man his age, who should be settled, successful, instead having to walk through water to view a dead stranger. Without the benefit yet of breakfast, even coffee, or the touch or voice or simple presence of a loved one. Was it some wrong turn he took in life? Or an accumulation of smaller moves–a pattern, an attitude? Perhaps with Bing, his lack of solutions when the son went wrong, then the blame of his wife and his seeking refuge in business, a failed refuge and a failing business as well. It was good he had this Hedges to talk with, a man who'd done decently in business, who wasn't ruined by family. He gave Wang a link to sanity, more meaning to his coming here, some justification.

The body was curled sideways, a hump in the shallow water. It was an elderly male clad in black or dark blue swim trunks. Though the face was partially in the sand, there were no signs of violence, so Wang could see he was Caucasian. Perhaps a vacationer in the Kingdom, out too far swimming, or maybe from a cruise ship, or a sailing mishap. Now, however, just nothing. Another who'd taken wrong turns, or maybe just one–a fatal error–and wound up here at this island. Lying inert at my feet now, thought Wang, he maybe had many friends, a loving family, a good business or professional career. Perhaps he enjoyed traveling, many other pleasures, made many right decisions until this last one. But then, maybe all that went before just set up this final choice, opened a door to meet me here on this island, unfortunately dead like this. I too am in a bad state, have made bad decisions to go with bad luck, but at least I stand here alive. I live as I meet this man who is dead.

Returning to the model, Wang first started the coffee maker and then phoned the Kingdom. Though he shut the blinds, the image of the body in the water remained in his mind, so breakfast would be delayed further. He told himself he'd transferred responsibility, he needn't fear involvement, but he'd long had trouble with involvements, with extricating himself. He was the first to find the body, after all. How could he prove what he'd been doing, what he didn't do? His aloneness here made him vulnerable, sometimes desperate. Too bad Hedges was away, but then his being here might be worse. Conspiracy theories!

Wang's fears proved to be groundless. A police launch docked about an hour later with a trio of officers in stiffly starched uniforms. Their leader, Captain Vua, still in his twenties and inappropriately smiling, thanked Wang profusely for his quick action in calling. He eagerly led the others to the scene in question where, without regard for their neat uniforms, they made short work of recovering and bagging the body for transport. In the end, it wasn't much different from the weekly trash pickup except that police performed it.

"We will investigate," Captain Vua promised. "Please have Mr. Hedges call if he has any information. Good day, sir."

Grateful as he was to have the matter behind him, Wang didn't question the brevity of the police action. For them, he supposed, it was a common thing. Life was tenuous. When he related events to Hedges later, however, the home owner was puzzled.

"They didn't investigate the scene, want to question me?"

"No. Seems it's up to you if you know anything."

"What about our neighbors?"

He gestured toward the research project. Wang looked to the trees beyond the fence, shook his head.

"He washed up on our end. Beyond us, just the sea. It's up to them, the police, to find where he comes from."

That evening, as the red light of sunset flooded his cottage, Hedges was restless. He could still sense Livia's warmth, didn't mind the sporadic nature of their relationship, but the body washing up lent a new perspective. How far was he himself from the fate of that man? Was he still living as if he would live forever? He needed to take things seriously, to take *something* seriously. Yet what, in the end, was there? In thinking it out he was forever piecing together fragments, missing somehow the great center, the source of the patterns our lives take. And these lives are so limited, so short in time despite vast stretches when we seem to be immobile, tied to frustrating sameness, suffocating culture. Maybe it would take a better world for him to be focused and serious enough, at least with Livia. Or maybe it was he himself who would have to be better, but how do you change basic nature?

He decided to take a walk. Not down the beach toward Wang's abode, his usual route, but along the rocky southern coast of the island.

It was only a short distance to where the rocky shore bordered the research project. The fence was not continued down to the water, the rough coast apparently considered a sufficient barrier. Hedges had to pick his way carefully, his gaze downward until he came to a point where the sea intruded between the larger rocks, forming a mini-archipelago.

He moved inward, avoiding the water line, toward the scrubby trees and undergrowth above. The sun had dipped below the horizon, the afterglow sending a salmon shroud over the rocks in the water, their long shadows reaching back toward Hedges. Relaxing, he looked out over the orange sea.

"Hello," came a voice.

Unsure he'd heard it, Hedges frowned curiously as he viewed the glowing rocks, their interspersing inlets. Was it the sea lapping?

"Over here."

He looked back over his shoulder, toward the rough growth above. A figure in white was seated at the edge, legs folded to one side. She had long black hair, still striking against the dimming sky, and pale features that were lambent in the sunset. Her eyes somehow shone as they met his stare. She smiled. Hedges stepped closer.

"Hello," he answered.

"Do you live here, on the island?"

"Yes, several months now. Irv Hedges."

She accepted his hand, her own very smooth and cool.

"Noelle. I work in the labs."

He saw now that her garment was a lab coat. It hung loosely on her slender form.

"Guess that's all sort of hush-hush."

"Yes, hush-hush."

She looked past him toward the horizon, took a deep breath. He glanced back at the deepening colors.

"Beautiful evening," he said.

"They're all nice here, most of them."

"Been here long yourself?"

"Going on a month now. Still adjusting but–"

She looked away slightly as if distracted.

"It's nice," she finished, but didn't look back.

"Like to walk a bit?"

"Sure."

They moved off in the direction Hedges had been taking. The ground rose toward the eastern end of the island, the hill around which the choppers flew.

"On your break now?" he asked.
"Yes, sort of. The hours are flexible."
"That's nice."
"Actually, we're always working. I mean, unless you leave the island."
She seemed to say more, mumbling, Hedges not catching it.
"Excuse me?"
"Oh, nothing. Never mind, that's just me."
He let it go. She deftly stepped ahead over rough terrain.
"So are you retired?" she asked, turning to face him.
He paused a moment to take in her face, animated now in its paleness.
"Yeah, that's me," he said, "an old retired guy."
"Oh, now–"
She looked off again to the sea. He followed her gaze, was reminded of the body that had washed up.
"There was another old guy today, apparent drowning victim. Older than me, I guess. They fished him out of the cove."
"Today, you say?"
"Yeah. I was gone at the time but I heard about it from Wang, the caretaker."
"He was swimming?"
"I suppose. He was wearing swim trunks."
Her face settled in reflection.
"I think it's Mr. Talbot. He was a visitor here."
"Oh, I'm sorry."
"I hardly knew him. He was here on business, sort of."
"The police from the Kingdom will want to know."
"I'll inform Jens or Dr. Numerian. No need to worry about it yourself. They've maybe been in touch already. Probably they have."
Hedges was struck by her coolness, but he shrugged it off. He didn't know the story on this, after all.
"Well, I hope it works out all right."
They'd progressed to a rather high point, with some

buildings coming into view and, near the eastern edge of the island, the heliport.

"We'd better head back now," she said. "There's the guards."

"Guards? Armed?"

"Yes, just a few. It's a sensitive project."

They worked their way down the slope, tricky in the gathering twilight.

"Did you come here by yourself?" he asked on a pause. "Or is there family?"

"My husband died. A stroke they think, stress-related. We hadn't had children yet. That's why I'm here, I guess. This was his work, too."

"I'm sorry," Hedges said again.

This time she acknowledged his sympathy, nodding, then resumed the trek downward. Hedges occasionally heard again the murmur, or mumble, of undirected statements, but he said nothing. He waited until they were back where they'd met, then asked if she'd like to meet again. She looked around at the darkened stones, the black water.

"Maybe I can get you a visitor's pass," she said. "It wouldn't get you far, reception and the lunchroom, but it's better than nothing. Or we can just meet here, by the boulders."

"Sounds great."

They said goodbye and Noelle passed into the trees and shrubs atop the litter of rocks. Hedges followed a few steps, watching her progress, but she was quickly lost to sight. He stood for a moment in isolation, assuring himself that yes, he'd met a woman here tonight and it had gone well, despite no preparation. She was young and yet there was something classic about her, a level of quality that had always eluded him. The drive in himself to be separate had been weakened, he thought, but he had to be realistic. He was still living as a loner, was alone right now for the scramble back to his cottage. He'd better be careful on these rocks or there would be another body for the police boat.

He picked his way slowly toward Reverie Cove.

12.

In a shady corner of the hospital grounds, near a garden of aromatic flowers, Livia sat with a supervising physician. It was mid-afternoon, but they were shielded from the worst heat and a light breeze was blowing. Water trickled before them in a small fountain.

"The autopsy will likely be perfunctory," the doctor said. "It's clear enough he drowned while swimming. I doubt we'd be doing it if he weren't a foreigner, if there weren't a tourist industry to protect."

"Yes," Livia acknowledged, "I can appreciate that."

"Of course, it's important to *you*, the Ministry of Commerce. I too can understand."

Livia smiled, turned from the fountain to look at him. He was about her age, but starting to look careworn.

"I'm glad of that. You've always seemed so reasonable. A really elite citizen, not just a member of the club."

He briefly returned the smile.

"Thank you. But I'm a doctor and senior staff member. There are ethics that guide us, that should carry over to our lives in general."

Livia nodded. She should come to the point, she thought. His time was limited.

"I'm sure Dr. Numerian could appreciate that."

"Who?"

"Head of the project where the drowning happened, an E List member."

"Ah, yes." He eyed her warily. "He has an interest in our autopsy?"

"Well, Mr. Talbot was his patient. I suppose he got to know him somewhat. Anyway, he's concerned, as are some others–the project, the company–that there might be unnecessary problems, embarrassment for the family, if the body is released as it was found, as it is now."

"I don't understand."

"There was something about the treatment he was receiving, how it affected his vital organs. It would be better for all if they weren't there after the autopsy, if they just went out with the medical waste. And of course, if absolute secrecy were observed."

The doctor looked at her blankly.

"Are they hazardous, these organs?"

"No."

He shrugged.

"An odd request. But from a fellow physician, obviously of stature. I suppose I can respect his judgment. Of course, there'll be expenses involved."

He glanced at her sidelong, then studied the fountain. Livia removed an envelope from her purse and touched it to the doctor's sleeve. He moved it to an inside pocket of his jacket.

"Thank you for your understanding," Livia said.

* * *

Mr. Ulib lived outside the city proper, at an elevation, though not so far from Livia's neighborhood. The veranda of his mansion gave a panoramic view of the city and adjoining sea, down to the shipyard and beyond. He stood now admiring it with Hedges at his side, the ice in their cocktails reflecting the evening light. The deputy trade minister was almost as tall as his guest, and much heavier. He wore a cummerbund and medals in keeping with his position. Livia was with the other guests inside, having introduced Hedges and then kept others away from him and her boss.

"So," said Mr. Ulib, "why copper pipe fittings?"

"It was a family business. I took over from my father."

"No, I meant why copper. Why not a different metal? Certainly there's cheaper."

"Well, it's long-lasting, versatile, resists corrosion and pressure. But I would always point out its non-permeability. It gives the best possible protection against contaminants to a water supply. Nothing gets through–no germs, fluids, organic substances–nothing. And they can't weaken the copper in its service."

"Hm. And you made them in all shapes and sizes?"

"Oh, yes. We carried the full range of diameters and wall thicknesses, with fittings for making bends and turns in the pipe, for joining or branching the pipe, various types of couplings, slip couplings, adapters–"

"The whole shebang, we might say."

Mr. Ulib showed his smile of prosperity, which Hedges discreetly returned.

"Yes. The whole shebang."

Ulib nodded, his gaze falling on the E List pin Hedges wore on his lapel. He'd decided to give in and join after his encounter with Noelle on the island. It was experimental, he told himself, a test of his new impulse toward connection. The pin, a red enamel *E* topped with a crown and flanked by palm leaves, now graced the old blue blazer Hedges had worn to funerals and traffic court back home. He hadn't explained his change of heart to Livia, instead giving Mr. Ulib's party as his reason for joining. He wanted to fit in, he'd said, and also to not embarrass her by being a hold-out.

"Good to have you with us," said Ulib. "An elite citizen officially now."

He raised his glass and Hedges reciprocated. They looked out over the coastline, the familiar colors of post-sunset.

"So," Ulib continued, "you're retired completely now? No further connection with the industry?"

"Yes, I sold out. I don't retain any interests."

Ulib nodded thoughtfully.

"That makes you the only non-commercial resident of Progress Island."

"Oh? Isn't the research firm a non-profit organization?"

Ulib laughed, a note of cynicism trailing.

"Hardly. Their funding is rather nebulous, but their field, immunology, touches on some of mankind's great concerns, therefore on lucrative industries. It's a long time since Dr. Salk. Any cures discovered out there will come at high prices to those who want them."

"They're developing medicines, or some sorts of cures, for profit? To hold the patents, force people or countries to pay a lot to use them?"

"Such is our modern age. Nothing is free. Not even what one might expect in the name of human decency."

"Did you have any qualms about letting them in?"

"We don't know exactly what they're working on, or of course their methods. It might all be for the best, necessary, and above-board. They can certainly progress faster than universities and socialists. They have focused management, the big money behind them."

"And their location here–just for secrecy?"

"We assume that, officially at least. To protect the eventual patents. But, as I say, we don't know exactly what they're doing. I suppose we haven't wanted to."

And so, Hedges thought, Vasquibo finds the Kingdom accommodating, freeing them from constraints they'd find in other places. Is this what's necessary for progress? He smiled as he thought of Deville Associates, floundering with their development on his end of the island. The backside of the cutting edge. Yet also the catalyst to whatever was going on.

"I heard you had some contact with them," Ulib continued.

Hedges recalled Noelle in the orange afterglow.

"Just a little. Met one of their workers out walking."

"Yes. She reported it to Dr. Numerian, of course."

Things get around here, Hedges thought.

"Of course." A hesitation. "Anything new on the body that was found?"

"He was Dennis Talbot, a visitor at the project. He apparently drowned while swimming, but the body is being held for further analysis."

"Family?"

"Vasquibo is doing the contacting. He was well known to them, evidently. There on some pre-arranged business."

Hedges caught a sudden tightness in Ulib's voice.

"I wanted to ask you," the official went on, "whether you learned anything in your conversation–with the worker, I mean, on the shore. Anything about what they're doing that seemed–well, unusual. Perhaps extraordinary."

Hedges did the mandatory reflection, but all he recalled was the pale, glowing image of Noelle in the changing hues of dusk.

"No, I'm afraid not. She herself said it was all secret."

"You'll be seeing her again?"

"Probably, I think."

"I'd appreciate your letting me know whatever you learn about their methods. Specific actions, procedures. We might as well be candid with each other. We should both know what they're up to."

Hedges didn't like the sound of this, but Ulib was a big shot here.

"Okay, sure. But I'm not looking to get real involved. I'm just an old retiree."

Ulib laughed.

"Understood. But it could be important, Mr. Hedges. Just so we're straight on that."

"Straight, right. But what about Dr. Numerian, the head guy? He's E List and all. Can't you just get what you want from *him*?"

Ulib shifted uncomfortably.

"He wears the pin, it's true, but also the 'secret project' cloak. He's an Elite Citizen as much as it suits his purpose, or rather Vasquibo's. There are others no doubt, far away, with more to say in things than Dr. Numerian. But he's the one we have to deal with, and sometimes Jenssen, his engineer. They're soldiers of their company, no matter what they say to you. You cannot trust them."

"Sorry to hear that."

Ulib looked in his glass, now empty, swirled the dregs of ice.

"Yes, well, you were a man of business. You can understand. Perhaps we should go for fresh drinks now."

He hesitated, however, as they were about to enter.

"By the way, there were several visas issued for people to join your community, to share in your dreams at the cove." He laughed. "They'll be arriving soon."

"Really? But there's been no more construction. Where will they live?"

Ulib shrugged.

"Who knows? But one is the receiver for Deville, so he'll be in charge. We took care of a dead body, but this receiver should handle the live ones."

They turned into the large parlor, where Hedges caught Livia's eye across the room. He recalled her promise to leave early, knew he wouldn't hold her to it. They'd go when she was ready, when she thought it was proper. He'd be an Elite Citizen for her.

13.

In an airliner high above the ocean, Fauss reclined with his eyes closed after downing several beers. He'd peek sometimes at the couple with whom he was traveling, the Hoagles, who were across the aisle and several rows up. He didn't want to deal with them for a while, their questions and comments about the Reverie Cove mess. The man wasn't so bad but the wife was a dingbat. Let them think he was drunk for now.

"I must have dozed," the woman said, raising her head. Her red curls were disheveled from the long trip. "Do we have much farther?"

"Still a couple of hours," her husband answered, "then our connection in Auckland. A small plane, no doubt." He sipped his chardonnay, its color that of his well-trimmed beard. "Then we still have a boat or hydrofoil or something after that."

"God. You did find yourself a hideaway, Kurt."

"Can't be helped, Chloe. You know that."

She looked out her porthole.

"I'll miss them all. The quality people, the real life."

"It's only for a season. We'll see the house is built, put it in order, then have it for—well, our retreat in the future."

"A refuge, you mean. *Yours*."

Kurt gave her his mature, philosophic look.

"Some friction is inevitable in life. It goes with success. I take a discreet approach: withdraw for a while and let the lawyers work it out."

75

Chloe pouted.

"Are there things to do, anyway?"

"Of course there are. For one thing, there should be plenty of exotic birds to add to your list. Those binoculars will get a workout."

She didn't respond. Though in fact a birdwatcher, mention of the exotic aroused her thoughts of attractive men. She let it pass, turning her smile to the porthole.

Fauss noticed them talking, hoped they'd keep each other busy. He didn't want someone hanging over from the aisle, grilling him with questions, perhaps guessing his intent to delay their house. He had to watch the cash flow. He considered a restroom trip, decided to save it as an escape option. Settling deeper into his seat, he lapsed into memories of his adolescence: making the old chain-net clink with a basketball, catching a pillow-like softball against his stomach. Always a dirt stain there on his shirt. Simpler times.

* * *

Jens Jenssen stood atop a rise on the island, binoculars in hand. The rise wasn't as high as the hill to the south, beyond the heliport, but it gave a good view of the common area and dock, the sea beyond. Jens was awaiting the water taxi, ostensibly to pick up supplies, and had a three-wheeler in which to carry them. This would normally be a job for one of the guards, but today was different. Several new visas had been issued for people with Reverie Cove as their destination. Jens wanted to see them, perhaps meet them, supplement his computer data for the sake of project security. He'd prefer to be simply an engineer, as he'd been in his home country, but he understood the need for minimal staff, for secrecy, so he'd gamely undertaken this second role. There were only the four guards, after all, armed only with revolvers. The Institute didn't want to broadcast that something priceless was here.

Catching sight of the boat, Jens took his seat on the motorized tricycle. He was a husky man, low-browed, and could easily have passed as a regular policeman. He coasted down the slope, hardly touching the gas pedal. He waited on the boardwalk as the water taxi docked.

"God!" someone shouted. "What a ride!"

It was a froggy-looking middle-aged man, leading the charge off the boat.

"Where's Wang?" he demanded.

"I wouldn't know, sir," Jens replied. "I'm with Vasquibo."

"Oh. Well, he's supposed to be here. I'm with some people, new owners for the Cove."

"You're with the Deville company, sir?"

"God, no. I'm its receiver."

Being addressed as God began to irritate Jens. He held out a hand to his squat new acquaintance.

"Jens Jenssen."

"Edgar Fauss," the receiver replied.

A tallish woman, rather spindly with curly red hair, was alighting on the pier. She gawked about wide-eyed, her open-mouthed smile greeting all she saw. Behind her, in the boat, a man was assisting the driver with luggage and packages. He also was tall, with short-cropped blond hair above a high forehead and matching short beard, well-trimmed. He had an intelligent cast to his face. Someone, Jens reflected, that he might raise a stein with.

"Wow!" the woman intoned loudly, giving sound to her facial expression.

She was looking at Fauss, but the receiver had spotted Wang approaching in a golf cart and paid the woman no attention. She shifted her gaze to Jens.

"Talk about absolute minimalist. Welcome home, Chloe!"

Jens gave a slight smile and walked past her toward the boat. These first two were nothing, he could see. The driver was finishing with the blond man, chatting as he received a tip, but he recognized Jens and quickly attended to the supplies.

"Moving in today?" the engineer inquired.

"Yes," replied the blond man. "Will we be neighbors?"

"In a way. I work for Vasquibo Institute, in the research plant up the road there. Jens Jenssen, chief engineer."

They shook hands.

"Kurt Hoagle. I'm an engineer myself, but software. Temporarily retired."

"Giving it a try, hey? Nice to have the option."

"Well, we'll see how it goes. You've met my wife?"

"Yes, briefly. Charming lady."

Hoagle nodded, saying nothing.

"Well, I'd best let you get settled. We'll be seeing each other, I'm sure. It *is* an island."

Provisions loaded, Jens rumbled back toward the compound. The people headed for Reverie Cove, in the opposite direction, were progressing more slowly. Jens smiled at their disorientation. They seemed harmless enough, just so none of them became a nuisance. The software man was probably competent, being able to retire here, and might be a resource in a pinch. It'd be a tough request, though, with their security needs. Much obfuscation of purpose and methods.

He sighted Dr. Numerian walking among the buildings, stopped the tricycle. He related to his superior his impressions from the pier. The older man nodded appreciatively. He was smaller than Jens, wiry in build, his graying hair combed sideways.

"It's good you checked them out. Some new donors are arriving tonight on the pad."

Jens looked out toward the heliport.

"I'm getting uneasy about that. We can't keep that up long-term. The organs should be harvested off-site."

"Now, Jens. We want maximum control of the process. And optimal conditions, of course. Fresh beats canned any day. You know that."

"Yes, doctor. But people might be watching now. The Talbot incident—"

"We had a breakthrough there—or should have—to put us much closer. Then we wouldn't need all these chimps, necessarily. Talbot blew it. He maladjusted, got too cocky. We can only hope—believe—that it's not an inevitable side effect."

"What about the body? The relatives must be anxious for a funeral."

"Our girl in the capital will handle it, bribe someone to get it released."

"The organs might possibly be a problem. Second autopsy or something."

"Those will 'go missing,' as they say–a small country's inefficiency. More bribe money out the window, but what can you do?"

"And the silence of the autopsy crew?"

"They know better than to blab in a place like this. Swift retribution awaits."

Jens looked out over the compound, sighing impatiently.

"Such uncertainty. Too many variables cropping up. It's a godsend we have Noelle."

"There's nothing like a prototype," Numerian smiled. "There's no god involved, though. Her husband was just a man, like you and me. A scientist, yes, and a great one. Perhaps as close to God as one can get. But–"

He broke off as he and Jens locked eyes. Simultaneously, it seemed, they sensed a great new standing for themselves in relation to the universe.

"One of those off the boat," said Jens, "a clumsy fellow, kept saying 'God this' and 'God that' when addressing me. Until I put him right, of course."

After a hesitation, Numerian laughed. It was rare for him.

* * *

Rummaging in his suitcase, Kurt found the pouch of tobacco he'd packed. He was an occasional pipe smoker, chiefly in idle or especially busy times, and today somehow qualified as both. Chloe had located her small binoculars, handy for birdwatching and other nosiness, and was propped at the window of their room, peering out. They'd been given the master bedroom of the model pending construction of their own home.

"Any interesting species?" he inquired.

"Not yet. Just garbage-eating gulls, as far as I can see."

"Well, give it time. We have plenty of it now."

He waited a moment for her to turn, perhaps say something sweet, but she was lost in her observations. He sidled out the door to light up outside. Back at the window, Chloe watched a man across the cove emerge from swimming and approach his small cottage. The man was nude. Chloe watched raptly until he disappeared inside.

Descending the stairs to the living room, Kurt picked up on the conversation between Fauss and Wang.

"I really can't go more than a week on that," Fauss was saying. "In fact, I was actually thinking just four or five days. Just time for the prefab to arrive and be ready for you to live in. I'm a state corporation commissioner. I have a whole raft of responsibilities back there. I don't work for Deville. This is all extra for me, heaped on top of my real job. I'm not making anything here. I'm just falling behind in my other work, thanks to your employer!"

Wang was cautious.

"I understand, Mr. Fauss. I know you can't stay long. But the number of things I must deal with–seeing my daughter, my son's problems, the situation with our business–and then the travel time, considering the service I've given, the demands on me here, this location–"

Fauss waved his hands impatiently. Noticing that one held an unlit pipe, Kurt hid his own and continued toward the exit.

"Wang, this is business!" the receiver emphasized. "Your company's broke and I'm here to right the ship. Things *cannot* go on the same as always!"

Fauss continued as Kurt escaped into the breeze outside. The receiver had mentioned on board that he'd ease the living situation by granting Wang a short leave, with the caretaker to live outside the model on his return. The shortness of the leave had apparently become an issue. Moving from the model to a metal box couldn't have appealed to Wang either.

Kurt smiled as he glanced back at their bedroom window, but Chloe wasn't there. She'd mentioned wanting a shower, so no doubt she was shedding her clothes. She'd been good in the end about the move, understanding that it was practical–given the legal turmoil, the financial threats–as well as something he needed to do for a while. And it *was* only temporary, though it would be nice to have this for later escapes, should the need or want arise. The Kingdom and the island's autonomy provided legal barriers to the onslaught of corporate jackals.

He continued down the beach, enjoying the breeze off the cove, the sea beyond. He passed the unsold properties, large and marked with flags. Theirs was number 14, squarely at the center of the crescent-shaped coast. He'd chosen it for the direct vew of the opening to the sea, the world of intrigue and deceit beyond. A large, blocky *SOLD* sign had been pounded into the ground. Kurt smiled, thinking he might be the first to see it aside from Wang. But then, he thought, his gaze shifting to the far point of the cove, there was that hermit. Why would anyone move here to live alone? The waves constantly lapping, the sun glaring off the sea, the long stillness of the nights– haunting, one would think. A lure to craziness. Looking back over his property, he considered whether additions to their home might be feasible. A sizable office and work area, a lab even. The money was there, so why not?

A group of seabirds passed noisily overhead. Kurt watched them fly beyond the fence and into Vasquibo territory. Yes, he speculated, you could do anything in a place like this. Anything was possible.

14.

The overhead light was harsh but Noelle liked it that way, forcing her to focus hard on Terence's notes. Her assistant Anna was at her microscope, observing a new set of samples and making notes. They worked well together, both of them living for their work now. In Anna's case, it was a welcome escape from the limits of her national culture, while for Noelle things were more complicated.

It was no longer for content that Noelle studied Terence's notes, but out of sentiment, a need for emotional guidance, assurance that what they were doing was great. Terence had given his life, after all, for this work. He'd been desperate near the end, and reckless as it turned out, but what was he to do after the loss of funding? The newspapers liked to show the Animal Rights people with their signs, but Noelle knew it was the Lords and Ladies in government, paranoia about the national health plan, national solvency. And lurking behind it all, that crazy fear of challenging God. But Terence was too committed to let anything stop him, so he pressed on without adequate trials and became his own test subject. The flaws in the process were fatal to him, but he made her the beneficiary of their discovery. Now here she was, the end result for Numerian and team to bring about in others, making the process marketable.

Noelle got up and went back to Anna.

"How do those look? Any progress?"

"Yes, quite stable actually."

"Think we can try them on Popper?"

Popper was a mature chimp in the experimental animals unit, or EAU.

"I don't know. Maybe we should compare one more batch. Jens is getting nasty about bringing animals in."

"I thought they could defend using chimps. It's only illegal in certain countries."

"He says one thing will lead to another if people start poking around."

"Yes. Well, we don't want to rush things anyway."

She hesitated as Terence came to mind.

"I think I'll visit old Popper."

Anna laughed softly.

"Give him my best. Tell him—"

But Noelle was already walking off, talking unintelligibly in a low voice. Anna was accustomed to this and gave it no thought, returning assiduously to her microscope. She was comfortable working alone, knowing she wasn't really alone, surrounded as she was by the elements of superior new life—synthetic enzymes, carrier viruses, and transgenes suspended in precise temperatures and chemical environments, awaiting their roles in the project. With people like Noelle and Dr. Numerian, she was at home here and treasured her role, her escape from oppression.

Exiting the synthesis lab, Noelle walked under the moon to the EAU. The moon was high and brought out the glow on her skin, the pale, porcelain quality that was a minor side effect of Terence's perfected chromosome. Except it wasn't perfect, she reflected as she looked at her arm. This little glow might be seen as a positive, something people sought from cosmetics, but then there was that other—the run-on, like a car when it should be shut off. As if some level of thinking below the conscious insisted on expressing itself after she meant to stop talking. Perhaps here, with the expensive equipment, the many trials, her own and Terence's case histories, they would have real perfection. Of course, there was Numerian's part to consider, the surgical replacements on older subjects. But there was no getting away from it, this combination of strategies. It was clear from the beginning that, in order for the project to exist, to be funded, it had to be designed with marketability in mind. And it was older people who would pay the price, take any risks involved. Younger people couldn't see their own deaths, thought already that they'd live forever. And yet older people have old organs, unable to support the process as her own had, so there had to be replacements. Numerian demanded optimal materials, as well as optimal conditions, for his work as well as her own, so he brought in the chimps as donors. He was succeeding, Noelle had to admit, where she and Terence could not.

Closing the door behind her, Noelle walked slowly into the dim, indirect light of the EAU. She passed the cages of the new chimps, two males and a female, still curious about their new surroundings. Numerian preferred all males for the project, wanting as much consistency as possible, but perhaps the supply was dwindling. Next to them was Pundit, a mature chimp who'd served as a practice subject for Talbot's procedure. Pundit sat quietly, gazing serenely at the younger chimps, maybe feeling fraternal since youthful organs were in him. If only Talbot could have handled it as well, but his exhilaration at the change did him in. The human factor, perhaps, but then Pundit had another advantage: he was imprisoned.

She came to Popper's cage opposite the awakened dogs. Like Pundit, he was implanted with young organs, but he lacked the genetic changes effected in Pundit and Talbot. Those changes had been made to certain individual genes significant in the aging process. Talbot had had decades added to his natural life, which he promptly threw away. While scientifically a success, the work on Talbot did not accomplish the practical mission of the project, for which Popper would be the final stepping-stone. Like Noelle, and based on Terence's work, Popper was to receive an artificial chromosome to effect numerous genetic alterations at once. If successful on the chimp, the procedure would then be marketable to wealthy humans seeking unlimited natural lifespans. Any problems revealed by the Popper trial could be explained and fixed thanks to the rigid controls here, unlike the chaos in which Terence had worked.

"Hello, Popper," Noelle said. "How are you feeling?"

The chimp stared at her mutely.

"Ready for your big day? It's almost here."

Popper looked out through the door, perhaps anticipating food. He was on a special regimen of nutrients and hormones to optimize chances for success, but he got treats as well to keep his spirits up. He looked quite fit to Noelle, his eyes clear and coat full and shiny, his movements strong and smooth.

"Miss your buddy up there? Don't worry, you'll see him at exercise tomorrow."

The ethicists came to mind as she said this. They would hardly be satisfied that exercise, treats, and kind words were provided. And beyond this use of animals was the planned marketing to human beings, the implications for society when the procedure was utilized. Major adjustments would be necessary when some people didn't die. And where, some would ask, does God fit in? The reactions would be hostile without precedent, and world-wide. They wouldn't see at first how they wanted it for themselves, or for ones they loved as she'd loved Terence. Oh, well. The project was safe for now on this island near the Kingdom, and its finances were safe in similar places, cautiously nourished by the faceless consortium of investors.

Noelle looked around for the treat box, but didn't see it.

"Sorry, Popper. No treat today, I guess. Next time for sure."

She walked in a bit further to give the mice a glance, saw that all was well, then made her way back toward the exit. Having talked to Popper, she could now see more clearly the change in Pundit's expression. His calm eyes gazed from his upturned face with majesty, as if knowledgeable that his was a superior fate. What actually would happen to him was uncertain. Numerian was planning to move on to supplemental strategies once their main goal was achieved, including nanotechnology, which influenced the hiring of Jens. The engineer's estimates for additional staff and capital needed, however, were formidable, so Numerian was leaning toward a try at brain transplants. A healthy, superior specimen like Pundit could be implanted

A Truly Higher Life Form

with an old brain, which might then experience the world for a longer time.

Poor Pundit, thought Noelle, and turned to leave the EAU.

After she was gone, the chimps settled down and Pundit collapsed into a sprawl. The dogs relaxed their alertness, the mice continuing as always. Popper surveyed the scene, confirming Noelle's conclusion that the treat box was not available. He wasn't actually disappointed. Since the change they made inside him, with its aches and odd feelings, and with the shots and new food he got, his craving for the treats had slipped away. He took them and put them in his mouth, as was his habit, but then later he took them out. He'd grind a wet treat tablet against the lock mechanism of his cage, some of it entering the lock and the rest falling downward. It was a good enough adjustment, he felt, so it became another habit. He laid a hand on the lock now, gripping a bar of the door with his other hand. It had been closing with a softer and softer click. Wondering what he might hear, he tried to shake the door. Unsure if he heard a sound, he shook harder. The door swung open.

Popper sat for a while, gaping at the opening in his cage. There should be humans in the space. Tentatively, he reached out, then swung himself forward. Yes, the aisles were clear. He swung himself out and looked around. He ambled back to the mice cages, grunted, turned away in disgust. He came back past the dogs, who eyed him lazily. He gave a robust snort and one of them pricked up its ears. Satisfied, Popper continued on toward the front, the cages nearest the exit. The new chimps became excited, especially the larger male, as if sensing something afoot and wanting in. Pundit showed little response, giving only a sidelong glance from his sprawling position. It was he, however, that Popper attended to, not quite gloating but awaiting some recognition of his freedom, his superior status. None came so, disappointed, he turned away and ambled back to his cage, shutting the door with a very soft click.

He hadn't quite made it to the exit door, the latch he could open with a turn, eyed now by a smiling Pundit.

15.

Waves of heat rose from the tarmac as Wang crossed to the nondescript terminal. He could see from the wide-open doors that the air-con wasn't working. There was still some relief as he escaped the sun, but this allowed him more of another feeling, a familiar emptiness. The joys and trials of being with his family were again past, and he was again reduced to his servile role in this foreign place. He wished he could see more of Tia, his daughter, but it was mostly for her that he labored here. If she couldn't get into a medical field, he thought, then perhaps pharmacy. That would tie in with the family business.

He joined a short line at the immigration desk, showed his documents. The sweating officials had been laconically stamping visas, but now there came a change in their demeanor. A list was consulted, an outdated computer checked, a guard called over.

"Please stand out of line, sir. The officer will take you to a waiting area."

"I don't understand."

"Your data tripped an alert. We must notify the national police."

Wang cooperated, not especially worrying. He'd read and heard of many such mix-ups with the heightened security. It was easily enough straightened out. He also had an American official, Fauss, on Progress Island to vouch for him.

After about half an hour, Captain Vua arrived with a colleague.

"Well, Mr. Wang," said Vua, "how was your trip?"

"Okay until now, Captain. It seems there's been some mistake."

"Ah. Perhaps so. However, there's also been a grave development since you left. The case of Mr. Talbot, the unfortunate man you found. You recall?"

"Yes, of course."

"Of course. Well, this is rather gruesome, Mr. Wang, but his insides, you know, were missing from the body. We have an international complaint to resolve."

"His insides? Gone?"

"Yes."

"Well, I–how should I know about *that*?"

"I don't know. We simply must investigate. You see, you were the last one with Mr. Talbot–with his body, at least–before it was in official custody."

"I know nothing except I saw him there–dead–and called you out. Mr. Hedges, who lives out there, he's a witness!"

"Yes, he came in later. But I'm afraid we must detain you, Mr. Wang, while we sort things out. There's international interest so we must show an aggressive response."

Wang protested but to no avail. Vua assured him that he'd be well treated, he'd be reunited with his luggage at the jail. The captain would personally threaten the airport staff against any pilfering.

* * *

Hedges was in the water off the south coast of Progress Island. The sun was high, not the most pleasant time for a swim, but he'd wanted to escape the commotion at Reverie Cove. A work crew had arrived and was preparing the prefab to which Wang would be moving. It was on property 18, not as convenient for trips to the dock, but Hedges would be a closer neighbor. The new residents in the model apparently preferred privacy, at least one of them. Hedges had met the husband, Kurt, out walking in the dark, but they'd only exchanged a few words. He seemed well-educated, perhaps a bit conceited, but Hedges sensed a commonality that had led them both to come here.

A slow, awkward swimmer, Hedges enjoyed his greater buoyancy in salt water. He'd taken care as he passed the place he'd met Noelle, its indefinite shoreline and profusion of jutting boulders. He wondered if they'd contributed to Talbot's fate. But there were currents farther out and Talbot was an old guy, and he was unmarked except for surgical scars. He'd just misjudged, taken on too much, something it wasn't in Hedges's nature to do.

He decided to swim back.

Casually, watching the sparkles on the water's surface, he proceeded around the point on which his cottage was located. He'd worn swim trunks today since more people were around. He preferred to get out in the cove rather than on the outer shore, feel the fine sands welcoming his feet. Churning into the cove's mouth, he noticed the three men who were still occupied with the prefab. Closer, however, and maybe distracting the crew, was a red-haired swimmer even more awkward than himself. It took him a moment to realize she was the wife from the model, whom he'd seen only from a distance thus far. Having paused between the points, Hedges felt obliged to approach and greet her before going ashore.

"Hi!" she called. "I'm Chloe!"

"Irv Hedges," he panted as he stopped in the water.

"You must be the hermit."

"Hermit?"

"That's your place there?"

"Well, yeah, but–"

He saw she was giving someone else's assessment. Glancing toward the model, he felt uneasy about the receiver, Fauss.

"I'm just a regular guy, actually. I don't mind a bit of company."

Her smile was wide and open, giving her a rustic look beneath her wet curls.

"Were you getting out just now?"

"Yeah."

"Mind if I rinse in your house? That awful little man is snooping around in ours."

Hedges felt vulnerable, not quite in control, but what could he say?

"Sure, no problem."

As they waded up, he mentioned his encounter with her husband.

"Kurt? What did you think of him?"

"Well, we only talked for a minute. Nice to meet you and such."

"Yes, Kurt is complicated. Takes a while to get to know, not to mention understand."

Hedges opened the cottage and directed her to the shower, inviting her to use his robe afterward. To avoid any questions of propriety, he told her he'd be outside, having a look at the prefab work.

"Thank you," she said, smiling with her eyes as she held the bathroom door.

Hedges grabbed a tee-shirt and got out of the cottage.

The crew was finishing up, one of them already walking down the beach toward the common area and dock. Hedges suspected they'd been dawdling to watch Chloe cavort in the water. He waited while the others left and then sidled toward Wang's new home. It wasn't much, he found, not much better than the office shack one might find at a construction site. Maybe that was the idea, to get further use from it when more houses were built here. It fit with the apparent shrewdness of the receiver. There were no copper pipe fittings, Hedges noticed. Prices must still be up.

When he guessed Chloe must have finished her shower, Hedges drifted back toward his cottage. He reached the patio in back and took a few tentative steps to the back door. He peeked in its window. There was movement–Chloe, of course–coming into focus as his squinting eyes adjusted. With arms raised high, she was carrying the two parts of her wet bathing suit around the cottage, perhaps seeking a good place to dry them. She was nude.

Hedges slipped away as quietly as he could.

Across the cove, in the living room of the model, Fauss stood at the phone while Kurt puffed his pipe on the couch.

"Well, do you actually know anything about the body? Why do they want to hold you, then? Missing *what*? Organs–like out of the body? For Chrissakes! Uh-huh, family in Australia, consulate, better investigation. Their tourist business, right. Well, I'm not forking out any bail money, Wang. You know we'll never see it again from these characters. I'm the receiver here. I can't let a bunch of pina coladas put the squeeze on me!"

He was soon off the phone, leaving Wang unaided in his predicament.

"Damn!" he exclaimed as he returned to his end of the couch.

"I take it," Kurt ventured, "Mr. Wang will not be returning on time."

"Damn, damn, *damn*!" Fauss answered. "Now I'm stuck in this crappy place because some tropical bozos don't know their asses from holes in the ground!"

Kurt decided to let him stew awhile, considered taking a walk. But a few more shouts and violent gestures seemed to lift Fauss from his fury, at least temporarily, so he was free to return to their earlier discussion. He even took out his pipe.

"Anyway," he said, "getting back to your, uh, idea. We have a contract in place, right? You got in under the wire with Deville. But the changes you're talking about would add hugely to the cost of construction. I can't have a lot more cash flowing out to the contractors. I already have to sweat their overruns. I can't free-wheel like Deville did. As receiver I have to plug the dike, take no risks. I have to be Scrooge."

"Couldn't I just deal with the contractors myself? On the additions, I mean. I could negotiate, watch overruns et cetera myself."

"Sure you could, post-construction. After I have Deville out of the picture."

"But that would be much more expensive. How about a rider on our contract in which I shoulder the additional cost?"

Fauss shook his head, sage now amidst his pipe smoke.

"No can do. The costs would be impossible to keep

separate, plus I'd be setting Deville up for liability in case you defaulted. The judge would nail me to the wall."

Kurt frowned.

"I can provide ample financial references, if that's the problem."

"Actually, it's not just financial. This development, Reverie Cove, is supposed to have a certain character. Something like, I don't know, peaceful seclusion for retirees or people getting away from it all. It was clear in their pitch, choice of location, the set-up of the place. What you're talking about–labs, equipment, a pro office–is at odds with all that. The additions would encroach on the planned space between the properties. You might see fit to bring in employees, and what about additional waste? See what I mean? It wouldn't be Reverie Cove any more, except in name only. And the name would become a mockery."

Kurt took a puff himself, studying the owlish man beside him.

"You don't seem to have many dreamers arriving anyway."

Fauss gave a grim smile.

"This place wasn't my idea. I just can't have screw-ups on my watch."

They both puffed in silence.

"Look," Fauss continued. "You want my advice? Given the incompetence at Deville, I'm not sure this development is legally sound and met ethical standards. If you wanted out of your contract, there's probably some wiggle room."

Kurt took a moment before responding.

"No, I don't want to wiggle, Edgar. Construction may proceed, and as soon as possible. The existing contract, if that's the best–"

The phone rang again. Fauss jumped to answer it, as if welcoming the interruption.

"No!" he was soon shouting. "Absolutely not! I expect a swift hearing or questioning or whatever so he can get back to work. And think on this, friend: any bad press about holding foreigners and your tourist business takes a hit! Lots of money lost for your country and who's gonna answer for *that*? You, right? Think about it. Now I want that man released and I'm not gonna pay any phony bail to you or anyone else!"

The conversation proceeded while Kurt reflected on the couch. Across the cove, Hedges sat in the shade of the prefab awaiting Chloe's exit from his cottage. He didn't know what she was up to, and he had no inclination to find out. At this age, this stage of life for him, when he'd finally resolved his penchant for isolation, someone like Chloe was a threat, caused panic. It was foolish, he knew, from an objective standpoint, but then *he* was foolish, always had been, and unavoidably so. But he'd accepted his nature and even balanced it here with his visits to Livia. He was at peace, needed nothing more. And yet, it suddenly occurred to him, while he had no use for the "more" represented by Chloe, there was no denying the enchantment he felt in his meetings with Noelle.

Chloe emerged from the cottage, dispelling his thoughts. She was wearing his royal blue robe. Her swimsuit dangled from one hand, apparently still wet. She sauntered toward him, not so much coy now as something else, perhaps insouciant. Was she miffed?

"Sorry I took so long."

"Hey, no problem."

"No problem? Really?"

Hedges felt a welling irritation. He kept silent.

"Okay if I wear your robe home?"

She held up the damp swimsuit for inspection.

"Sure, go ahead."

It sounded wrong to him, as if he were ordering her to leave. But he'd been civil, hadn't

he? Considerate. What more could be expected of him?

She started to smile but suddenly turned and walked off.

"See you," was all she said.

Hedges watched for a moment, then headed for his cottage. He, too, needed a shower, the salty sea having dried on his body. He felt the dry oozing of the fine sand at his feet, somehow lacking its usual degree of comfort, intimacy. He found that Chloe had left the door of the cottage ajar with the air conditioner running. She'd also had a snack, an empty yogurt container and spoon lying on his table amidst a galaxy of toast crumbs. There was also a wine bottle, empty now but half-full of Cabernet when last he'd seen it.

Hedges turned off the air-con to save the solar cells. Returning to the door, he watched Chloe on the other side of the cove, still walking in his robe. I am what I am, he thought. No more, no less. You might not like that but nothing's going to change it.

But again Noelle's image flitted in his memory.

16.

A tricycle stopped before one of the government buildings in the center of the capital. Livia alighted, paid the driver, and greeted guards to whom she was familiar. She wore a shiny rose-colored dress today, her hair tied back loosely with a matching velvet band. She removed her hat as she entered the building, having worn one, as usual, against the sun rather than for fashion. She ascended a wide stone staircase, worn toward the center from generations of use. She passed a few office staff, her nominal coworkers, on her way to Mr. Ulib's office at the end of the hall. It was unusual for him to call her in, disregarding her appointments, but they both knew her loyalty made that a non-issue. She opened his door and entered.

Mr. Ulib wore expensive suits in the office, as he did at social and government events, but without his cummerbund and medals. Such items, he'd confided to Livia, did not impress foreign business people, and perhaps even marked him as antiquated. He sat now behind his expansive desk, accompanied by a young police captain who turned in his chair as Livia entered. Livia recognized him.

"We're just finishing," Mr. Ulib informed her. Then, to the captain: "You've met Miss Poe, my special assistant?"

"I think so, yes, at a function or two."

"You recall Captain Vua?" asked Mr. Ulib.

Livia murmured her assent, exchanging polite smiles. Her strongest memory of the captain, however, was of his wildly dancing with a woman who looked like a prostitute. He'd been out of uniform and more or less drunk. It was in a club Livia visited incognito, her hair in a dowdy arrangement and her face behind garish dark glasses. She occasionally went out this way to spy on the world, to see what was going on without having to play her role. To relax. At this particular club there were often quality people–lawyers from the justice ministry, medical people, professors. This was an off night, however, made more so by the arrival of Captain Vua and his group. As his grotesque performance ended, he noticed Livia watching from the bar. Struck by her look of tacky aging, he turned away with a sneer and went to join his friends.

"You look most beautiful today," he said now.

Livia murmured thanks, reminded again of the shallowness of sunny smiles.

Once he'd gone, shutting the door behind him, Livia sat before the desk. Mr. Ulib settled into his gravest mien.

"There is clearly a problem," he said. "Complicated. Threatening."

He hesitated, his lips pressed together, his gaze past her shoulder.

"Can I help?" Livia ventured.

"Unfortunately, not much. You've been quite valuable, but this involves the darker side of things. We're on the defensive, it seems."

He looked at her directly.

"I'd like to think it was just incompetence, bad as that is. Then it might be fixed and explained somehow, smoothed over. But this release of a body–Talbot, from Progress Island–with parts missing inside, questions about the death, nobody knowing what happened–it smacks of something else. Captain Vua is in charge of the investigation. He led the recovery detail that brought the body in. They've detained the man who called them, who found the body, a caretaker out there. He's clearly not at fault, has no more information, but they're holding him to show we're doing something. It can't go on, of course. We'll need a real solution. Our commercial standing is quite fragile in the world. We can't afford international scandal."

Was she here, Livia wondered, to commiserate? Was it simply her presence, her listening, that Mr. Ulib had summoned her for?

"You said there wasn't much I could do about it. Was there something small, then? Any way I can help, you know I'm ready to act."

Mr. Ulib smiled, seeming for a moment his usual placid self.

"I know that, of course. But this is beyond your purview, Livia. I don't need you to act, actually, but to refrain from what you've been doing."

Livia froze, dreading his knowledge of her secret.

"Sir?"

"I know your work on the E List has meant much to you, as it has to me also, of course. The ministry is most appreciative, as is the palace. But this situation with Talbot suggests a possible misuse of influence, a need to tighten the reins. I don't like to think an Elite Citizen has abused the pin's influence, but I'm afraid we have to consider it, protect against it in the future. As of today, recruitment for the E List is suspended indefinitely, as are the meetings and activities of the members."

Livia relaxed a little, unsure what to say. She settled for a look of disappointment.

"I've spoken with a colleague in the culture ministry," Mr. Ulib continued. "The palace has been wanting to expand our music programs, send students abroad to compete. There's a desire to have a national orchestra some day. With your teaching background, we think you'd do well in coordinating the program, bringing together the students, teachers, and parents to raise the standards. Later will come the international arrangements, the good will and attention to detail that you're so good with. I'm sure you'll be fine in the position, Livia. You should do well. Your salary will continue on the same level."

Livia relaxed some more, allowed her downcast look to melt to tears.

"I'll miss working with you, Mr. Ulib."

"I'll miss it also, Livia, but I'm sure we'll be seeing each other sometimes. And before I forget, I must ask you to contact me if you hear any more about Talbot. You may bypass Captain Vua. I have little confidence in his handling this. He only has his commission, not to mention his rank, because his father is a senator. Otherwise he'd be working in the casino. You also need not report on what your friend Mr. Hedges says. He and I have a separate understanding. He seems like a fine man."

He smiled fondly with this appraisal, eyes lingering on Livia's.

"Yes," she replied, "he is."

Leaving the building later, Livia was disconcerted. She'd grown used to her work routine, made it part of her identity, and now it was gone. She turned to take a farewell look at the entrance. One of the guards, misunderstanding, stepped forward and hailed a loafing tricycle driver down the street. Thus Livia was hustled on her way.

She was driven out of the city center and through the commercial ring, skirting the waterfront. She passed the turn for Poseidon's, where she was wont to meet Hedges, and continued toward the city's tattered edge. Near the turn for the airport was another cluster of businesses. She had the driver stop before a clothing store, waited as he drove off, then walked a short distance to the Big Gong restaurant.

It was gloomy inside despite the curtains being open. An elderly couple sat by the window in front, having tea. The only other customer was a big man near the back, eating from several plates with beer bottles next to them. A wraith-like waiter moved in the shadows. Livia allowed her eyes to adjust, then approached the big man as he watched her.

"I got hungry waiting," said Jens. "What did he want?"

Livia hesitated as the waiter drifted near.

"Just tea," she told him.

She then related to Jens her conversation with Mr. Ulib. She spoke calmly until describing the change in her job, unable to control her sense of loss. Her voice wavered and trailed off, but Jens didn't seem to notice, having his own priorities.

"So there's no specific person they suspect?" he asked. "Our man and whoever helped him are as safe as anyone else?"

"Yes."

"What about money? Do you think he'll want more?"

"I don't think so. He'd be in danger himself if he talked."

"Yes, well, just in case—"

He slid an envelope across the table to her.

"I don't think this will be necessary."

"Well, you'll be ready if it is."

Jens called the waiter to clear his dishes, ordered another beer.

"Dr. Numerian appreciates your help," he told Livia. "I believe he mentioned a work visa for you, Europe or America. If things are getting awkward here for you, perhaps we should move ahead on that."

Livia sat up, tried to focus on the proposal, the reality of such a great move.

"Well, what do you say? It would be good for all of us. You'd be safe from investigation and they'd have no link to the project."

"Yes, it's something I want. It just seems so sudden."

"It will always seem sudden. Every great change seems sudden. And drastic, perhaps. But that's what makes it great, its effect. That's why you should want it to happen."

While they conversed in the Big Gong, Mr. Ulib stood at a window of his office in the ministry. His gaze took in he street below, the stone buildings, a bit of sea, the endless sky with its haze of heat. He missed the old life, he realized, the years before technology and economics made the world smaller. He saw himself as a boy, playing with others of his class in the dusty byways, the fragrant gardens. The older generations looked on with hope, relieved that the ravages of war had passed them by. Now he and his country had come to this, shrinking roles that were nonetheless vulnerable to foreign or domestic sabotage. A single incident could spotlight their insignificance, expose their culture as anachronism. With an even worse economy, with disaffection of youth, the Kingdom would be humiliated, a vassal state. He and his colleagues could do little to stop it.

A bird crossed his view, winging up over the buildings. Mr. Ulib watched it pass from sight, replaced in his thoughts by his condo in California, an overseas investment that was now something more. Yes, he thought, I could live among men like Hedges, solid men of business who needn't fear humiliation. Men whose visions are free from uncertainty, obstacles. Leaders. Beacons of rational thought and actions.

17.

Chloe stood in the doorway of the model, looking out at Fauss floating on his back in the cove. She felt rising disdain as he rippled the water with his arms. Behind her the door of the microwave stood open, the remains of an exploded fish steak inside, courtesy of Fauss. It was the second time this week. The other time she had an incinerated calzone to remove before she could have her lunch.

There were many irritations from the man. It wasn't herself, she thought, because she lived with a man she accepted and loved in her way. But Kurt was neat and clean, even stylish, and considerate almost to a fault, whereas Fauss was an obnoxious pig. Besides the kitchen, he always left the bathroom a mess, soiling all the towels and using much of her shampoo. Once she'd returned from birdwatching to find her underwear rifled.

"Try to ignore him," Kurt advised. "He'll be gone any day now."

But the caretaker was still in jail so Fauss was staying longer. Anyway, how was she supposed to ignore him, with those things he did? That might even have been him the other night, rustling around the half-bath window while she was in there–a peeping Tom! And then he had the gall to try to badger Kurt through her, push him into cancelling their construction. That had been another time when Kurt wasn't around.

"You don't seem happy here," Fauss had said with fake sympathy.

She gave him what must have been an ugly look.

"I mean," he went on, "you've hardly arrived and it seems you're ready to leave."

She gave a half-shrug, looked back at her magazine.

"It was Kurt's idea. A retreat for when he needs it." I just go along, she thought to herself but wouldn't say to Fauss.

"Guess it's kind of rough for you," he persisted nonetheless, "an isolated place you really don't want to be."

She crisply turned a couple of pages.

"I'm fine."

"You can easily get out of the contract, you know. I have full authority to approve."

"Talk to Kurt!"

"What's that magazine you're reading?" he asked after a pause.

"A catalog," she almost snarled. "Copper pipe fittings."

Chloe wondered now if she should confront him about the microwave. However burdensome, it wasn't close to being the most serious of his offenses. She didn't want him to think the bathroom peeping and underwear fetish were no big thing for her, maybe even turned her on. She'd better hold her fire, she thought, perhaps complain to someone else.

She turned away from the floater in the cove and prepared to make a salad.

* * *

The door to Popper's cage in the EAU stood wide open. Most of the animals were indifferent to this, but Pundit stared with consternation at the door of the building, not fully closed. It was evening, as it had been for Popper's other forays. Pundit had seen him discover the means of escape, then go outside for increasing periods, always to hurry back. Tonight, however, he'd been out uncomfortably long. Pundit was growing restless, envy stirring in him as the other's freedom grew.

Outside, Popper ambled to the edge of the compound and toward the southern shore. He kept glancing back at first but, catching a familiar scent, scuttled eagerly toward a growth of small trees and shrubs. It gave way to a descending litter of boulders that eventually dotted the sea, but Popper stopped short in the bushes. There was another scent now, and another voice talking with the small human who was kind to him.

"So I was just drifting," Hedges said, "though I guess I looked different to others. Purposeful and such."

"But wasn't there one you cared about most?" Noelle asked. "One you couldn't forget even if you wanted to?"

"I just remember fragments of relationships. Together they might make a whole, but–no, no. There was never the advanced stage, or stages. Where a relationship dominates your life."

"Not that it's good, necessarily. That dominating love."

"No. Maybe that's what I was afraid of. Getting cut off from the rest of life, missing out on things."

"Missing out, yes. There can be so much to life."

"And so little time, as they say."

"So the problem, do you think, may be life itself? That it's too short?"

"Well, yeah. For some people, anyway. There's also *quality* of life, of course. Time moves pretty slow when it's not there."

"But if you have the quality, or it's available to you, then the issue becomes to live longer. Doesn't it? Perhaps as long as you can?"

"Well, sure," Hedges chuckled. "Sky's the limit."

Sensing that his friend wasn't in danger, but also was not available, Popper slunk back from the scene. Behind the cover of brush, he ambled westward toward taller trees on the far reach of Vasquibo's property. He eventually came to the chain-link fence with Reverie Cove beyond. He surveyed the moonlit expanse of land, the gentle sweep of water it enclosed. He noted the two small buildings, the prefab and Hedges's cottage, both dark. The prefab stirred a memory of his cage and he glanced backward, momentarily anxious. But he was energized by discovery so curiosity prevailed, especially when he saw lights to the northwest, the model standing on the far point. Staying to the clear strip by the fence, Popper continued his exploration.

Coming from the opposite direction, puffing casually on his pipe, Kurt reflected as he walked past the properties. The emptiness here, the delays in development, the incompetence, would eventually grate on Chloe. Remoteness, seclusion, even for a little while and with pressing purpose, weren't for everyone. He couldn't expect her to be patient and appreciate its value. It was, after all, her unlikeness to him that he'd found attractive, that was her value. For him and for society she provided a forceful balance to his intensely ascetic, fanatically private nature. She liked the security he offered, the modest celebrity, but her need to leave would accelerate and he would have to accompany her. Her flirting tendency was an outlet for her, might have helped keep them here, but the lack of prospects only frustrated her. She found Fauss repulsive and the hermit was some kind of crazy virgin. Kurt had been amused at first when she'd appeared in Hedges's robe, but Chloe soon put him right.

He approached the prefab, Wang's imminent arrival coming to mind. Perhaps, he thought, a more promising target for her. But what's that—up by the fence?

A bulky form was moving through shadows of trees on the Vasquibo side.

Must be one of the guards, Kurt thought. Looks like he's drunk. Well, Jens said they'd economized in hiring them. You get what you pay for.

Earlier in the day, Kurt had been Jens's guest in the lunchroom of the project. Jens had expressed belief in the use of nanotechnology to prevent entropy in the regeneration of human cells. The tiny robots or organisms infused into the subject might be self-replicating, but would in any case be subject to wireless control from without. Current financial limits kept the project from developing this strategy, Jens confided, but Kurt's involvement might speed things up. Kurt found it mildly interesting, said he'd think about it. Before he left, Jens led him to a corner of the reception area and talked of something else, ideas of Dr. Numerian. Either to supplement a brain transplant, or to program the new brain of a clone, Kurt might assist with mind transfer, the scanning and mapping of a subject's brain to produce complete files of his thought processes, memories, et cetera. Kurt had nodded thoughtfully, seeing the promise in such an application of his software skills. Success would be quite lucrative.

And our fame would skyrocket, he thought now as he walked. Chloe would be pleased, bubbly with joy. She could throw parties, flirt with big shots, stand in for me on talk shows. Perhaps if I float it by her, she won't mind hanging tough awhile on the island, or returning when Vasquibo is ready for me.

He came to the end of the fence near the southern shore, noticed that Hedges's cottage was dark.

Guess our hermit goes to bed early, Kurt thought. Damn him for his purity! Or is it purism here? People have no idea how their idiotic ideals can get in the way, the damage they can do. What an idiot!

He rounded the edge of the fence and found increasingly rocky, uneven footing as he traversed the southern shore. He had to pick his way carefully, his gaze downward except when he paused to view the sea, indigo under the moon. He felt a comforting solitude as his gaze pierced endlessly into infinity. Moving on, he noticed the sea intruding between the outermost boulders, forming a tiny archipelago. He moved inward, toward the rough growth overhead, but soon realized he was not alone. Two voices, male and female, carried to where he crouched near the brush, then ducked into it. He was loath to interrupt a tryst. From his vantage point he was shocked to recognize Hedges, the supposedly purist hermit. Wondering what sort of woman had managed to entice him, Kurt strained awkwardly for a better view. He almost dropped his pipe as he caught sight of Noelle, her face and hands luminous under the moon, her white garment drab by comparison, her rich fall of long black hair, the flash from her eyes.

"I shouldn't have told you so much," she said.

"You can trust me," Hedges replied.

"But can you handle it, the knowledge? Most people aren't ready for it. Not till there's clear, concrete proof. Irrefutable. But I wanted you to see—you know, that you have options."

"I appreciate that. I don't think I can use them, but I appreciate your telling me. And I appreciate *you*."

A hesitation.

"I don't see what can come of this," said Noelle. "I mean, I'm not clear."

"Neither am I, but–"

Hedges seemed at a loss.

"Maybe," Noelle ventured, "we can just share our uncertainty, go down a foggy path together, like children in a strange garden."

Hedges laughed uncertainly.

"Except we're not children," he said. "Especially me."

"But maybe something like it, if you want. The extra life ahead, unending even, and a *better* life–"

Her voice trailed off in a tone of entreaty.

"For *us*?" Hedges finished.

Noelle answered by raising her hands, holding his face when he came forward. They kissed, a profound statement of unity in the moonlight.

Unnerved, Kurt backed into the brush. Above the rocky shore, he moved westward toward taller trees and the boundary fence. What in the world, he wondered, was going on there? Like a goddess she was–glowing in a lab coat–offering eternal life to that nutcase. Kurt recalled his talk with Jens, considered the secrecy of this place, its shadowy backers. He didn't have the full story on this work, but he sensed it was big and he well might want in.

He worked his way around the edge of the fence, back into the Reverie Cove development. Still excited, he relit his pipe and puffed with vigor as he strode northward close to the fence. There was a rustling of brush as someone approached clumsily on the other side. That guard again, Kurt thought. The thick form slowed as it passed him, indistinct in the shadows of trees.

"Good evening!" Kurt declared crisply.

The only reply was a robust snort.

"Good Lord," Kurt muttered, "what an animal!"

He quickened his pace as Popper continued to his cage.

18.

Sweating profusely, Fauss marched through the city center with Wang at his side. It had taken some time to secure the release, and Fauss was angered by the byzantine procedures. Having not received payment, the authorities had insisted Fauss pick Wang up in person, taking full responsibility. The receiver had to complete many forms and they even took his picture. It was finally behind him but irritation lingered, leaving Fauss disinclined to commiserate with Wang. Fauss also had other business here, wanting to make the most of the trip.

"Maybe we should take the tricycle," Wang suggested. "It's very far to the water taxi."

"We're not going back yet," Fauss replied. "I have to see a deputy minister."

"Do you have an appointment?"

Fauss frowned at his companion as if he'd said something senseless.

They arrived at the building and breezed past the outer guards, though one turned to watch until an inside guard met the visitors. They were patted down and allowed to proceed. They soon found Mr. Ulib's outer office, a surprised assistant trying to handle Fauss's intrusion. Overmatched, the assistant checked with his boss and waved the visitors forward, but Fauss raised an arm before Wang.

"Confidential," he stated glibly.

A Truly Higher Life Form

Wang took a seat next to a potted palm.

Within his office, Ulib was expansive, welcoming Fauss and even offering a cigar.

"Thanks, I have a pipe."

"Feel free to light."

Ulib lit up himself, so Fauss brought out his pipe and added his smoke to the billows. Though soaked with sweat and not relishing heat, he wouldn't allow Ulib to seem more relaxed.

"So," said Mr. Ulib, "have you progressed with your work here?"

"Yes," Fauss answered, "I'd say I have. But I'm not finished yet."

He hesitated but Ulib was impassive, nodding slightly behind his desk.

"So you have more to do?"

"I might. I *very well* might. Oh, I've stopped the bleeding, financially I mean, but there's the question of how Deville got into this. This financial *mess*."

"Ah. But surely that's very complicated. They have many other holdings, correct?"

"Yes, and they're being dealt with. But this was by far their shakiest venture, the *coup de grâce* to their financial functioning."

"Sounds rather melodramatic," Ulib smiled.

"It's a serious matter!" Fauss retorted, then caught himself. He had to be smooth on this.

"The thing is," he continued, "I'm not convinced the original purchase of the island, the joint purchase by Deville and Vasquibo, was entirely valid. In fact, it's highly flawed."

Mr. Ulib held his cigar before his face, raised his eyes as if considering.

"What do you mean?" he finally asked.

"Well, there was no real title search. The only history was conveyance to you by another government entity, the official essentially a colleague. And I understand there's this fraternity between you, the 'E List,' creating even more of a conflict."

"The Elite Citizens List has been dissolved."

"Well, it wasn't at the time of the sale. And anyway there's more. The purchase resulted in tenancy in common, immediately followed by an order of partition. The tenancy in common didn't last a single day, so it's questionable whether it legally existed at all. And if it didn't exist, then neither did the sale."

Mr. Ulib shifted in his chair.

"Mr. Fauss, a judge of the Kingdom was present to sign the order of partition."

"Fine, but did it *mean* anything? Were they the *legal owners* yet?"

"It seems you're grabbing at straws."

"Yeah? Well, try this one. What about the lenders for Deville and Vasquibo? You went ahead with partitioning without advising them, getting their okay."

"Vasquibo was fully financed by their investors. Their attorney had full authority."

"Yeah? Well, that wasn't the case with Deville. And now they're gonna take a bath!"

I could use one myself, Fauss thought. He had to restrain himself, stop sweating.

"Deville got the smaller share of island," he continued. "For sure the lenders would've wanted a say on that. You shrunk their collateral."

"The agreement was between the co-tenants, the purchasers if you will."

Fauss sat back, puffed his pipe, he and Ulib eyeing each other through swirls of smoke.

"I assure you," Ulib smiled, "the sale was entirely valid under our laws."

"The document signed by the prince," Fauss fired back, affecting coolness.

"The order of autonomy for Progress Island?"

"Yes. I noticed it was dated the day before the sale."

"So?" Mr. Ulib frowned. "All the documents were prepared in advance. A signature from the palace requires an appointment, so we got it the day before."

"Still," Fauss insisted with half-closed eyes, "the island was then autonomous before the sale. So the mainland did not have legal authority to sell it."

Ulib laughed at this.

"Oh come now, Mr. Fauss. It was clearly a matter of necessity under our laws and customs, which *are* the deciding authority here, you know. And who on the island could have exercised autonomy the day before? The sea birds? A marooned rodent or two?"

Fauss felt the mockery, thought he may have gone too far. His old pushiness might be surfacing–the urge to show all he knew and get credit for it, as he once tried to please his teachers. But he had one more card to play, albeit a weak one, and he couldn't stop babbling.

"Then there's the fishing rights issue," he said.

"Fishing rights?"

"They're being disputed in waters closer to Progress Island than to either of the countries claiming them."

"Well, what about it?"

"It should have been disclosed before the sale as a defect in the property."

Mr. Ulib gave Fauss a probing look, as if verifying he'd heard correctly, then yielded to a deeper laughter than before. He puffed on his cigar, laughing a little more as he drew it away.

"Commercial fishing at Reverie Cove! Is one of your retirees going to bring a fishing boat in, have the crew live with him? Would his neighbors enjoy the stink?"

"These are all solid points I've made," Fauss insisted. "I'd appreciate your cooperation in having the sale nullified and reversing the inappropriate transfer of funds."

He stopped talking, determined not to not water down his position further. Pinned by his owlish glare, Mr. Ulib sobered but, laying aside his cigar, assumed a sympathetic mien.

"Mr. Fauss, with all respect, we both know that is not going to happen. The transaction was entirely proper within the laws and regulations of our Kingdom, which are the only standards that apply here. In addition, there has been considerable building and other changes on the island, so it's no longer the commodity that was sold. You cannot exchange a pair of shoes after you wear a hole in them. I know you have a job to do here, and I respect that. I understand you had to give this a try. But it seems you've exhausted your points and I feel no compunction in, well, setting them aside."

Fauss was silent, seeing the game was over. He rose as if to leave, but Ulib raised a hand.

"There may be another way," he said. "A way I can help you."

Fauss settled back as Ulib touched the intercom on his desk.

"Hold any calls and don't disturb us for a while."

Ulib then got up himself.

"Excuse me a moment. I'll just stretch my legs."

He slowly strode to the window, viewed the city outside, then returned and, to Fauss's puzzlement, unplugged his intercom. Instead of returning to his chair, Ulib came to the front of his desk and sat on its edge close to Fauss, speaking in a hushed tone.

"Now," he said, "perhaps we can help *each other*, sir."

"I'm listening," Fauss replied gamely.

He tried to show no emotion as the proposition unfolded. It was an offer to buy Deville's portion of Progress Island as a new transaction, but with an odd stipulation. Somehow or other, Mr. Ulib was also to receive a worthwhile interest in the island project of Vasquibo Institute. Negotiation with the project was to be done by Fauss, with closing of the Cove sale dependent on his success. Mr. Ulib would remain in the background.

"You'll have your profits from the sale to influence them, and I'll give them a piece or two of the Cove as well."

Fauss was inwardly flustered by the plan, an anomaly in his way of doing things. He was a standard-procedures man who feared the least challenge on ethics. But this was a different place, much different, with its own ersatz rules, and he was desperate to untangle Reverie Cove and Deville Associates. He couldn't just leave things a mess and slink away to retirement, exiting on a profoundly sour note. He was Edgar Fauss, after all, with his reputation as highly competent, his identity as an accomplished man, and these must be perpetuated.

"Let's talk some figures," he said.

In the outer office, sitting by the potted palm, Wang was talking on his cell phone with his son. He'd wanted Bing to know he was free, that his steady employer had come through, that Bing should now focus on stabilizing his own situation. But the son's opportunism asserted itself, presenting Wang again with a painful contrast between Bing and himself.

"No, no, what are you talking about, sue everyone? They would just throw me out of here, deport me. I couldn't get to my job, it would be gone. Sue *who*? The company? About the bail, the delay, I see. Well, I don't know it was their responsibility. And again, the job would be gone. You have to be careful, Bing. You don't throw away something steady just to try a quick grab. Things don't work that way."

On the other side of the palm plant and a little down the hall, Captain Vua stood listening with an eavesdropping device. He was pointing a small wand toward the plant, a wire leading from the wand to an earphone he wore. He'd heard nothing suspicious, confirming the conclusion that Wang had nothing to do with Talbot's death or mishandling of the body. Vua continued to listen, however, since he had no other leads and it made him feel professional. It also occurred to him that Bing sounded rather sleazy, that an Interpol check might be justified. Even if it turned up nothing, thought Vua, the check would enhance his investigation, give it some class.

The door to Mr. Ulib's office opened. Fauss came out striding purposefully, chin raised and holding his pipe. Vua put away his device.

"Let's go," said Fauss to Wang, barely breaking stride.

He breezed past Vua, paying him no notice, but Wang gave a nervous nod. Vua answered with about half his usual smile. He followed them until they disappeared down the stairs, soon to be trailed by a man outside. They'd be returning to the island, Vua saw, so he could turn his thoughts again to the sports car he desired.

19.

Jens stood at the boundary fence, viewing the remains of sunset through the chain-link. This was where Kurt encountered a drunken guard, he'd said, though that was in full night and with the moon blocked by overhanging trees. Not enough to confront someone on, Jens thought. Too bad. He'd wanted from the beginning to have a better-trained unit, but there was parsimony when the project was first launched. It might soon become possible, however, as the value of what was being guarded became obvious.

Viewing the fiery sky beyond undeveloped Reverie Cove, Jens reflected on how he'd been doing well in his home country, how his coming here had been questionable. He was living comfortably, with a solid and developing career before him. The Vasquibo project appeared quite speculative. But, as an employee, he'd had no proprietary rights to his work, no matter how significant, and he was living in a socialist state. The offer to join the project was a chance to rise higher than he possibly could back home.

"Once in a lifetime," he commented aloud.

There were bumps in the road, of course. Financing to date hadn't been focused on the strategies he'd have preferred, ones that drew more on his talents and experience. But he had confidence in Numerian's precision and skill, and in Noelle's knowledge and commitment, so he expected to share in great success. In the meantime he'd apply himself assiduously to his duties as assigned, including this involvement with security.

Turning from the fence, he started back the way he'd come, toward the dock and path to the compound. Seeing the play of reddish light among the trees, however, he decided to take a shortcut. He was just emerging on the other side when he noticed two figures in the distance, standing close and conversing. One of the guards and a woman in lab coat.

"Off-duty, I hope," Jens muttered.

He watched from the shadows as the guard raised a hand to the woman's shoulder. She didn't respond physically though she was speaking to him. The guard removed his hand and looked down, the woman continuing to speak. Feeling suddenly foolish, Jens turned from the scene and crossed the field diagonally, away from the conversing couple.

He'd definitely have to pursue that replacement of the guards, Jens resolved. He'd revisit it with Numerian, stress that Vasquibo must agree with the need. Numerian himself could well appreciate loose ends, loose cannons.

* * *

"Pundit was bad today," Anna informed Noelle.

She'd just entered the synthesis lab, dust showing on her smock and her hair.

"What happened?"

"He started throwing dirt at Popper, scooping up big handfuls. He wouldn't stop and Lun couldn't restrain him. He had to call Rano and they were wrestling with him. I stayed with Popper and got dirty too."

Lun and Rano were two of the guards, Lun usually escorting Anna during the chimps' exercise sessions.

"Are you all right?" Noelle asked.

"Oh, yes. Just dirty. I don't know what's got into him lately. They used to get along just fine. Even after the transplants, at first."

"Well, Popper's been sort of–I don't know–aloof lately. He

won't eat till you leave, just leaves the treat pellets. It started before he got the chromosome, but maybe it's become nuanced in some way, a difference we don't see but Pundit picks up on, resents."

"Are his metabolic figures still okay?"

"Yes, and so are Lipper's."

Lipper was the smaller of the two new males. As a control, he too had been infused with the new chromosome received by Popper.

"So, except for Pundit, we're agreed on the success."

Noelle hesitated, fingering the edge of Terence's notes, thinking of Hedges.

"We need to observe," she said. "The objective is human recipients, mostly transplant patients, and solid marketing potential. We have to be sure, as sure as we can be."

Elsewhere in the compound, Livia sat with Dr. Numerian in his office. The doctor was edgy, as always when taken from his work, and he had Edgar Fauss waiting to see him next. But for now it was enough to deal with this lovely woman, to be gentle in counseling her out. The project was an overriding priority that had to be protected. In another place, at another time, he would have enjoyed continuing to see Livia. But here and now, with a budding investigation by petty officials, he wanted her out of their reach, which unfortunately meant out of his.

"You won't reconsider on Europe? Particularly in Jens's country, you could have a much better arrangement."

"No," Livia answered, "I've thought it through."

"Very well. Jens will be at the Big Gong with everything you need, and he'll accompany you to your flight. You're prepared to travel light?"

Livia couldn't help reflecting. She'd be abandoning most of her wardrobe, perhaps a large part of her identity. Today she wore a sleeveless peach-colored dress for the last time. But she had to sacrifice to avoid raising suspicion.

"Yes, and my papers are all in order. I'm ready to go."

Numerian regarded her.

"You're leaving the place that was your home for so long,

A Truly Higher Life Form

the people you know. Who knows when you can return? Vancouver is a cold city, though there are worse there. It might be difficult to move south, over the border. You might have to marry an American. I can make no promises for after this relocation. You are sure you accept this?"

"Yes."

Numerian allowed a rare smile.

"Then we are finished. I don't know if we'll talk again. The work here will take most of my time and energy for a long time. But I wish you well, Livia, and thank you for your help."

"Thank *you*, sir. Good-bye."

As she passed through the reception area, Livia noticed a pudgy man with glasses scowling at her. One of the guards stood nearby, dividing his attention between Fauss and the entrance to the compound outside. Security was spread thin today, Livia thought. The guard noticed her and murmured something to Fauss, who aggressively snatched up his briefcase and stomped toward Dr. Numerian's office.

Outside, Livia descended the wide path into the common area. It was a pleasant day on the island, the sun warming her shoulders with a soft caress, the sea breeze gentler than she'd expected. She attended to the sound of her steps as she crossed the landing area, her heels on the wood. The tropic buzz was her only accompaniment. How strange it seemed at this moment that she could be at the center of some sort of intrigue. She was innocent, of course, of any evil intent. She'd done as she'd always done to make a life for herself, get by in this backwater of the world. This time it meant taking flight, but it was clearly a necessary step, something she'd have done in her youth if she'd known better and had the means.

She continued down the path on the other side, into Reverie Cove.

What, she wondered, could she say to Hedges? He wasn't just some businessman she was cutting loose. In a way, he was the inspiration for this, her big step. He'd given her perspective on life, a sense of possibilities beyond the Kingdom. We have limits in our natures and in time, but we can accept these limits and grow with what we have, reach the best possible state.

He himself had made a radical change, moving here. She was doing the same in the opposite direction. She'd been refreshed by his attitude, she realized, even before this opportunity, this necessity, took form. It was at the core of her feeling for him.

She passed the northern point of the cove, the model off to her right, reached the beach and turned southward. She walked the path that fronted the properties, a ridge of firmer footing above the sand. She'd worn a smaller-brimmed hat today, anticipating more of a wind, so her view was unimpeded. Dr. Numerian, she realized, had of course been right. She would naturally feel some regret on leaving here. There were so many details that she was used to and were part of her–in her apartment, her work, her memories. She still had her sisters here, and old school friends, the friendly greetings of people who respected her. But then, too, as dusk closed in and shouts rose here and there, and on uneventful weekends, the Kingdom could seem such a small, stagnant, suffocating place. The tacky clubs, children playing in the dirt, tinny music on the street, the smells, the corruption, the archaic and useless customs, the absurd royalty. All of it unchanging, Livia thought, at least during her lifetime. What good was it to be respected in a place that itself had no respect in the world?

She eventually passed the prefab, where Wang was working on the door. He quickly returned her wave and went back to his task. Thinking he might be out of sorts, Livia continued on to Hedges's cottage.

"Ah," he greeted her, "now my day can start."

His usual easy smile, pool cue lightly held in hand.

"Hey," he said, "what's the matter?"

She hadn't moved or spoken, the tear she'd shed her only expression.

"Nothing," she managed.

"The wind maybe," he said, "a little sand."

"Must be that."

He stood aside and closed the door when she'd entered.

"A little calimansi, then? Or maybe a beer?"

"The juice is fine."

They sat in the living room on his couch, leaving space

between them as always when they met. A mild breeze passed through the screens as if they were outside.

"Mr. Wang was very busy," she commented. "Seemed he didn't want to be bothered."

"There was a break-in there. He's replacing the lock. He lives there now since they kicked him out of the model."

"Kicked him out?"

Hedges explained about the Hoagles and Fauss, who was staying longer than expected.

"How awful," Livia responded. "And then the little hut they give him is damaged. I can see why he's not so happy."

"Actually," Hedges grimaced, "that's not the worst of it."

"Oh?"

He hesitated.

"There was a big pile of feces he had to clear out. Sorry."

Livia looked at him wide-eyed, set down her glass.

"God! Who could have done something like that?"

"The people in the model think it was one of the guards from the project. Kurt, the husband, says he saw one of them drunk around here."

Livia shook her head.

"Will you be all right?" she asked.

"Oh, sure. Whoever it was won't come around again. They went into Wang's place because it was empty. He was still tied up in the capital."

They recounted the events leading to the investigation, eventually coming to Livia's new role and the demise of the E List.

"Do I have to return my pin?" Hedges smiled.

"Not that I've heard. You can keep it as a memento."

There was a catch in her throat as she said this, but Hedges didn't seem to notice.

"I don't suppose they're issuing refunds," he continued.

She smiled coyly, as if reminding him that this was the Kingdom.

"The official position is that it's suspended, not abolished."

"Ah, I see. Well, that about covers everything for them."

Livia kept her eyes on her glass as she swirled calimansi juice. She had to get down to business, she knew.

"Mr. Ulib happened to mention—"

She hesitated, not wanting to equivocate with Hedges. But his eyes were waiting, trusting whatever she would say.

"He said you were, you know, reporting to him what happens here on the island."

Hedges seemed surprised at first, then nodded, adjusting his sprawl on the couch.

"That was at the party, when we went to his house. I thought it was part of the E-List thing so I went along with it. And it was info on the project he wanted, not anything about *us*. But how would I know anything about the project? So, of course, I never had anything to report."

Livia waited a moment, drawing on her will.

"I wanted to ask you, well, if you could keep it that way."

He gave her a puzzled look, then chuckled.

"I don't see why not." A hesitation. "Is there something you want to tell me?"

She leaned toward him but stayed on her end of the couch.

"I just don't want you getting involved in whatever's going on. If it's something not so good, you might be hurt. Promise me you'll stay out of it, Irv. If you happen to discover something, don't report it to Mr. Ulib. Please."

Hedges again looked puzzled, deeply this time.

"Sure, but—"

She moved a bit toward him, close enough to take his hand.

"It's important to me," she said.

He smiled. She'd succeeded. She could move on, quickly while she still dared.

"Will you ever go back, do you think?"

"Back? You mean America?"

"Yes. Do you want to at all, deep down?"

"Well, I don't know. I sold everything to come here. Made a clean break. Maybe for a visit, I guess."

"But there must be things you miss, the day-to-day life you knew."

"There's things I'd miss *here*. There's you."

She smiled, almost kissed him. But she held herself back. She knew she should tell him everything, but also knew she couldn't. She could afford no risk.

"I only ask because, if I were to emigrate some day, I think it would be to where you came from. If you were also there, of course, it would be so much better."

Hedges cogitated a bit.

"I don't know what to say. Maybe when I visit, if I do, we could go together and I could give you the tour. No harm in thinking about it."

"No," Livia smiled, "no harm at all."

She kissed him quickly and pulled back.

"Want some more juice?" he asked.

"No, I have to meet the water taxi."

"Ah, this was a day trip."

"Yes. You know I wish it weren't, but these new duties of mine, the hours—"

"I understand. No problem, my dear."

He seemed to take it so easily, she thought. Was there even relief in his voice?

They kissed again when she left the cottage, Hedges watching as she set off down the path. She looked back once and they exchanged waves. Wang was nowhere in sight, his tools picked up and the new lock securely fastened. It flashed in the sun as Livia passed it. The warmth on her shoulders was comforting and she felt a peaceful sense of accomplishment, of moral victory, a setting right of the misdirections her life had taken. There was even, as she felt the breeze off Reverie Cove, a hint of adventure in the air.

20.

The Ulib mansion was locked and quiet, with minimal lighting, its customary state for the late hour. Mrs. Ulib was asleep, resting for travel the next day, but her husband was in the library standing over drafts of letters he'd written. He held a drink and had already drunk more than he normally did. This would have to be his last, he thought, though he was still stirred by the anger he'd had to control while writing.

"He was very upset," his assistant had said, referring to Numerian's call.

"A simple misunderstanding," Ulib assured him. "I'll clear it up."

But word was out, misleading though it was, and rumors spread quickly in the capital. When Numerian had turned down the proposition, Fauss threatened to nullify the original Progress Island purchase, citing the factors he'd given Mr. Ulib. A proposal of mutual advantage had thus transformed to an issue and possible scandal. The career and reputation of a deputy minister were in the cross hairs of lunatic fate.

"I'll be up a little late with something," he'd told his wife. "But don't worry. I'll be fresh in the morning to see you off."

Among the drafts on the table was a memo to his staff at the ministry. It advised them of the scurrilous nature of Fauss's statements: Ulib had sought to know if Vasquibo stock were available, Fauss was angry at not getting his way, Fauss distorted Ulib's request to gain revenge. Simple enough. No doubt they'd been gossiping on their own already, but this would provide an official response to give callers. He presented the same scenario in a follow-up letter to Dr. Numerian, augmenting his phone response. Fauss must be seen as the deal-maker, or attempter, the driving force in the ill-fated proposal. Ulib had also prepared a letter to his nominal superior, a brother-in-law of the king, adding a note of apology for any shadow, however slight and ephemeral, that might fall on the ministry. He took a much firmer tone, waxing indignant, in his complaint to Fauss's commission in America, researched on the Internet by an assistant. If he were lucky, Ulib thought, they'd provide a conciliatory reply he could use.

Still feeling agitated, he carried his drink from the library to the main parlor and the now-locked doors to the veranda. Pushing aside a curtain, he peered into the deep tropical night. He could see beyond the balustrade the sparse lights of the capital's nighttime commerce. It had been largely guided by his unseen hand, now employed in raising alcohol to his lips. Could it be, he wondered, that his judgment was slipping? To involve himself with someone like Fauss–how could it have happened? Maybe it was age, a decline in faculties. He would have to be more careful. He needed to assess himself and his future, make some adjustments.

He tossed off his drink and returned to the library to review his letters.

* * *

Shots in the night.

Hedges bolted upward in bed, hearing them clearly as sleep cleared off. Then, two or three seconds later, a final report.

Crouching instinctively in the dark, he looked out on the south coast. All quiet. He moved to a window looking out on the cove. No one around, Wang's building dark with the door closed, presumably locked. There were lights on the far point but that wasn't unusual. Someone was often up late there.

Hedges ensured his door was locked and went back to bed.

* * *

Wang was at Hedges's door in the morning. It was very early, the sky a soft pink and the sun still blocked by the island's eastern rise. Roused from sleep again, Hedges waited foggily for an explanation, but Wang himself was at a loss for words. Instead, he stood aside and pointed out toward the center of the cove, where a dark hump rose above the shallow water.

"Oh, no," Hedges heard himself saying.

"I can't go out there myself," came Wang's distant voice. "You can understand, I'm sure, after the other time."

Hedges nodded, then shook his head to clear it.

"We'll have to make a call," Wang continued, "but they'll want some information. A description."

They looked out over the peaceful water, the brutal flaw at its center.

"All right," Hedges agreed, seeing no other way. "Let's have a look."

They walked down the beach to the point nearest the body. Hedges waded in, receiving an unaccustomed shock from the chill dawn water. It settled into a vague sense of foreboding as he neared the dark form. A body, curled on its side on the sandy floor, but still dark at close look because—what was it? Unsure it was dead, Hedges kept his distance as he waded around to the face, blurred below the water. An ape, a chimpanzee or something similar, and dead as could be. Though light was meager, Hedges thought he saw a couple of fresh wounds and—could that be scar tissue, in a pattern on the chest? Hedges slapped himself, making sure he was awake, the situation existed, he was standing in the midst of it. Not finding himself back in bed, he turned away, waded back toward Wang on the beach. The caretaker was standing silently with arms folded, wanting no part of this adventure.

"It's an ape," Hedges informed him.

After momentary surprise, Wang was visibly relieved.

"Did you hear some shots last night?" Hedges asked.

But Wang shook his head.

"I slept very soundly. Catching up, you know."

"Yeah. Well, you better make the call. I can come on with the description."

"Do you think it's necessary? It's only an ape."

Hedges pictured the wounds, the pattern of scar tissue.

"There's a little more involved, I think. We better get them out here."

Captain Vua and team arrived an hour and a half later. Hedges saw them lingering as they passed the north end, talking with someone who'd emerged from the model. After some discussion, the group continued southward toward the spectacle. Wang stood at Hedges's side. They could see now that it was Fauss with the police.

"Relax, Mr. Wang," smiled Vua. "Your employer has explained what happened."

"Actually," said Hedges, "we're not clear on that ourselves."

"Very simple," Vua replied glibly. "There was an intruder by the house, this animal. It was a threat to the people inside, so Mr. Fauss shot it."

Fauss nodded in agreement.

"But, captain," Hedges said softly, "have you read my description of the body?"

Vua's expression stiffened.

"We will deal with that later, sir. As you can see, we are processing this and not leaving it for the refuse barge."

He turned to the other police and briskly gave orders. A bag for the body was laid out and Vua's men waded into the cove. They clearly found their task distasteful and were awkward handling the body. Captain Vua smiled at the onlookers.

"They are not trained for apes. You are getting special service today."

"Could they use some help?" Hedges offered.

"Do not trouble yourself, sir. They are well enough paid."

It occurred to Hedges that no one seemed curious as to why there was an ape of this size on the island. Wang wanted to avoid involvement, Fauss was grateful he hadn't shot a human, and the police were content for now with removal. Well, he wasn't about to take on the issue himself. The acknowledged hermit would live and let live.

To the north, through a window of the model, Kurt stood watching as he waited for the coffee maker to finish. He'd awoken to Fauss's voice nearby, excitedly talking to police about the shooting. They'd moved on by the time he was dressed, so he'd picked up the action with Chloe's binoculars. The body they were recovering was unconscionably decomposed for being only hours dead, or else it was some kind of animal. Kurt left the window and moved out to the veranda for a better look. As he began to raise the binoculars, he was alerted by his peripheral vision to several people outside the boundary fence, watching the body recovery from Vasquibo's side. Crouching back to the doorway, Kurt raised the binoculars and saw Jens Jenssen with one of his guards and the lab worker who'd kissed Hedges by the boulders. She wore a brimmed hat and was indeed very pale, but she lacked the glow she'd shown in the moonlight. She had a pained expression, while Jens appeared angry, the guard at a loss. They never turned toward Kurt since their attention was riveted to the scene on the beach.

This must involve the project, Kurt thought. There's been some slip, a loss of control. Jens might be interested in that dalliance by the boulders. A talking point anyway, a contribution I can make. They'll need to tighten the screws now. I can help and get a bigger foot in the door. What's to lose?

Kurt retreated to have his morning coffee, his shame for spying on Hedges and Noelle eclipsed by the prospect of gain.

* * *

The commission chairman sat at his highly polished desk, a scattering of documents before him. Clouded light fell from the windows behind him, which overlooked tree-lined boulevards. The chairman, husky and genial, middle-aged, looked up and smiled as an elderly visitor poked his head in the doorway.

"Come on in, Frank. Glad you beat the rain."

A Truly Higher Life Form

Frank entered spryly and took a padded seat before the desk.

"Haven't been in town for a while. Wore the suit with the least holes."

The chairman laughed.

"You're always welcome here, holes or no."

Frank nodded.

"Thanks, Don. But, ah, I guess there's some business. Right?"

"I'm afraid so. I don't mean to drag you out of retirement, but something's come up and, well, I decided I should get your input."

"My input? Sure, Don. Anything I can do to help."

The chairman straightened, looked down at the papers on his desk.

"Edgar Fauss. You were his mentor, I believe."

Frank's eyes widened.

"Why, yes. But that was a long, long time ago."

"Before my time," Don acknowledged. "But with the situation we have–a mess really, Edgar at the center–I need to tap into your relationship with him."

"A mess? Edgar? But he was always so scrupulous. No one more eager to please, at least where his standing was concerned, promotions and such. And he'd always been that way, it seems. He confided to me one night–we'd had a drink or two–that he'd been nicknamed 'brown' or 'little brown,' short for 'brown nose,' by his old schoolmates. It went on less openly when he tried to become a professor, and I suppose with the state when he first started. But he's nonetheless tried to do everything right with the commission. He's been assigned as receiver as much as anyone, I think."

"Which brings us to the current problem. Bear with me, Frank."

Don recounted the predicament of Deville Associates, Fauss's being assigned as receiver, his decision to focus on the Reverie Cove development.

"He felt he needed to go there, try and turn it around somehow, be super-scrupulous."

Frank gave a tentative smile.

"Yes, that's Edgar."

"Trouble is, he was due back a long time ago and," Don nodded toward the documents, "it appears things have gone haywire."

He bent over his desk and selected a multi-paged letter.

"We've heard from an attorney for Vasquibo Institute, the other outfit on the island. He says Edgar tried to muscle them into selling an interest in their business, using corrupt local officials and bribery. They wouldn't go along and so Edgar shot–yes, *shot*–a chimpanzee that was valuable in their research. There's a local police report attached."

Frank was open-mouthed but speechless.

"Then we have this letter from a deputy trade minister, name of Ulib. He's 'most indignant,' he says, about Edgar misrepresenting him for his–for Edgar's–own gain."

"What do those ribbons mean?"

"Nothing. It's just the way they do things there."

Don moved on to a legal document on long sheets of paper.

"This one has 'pain in the ass' written all over it. Someone named Bing Wang–yet another country involved–is suing everybody in sight for the unjust detention of his father, including Edgar and Deville for 'employee abuse.' Wang senior is apparently custodian at this Reverie Cove. He was being held on some minor charge, later dropped, and Edgar refused to pay the bail for him."

Frank's face was a mask of worry.

"Purely financial principles, I'm sure. Edgar's enthusiasm could sometimes cloud his judgment. I did my best with him but–"

"Well, he was outside the box on this next one, I'd say, and it went through the governor's office!"

Don held up some hand-written sheets and a typed directive with familiar letterhead and signature. Frank waited apprehensively.

"It's from one Chloe Hoagle. She and her husband have a house on order at this Reverie Cove. They're living in the model till it's built. Our guy has seen fit to plant himself in the model

A Truly Higher Life Form

with them, an extended stay now. Sounds like she's going nuts with him there. Complains about his personal habits–it gets pretty gross. Also his way of talking to her, obnoxious. She even says he's into, well, voyeurism."

"What! No!"

Don stared grimly at the older man.

"There's more, of course. The other concerns of Deville left unattended, Edgar's duties as commissioner on his colleagues' backs. But you can see where this is going."

Frank nodded reluctantly.

"I'm meeting Judge Nichols for lunch. I want you to come with me, Frank. Nichols remembers you, respects you, and knows about your connection to Edgar. It'll make it easier for him to pull Edgar off, assign a new receiver. Especially if you're the replacement."

Frank was alarmed.

"Me? But I'm retired! And how could I do that to Edgar?"

"It's for his good as much as anyone's. I could take it, of course, but that would look disciplinary to Edgar, and giving it to a younger commissioner would crush his ego. You're the most gentle recourse, Frank, the one he can live with best later. And we have to get him out of that *place*. That's what he needs more than anything."

In the end, Frank was convinced. The two men left the office together, resigned to entering the drizzle that flecked the room's windows. A wall clock signaled the imminent lunch hour and, with it, the end of the labored achievements of Edgar Fauss.

21.

Dr. Numerian was examining Pundit in the EAU, occasionally dictating a change in regimen to Anna. She took notes on a clipboard while Lun, the guard, stood nearby.

"He's been acceptably calm lately, you say?"

"Yes. No real hostility since we lost Popper. We've paired him with Lipper on the exercise and there's been no problems."

"Hm. Well, let's just bring him along metabolically. We'll see what direction we want to take later. We might try an incremental approach, give him another transgene, or–well, a totally different strategy."

He patted Pundit's shoulder.

"Back to your cage now, my friend."

He signaled to Lun, who came and led Pundit away.

"You're keeping an eye on the cage locks?"

"Yes," said Anna. "It seems it was just Popper. No imitators."

Numerian nodded somberly.

"We've taken a blow. But that just means we work harder, more carefully."

"I'll do everything I can, doctor."

"I know you will, Anna."

As he left, the doctor passed Lun, who was dutifully checking cage locks. The guard waited a moment after the door closed, slowly smiled, then casually walked back to Anna at the examining table. She smiled herself but didn't turn at first.

"Now, what are you up to?" she asked.
"We are alone here, Anna."
"Alone, hey? I see quite a few eyes on us."

Lun glanced around at the animals. He was the youngest and handsomest of the guards, shiny waves of hair atop his deeply golden features. He and his comrades were imports from another, much larger group of islands.

"Let's visit the town, Anna. You should take a break from this."

"They might not be friendly there just now. What happened to Popper, before that Mr. Talbot–they might be very suspicious, not want us around."

"So who knows? Just some police, some office people."

"Oh? I don't know, Lun. Word spreads fast in a small place. There's superstitions, fear. I wouldn't be comfortable there."

He looked at the floor, disappointed. Anna touched his arm.

"We're in a special situation here," she said. "We can't just do what we want. Not right away, I mean."

Lun drew a breath as he looked up.

"We think we will be gone from here soon," he said. "Seems Jenssen is bringing Europeans to replace us. To cover his ass with the company over Popper."

"Oh, I'm sorry."

But Lun shook his head.

"When it happens, maybe it can be good for us, you know? I can take you from here to my country. We can have a life where no one can bother us."

Anna smiled sadly. He didn't know she'd achieved that *here*.

"But Lun, there are many details. Besides my work here, I have no status in your place. I don't have good papers. They might not even let me in."

"I could come for you in the outrigger boat, with my friends. We'll take you over the sea at night and sneak into my village by the inlet. No one would see us in the tall reeds."

Bemused, Anna studied his earnest expression, tenderly touched his face.

"My friend," she said, "what can I say to you?"

Outside, Dr. Numerian had paused in returning to his office. He lit a cigarette and walked more slowly to the east, toward the heliport, getting beyond the buildings and gaining a view of the sea. He considered its vastness, immutability, and the futility of working to change much in the world. His wife in the distant homeland waited for his return, just as she'd always waited in their dull, melancholy city for him to return from studies, then practice, then teaching, then research. And now even here, in a place and time that had promised redemption, he was again sidetracked by the type of doltish bureaucrats that had been his bane. Disgusted, he flicked aside his cigarette. He'd do what he could to pick up the pieces, move on as he'd just advised Anna. Turning back toward the compound, he strode briskly to his meeting with Jens and Noelle.

They were waiting for him in his office, surprisingly relaxed he thought. He sat behind his desk, moved some papers aside, removed his glasses.

"Pundit's fine," he smiled at Noelle. Then, the smile fading: "I wish I could say the same about the state of our project." And to Jens: "Have you mentioned Hoagle's remarks?"

"Yes. Noelle bears them out, more or less, but there's actually much more to it. An opportunity, perhaps a great one."

He looked to Noelle, Dr. Numerian turning to her also.

"I've been with Mr. Hedges a number of times," she said in a clinical tone. "He's age 63 and appears to be in excellent physical health. Despite his solitary ways, he seems psychologically normal. I think he has reserve intelligence he can draw on. He's resourceful, and his judgment in moving here might well have been sound, based on inner knowledge of his own needs. He enjoys life and I believe he'd want to extend it."

Numerian's expression brightened. He reached to retrieve his glasses.

"And this assessment is not colored by, ah, personal involvement?"

"No," Noelle replied calmly. "The opportunity Jens

mentioned was *produced* by our 'personal involvement.' I am the reason he wishes to live longer than he would naturally."

"Hoagle said she looked like a goddess out there," Jens injected, "the moonlight and all. Hedges must think so, too."

"Well," Numerian grinned, "it's nice that others share our opinion."

He sat back and swivelled to one side, reflecting.

"He's a few years younger than our target population for marketing. Also not rich enough, but of course we won't be charging him. Ideally, assuming Popper was a success, we should do full organ replacement and then the chromosome. The larger male chimp is now primed as a donor, is he not?"

Noelle nodded.

"Laffer," she said.

"What?"

"That's his name, Laffer."

"Maybe we can afford to ourselves," Jens smiled. "We seem to be back on track."

"Just so we stay focused," said Numerian. "There's much to be done. We need to know, Noelle, how receptive Hedges is to organ replacement. Strictly speaking, it needn't be done, though it would lengthen his use of the chromosome. Carefully feel him out on that. Of course, he must know what he's getting into and the options must be explained."

Back in the EAU, Lun had left and Anna prepared to take the dogs out. She attached leads to two but would take the third out separately. He hadn't been keeping up since a recent hormone experiment. Anna felt compassion for the animals and was aware it could become excessive, but wasn't worried about it. Her motivation in her work here–the need for it, her colleagues, gratitude to Vasquibo–ensured her loyalty to requirements of the project. Lun was nice but, besides being younger, was proposing a type of existence that she'd long decided was fantasy.

Exiting the EAU, Anna and her charges walked to the hill on the southeast of the island. It was here that helicopters circled as they approached the heliport. Anna looked to the sea and then back over the compound, felt a warmth rise within her.

Only about fifteen people, she thought, and not even all this small island, and yet it's the world for me. She felt the wind in her chestnut hair, the lab coat flutter on her compact body.

"Still," she said aloud, "it's nice to be noticed that way."

* * *

In a city across the ocean, Livia arrived downtown and alighted from the bus she'd taken. She was still getting used to wearing a coat, even lightweight, but today would be good practice. She was going to take a "whale watch" tour on her day off. It was still some distance to the hotel lobby where the tour began, but Livia didn't mind the walk. It was good to be striding along here, a full adult again, after the week with her employer's children.

"Spare change, lady?" someone said.

"Help me out, ma'am?" said another.

She was getting better at navigating these stretches, but she'd take a different route on her return. It was nice enough here overall, but the last thing she needed was to be reminded of the world she'd left.

She noticed a disturbance ahead, slowed her pace a bit.

A crowd of mostly women was milling about outside a government building. A speaker was shouting into a megaphone from where she stood on a bench. She sounded angry but Livia couldn't get her gist. Others were cheering, however, some with signs referring to a public law, a policy, and respect for domestic workers. Livia noticed that the women were of various ethnicities, but the majority seemed to come from her part of the world.

"Come to join us, sister?"

It was a young woman in a windbreaker, some literature in her arms.

"No, I was just walking. I saw this so I stopped."

"It's about immigration policy, the injustice. You are familiar?"

"Injustice?"

"For domestic workers. The rule we cannot have our real professions. We are teachers, nurses, even doctors. But we must stay domestic workers because that's our visa."

She was a compatriot of the guards on Progress Island, Livia realized.

"Can you not go south, to the States?"

"That's very complicated, almost impossible. Don't you know that? That's why we're here. Are you just a tourist?"

"No, I work for a company."

"Oh, good for you. But can you still join our march today?"

"I'm sorry, I have an appointment."

"Well, here. Take a booklet. It's about our movement."

"I'm afraid I don't read your language."

"That's just the cover. The inside is English."

Livia wished her well and continued on to the whale watch. Clearly, she thought, one could do worse than take the course she'd taken. She too was a sort of domestic worker, but her employment with the family was under the aegis of Vasquibo Institute. She'd chosen it over another option, as a stepping stone, with a much better prospect for mobility than the women in that crowd. But it was good they could meet at least, speak and vent their feelings.

22.

The water taxi put in at its customary pier on the waterfront. Though Hedges had left messages for Livia via phone and email, she was nowhere in sight. He wasn't surprised, given their loss of contact. He strode past the waiting tricycles, one of which he'd normally ride with her, and headed on foot for the city center.

Hedges hadn't forgotten Noelle in his concern for Livia. His involvement with Noelle, though, and what it could mean for him, was something totally different from his friendship with Livia. Because friendship, really, was as far as he could go with Livia, no matter how intimate they were. There was his age, in addition to his nature, and the limits also of Livia's needs, which were subject to scheduling. Theirs was something mature and in the traditional world. With Noelle, however, there was something that challenged the usual boundaries on relationships and living in general. It was outside the scope of his experience, of most people's probably, and he felt compelled to follow through. Livia wouldn't like it, of course, so it would no doubt affect their relationship. But at present that wasn't an issue since he didn't even know where she was. And he was deeply concerned about her, felt the need to find her, his involvement with Noelle notwithstanding.

Hedges walked through the city's commercial zone, eventually reaching the banks and government buildings at its core. He asked directions to the culture ministry and soon found it in a less imposing building. A young man struggling with a copy machine directed him to a woman who might be Livia's supervisor. They talked in an open lounge area.

"Miss Poe is no longer with us. She was supposed to work with music programs, but she did very little. She only came in a few days."

"Have you heard from her since she came to work?"

"She sent a postcard from the Auckland airport. It simply said she resigned. Goodbye. Just like that."

Hedges looked away, tried to focus. A small indoor fountain trickled nearby. The supervisor, about Hedges's age, gave him an appraising look.

"You were close to Miss Poe?"

"I was on the E List," he managed. "We did E List business."

He thanked the woman and retraced his steps to the street. So Livia was gone, he kept thinking, and without even telling him. There was obviously much more to it, but why didn't she let him know? Maybe he hadn't really known her. They'd been close, but maybe just within a compartment of her life. The E List compartment, just as he'd told that woman. He was bothered by this thought, accelerated his pace to the trade ministry.

Perhaps noting his height and purposeful gait, the outside guards straightened as Hedges reached the building. The inside guard greeted him but didn't pat him down, accepting his claim to be a friend of Mr. Ulib. Hedges made his way to the outer office, sitting by a potted palm while Ulib finished with a trade representative. He seemed surprised to see Hedges, but was affable.

"We haven't had occasion to meet lately," he commented.

"I'm afraid I haven't learned much about the project, Vasquibo. That you don't already know from Captain Vua, I mean."

Ulib waved dismissively.

"Don't bother with that, Mr. Hedges. Apes in the water, what do we care? Just so they're not loose in the capital."

He laughed, then suddenly sobered.

"Of course, you had *that person* out there, now thankfully

recalled. We certainly don't need *his* type around here, a troublemaker."

Hedges nodded agreement, restless to move on.

"I was wondering about Livia," he said. "I haven't heard from her for some time and I haven't been able to contact her."

"Have you tried at her apartment?"

"No, not yet."

"It might be worth a try. I too haven't talked with her recently, and I suppose I had cause for concern. They called from the culture ministry and said she stopped coming to work. I had no explanation for them, I was very surprised. I hope she's all right."

"Would the police be any help?"

"No, I'm afraid not."

"But you must have some influence with them."

"Indirectly, yes. But they'd be no help on this. They don't really look for 'missing persons,' only take reports. And there's Livia's reputation we must think of."

"What about her relatives, her friends?"

Mr. Ulib's expression brightened.

"Yes, she has two sisters she sees, and their children, her nieces and nephews. Here, I still have her emergency card."

He opened a desk drawer and picked through a card file, pulling a card out.

"One of them is here on the main island, the other would cost you a boat trip. Another one, that is. I'll give you the address of the close one."

He copied it onto a message slip.

"It's across the island by the resorts. She has a little store there, I think. You take the airport road but keep going past the turnoff. Your driver should know."

Hedges took the slip.

"I suppose she might just be traveling," he ventured, recalling their last conversation. "An impulsive getaway."

Mr. Ulib looked dubious.

"Very unlike her, I'd say. Especially giving no notice at work, or to yourself for that matter. Correct?"

Hedges nodded in agreement.

"What about emigration? Did she ever express any—well, not plans exactly but, say, opinions about it?"

"Not to me," Ulib responded. "But then, that doesn't mean much." He smiled. "I'm sure that—given the right opportunity, something feasible for them—many of our citizens would emigrate."

Hedges discreetly feigned surprise.

"They don't like it here? The nice climate, the culture and traditions and all?"

"You can love your home and still want to leave it. The lure of another place, one that meets your needs better. Especially as one grows older."

"Yes, of course. I guess I should understand."

"It's simply one of the choices we make, freely or in response to crisis. Some might see it as destiny."

Hedges thought of Noelle, couldn't respond.

"I appreciate your coming to our country," Ulib resumed, "a successful businessman from a stable, powerful country. Also the responsible way you've conducted yourself. You're certainly an 'elite citizen,' with or without the pin!"

When he left the building later, Hedges boarded a tricycle and gave directions to Livia's building.

They moved out of the city center and through the commercial ring, then some shabby neighborhoods and vacant land, eventually arriving in the upscale residential area. Hedges had the driver wait on the street, which was quiet and had bowls of flowers hanging on street lamps. He rang Livia's bell in the building's lobby but, as expected, received no response. He repeated the exercise, then tried the door to the stairs but found it locked. There was no one in sight around the building or nearby. Hedges returned to the tricycle.

"Take me to Poseidon's restaurant," he told the driver.

Arriving at their familiar haunt, he let the driver go and sat at a shaded table on the terrace. With Livia he'd have gone inside, but he didn't want to get too comfortable now.

"An old-fashioned, sir?" asked a familiar waiter.

"Better make it a beer today. No, wait! I'll have a whiskey sour."

Livia's drink. As if she were there, a gesture. But everything pointed to her being gone, Hedges realized, and with finality. Perhaps the most he could hope for was to know why. The waiter came promptly with his drink, asked if he'd like to order food. Glancing over the menu, Hedges asked for basil mussels with sweet ginger pineapple, a squid salad on the side. He smiled as he spoke, thinking it an order that Livia might give.

"By the way," he added, "You know that lady I sometimes meet here?"

"Yes, sir. Very nice lady."

"I was wondering, has she been in here recently? Since the last time you saw us both?"

"No sir, I haven't seen her. Is there a problem?"

"No, no problem. I was just wondering if she's back from a trip."

The waiter smiled and went away. When he returned with the food, Hedges re-ordered the beer he'd canceled earlier. He needed to adjust, he told himself, to understand that the little world he'd arranged here for himself was not his final destination. His meetings with Noelle, her unique allure, and what she'd said about the project showed his life was not without promise. Though it didn't feel good now, Livia's absence might just accommodate a new and better scheme of things. At the same time, munching this food in their meeting place, he retained a strong sense of her, a relationship happier than his previous ones, albeit less intense. He needed to make a smooth transition, keep Livia in his heart as he moved forward toward–what? He wasn't at all sure, really. But, with Livia gone, he was more than ever driven to find out.

Finishing his meal, Hedges asked the waiter to call him a cab. The trip to see Mona, Livia's sister, would be wearing in a tricycle, especially in the midday heat after taking whiskey and beer. Hedges was again reminded of his age, his stage in life, and moved to stay in the shade. He soon saw a boxy limo arrive in front of the restaurant.

The driver knew the route and there was very little traffic, especially after they passed the turnoff for the airport, the cluster of small businesses around the junction. Hedges blinked at a flash of reflected sunlight from the sign of the Big Gong restaurant. They moved into a countryside with shanties and struggling farms, as well as stretches of scrubby growth, apparently useless. They passed a wetland area with children trying to catch things in the water. As they came to a gigantic hill of garbage the driver glanced back at Hedges.

"Almost there," he said.

They arrived among the resorts that neighbored the wide sandy beaches of this district. There were cross streets again, the driver turning into what seemed the main commercial stretch.

"You will try the casino while you're here?"

"No, just the one stop. Then straight back."

The driver grunted, evidently bemused. He soon located Mona's store and got out for a smoke while Hedges went inside. Small souvenirs and gift items, all quite cheap, were displayed throughout the interior. Hedges wondered how anyone could make a living here, then noticed a booth near the back festooned with lottery tickets, colorful and in various languages. There was also a chalk board with odds for boxing matches and a "game of the week," probably rugby. An old man with a soft drink was chatting and laughing with a young man behind the window. Hedges was about to approach them when Mona herself appeared through the postcards and sunglasses. He explained who he was.

"Yes," she said, "Livia mentioned you."

She looked younger than Livia, hair cut shorter but with facial similarity. She seemed less tall, but perhaps was fuller figured. A different sort of life, different work, could do that, Hedges reflected.

"This is your store, then?"

"Yes, with my husband. That is my son." She nodded toward the lottery window. "We have two others, another son and a daughter."

It occurred again to Hedges how little he'd actually known about Livia.

"It seems maybe Livia left the Kingdom," he said.

Mona was mute but held his gaze.

"I was wondering if you'd heard from her."

"Just one call. She's gone, yes, but she's okay."

Hedges waited but she didn't volunteer more.

"Any idea why she left? When she's coming back, if she is?"

"She–" Mona stopped to think. "Livia was disenchanted. Oh, not with you, or with any one person. She'd just gone a long time, not married and–well, she just got tired of things here, with the place. She had a feeling she had to get out. That's how I understand it."

"Think she'll be back?"

"I don't know. I'm sorry." She glanced toward the back of the store. "Wait, there's something I can give you. I'll be right back."

She returned with a key.

"It's for Livia's apartment. She left it with me long ago. She said when she called to go and take what I wanted, that there wasn't much. You can use it if you want, see what you can find about her. She wouldn't mind, I think."

Hedges was moved. Livia was gone, but here was this kindness through her sister.

"I'll get it back to you," he promised.

The drive back to the city was pleasant for Hedges. Though Mona had essentially confirmed his fears, there was enough of Livia in her to soften the blow, to make it manageable. Then there was this key, turned in his fingers as ragged fields slipped past. A trust between the two sisters, now passed on to him. So he was still involved with Livia after all.

They reached her building and Hedges dismissed the driver, the cab fare grown quite high. The key was the type that opened both stairway and apartment doors. A strange, suggestive stillness hung in the air as he entered Livia's abode, emphasizing her profound absence. The light, modern furniture sat as always, the bed was made in the bedroom, and many of her clothes remained. Hedges could see, though, that many smaller items were missing. A notable exception was a "Home Sweet Home" sign he'd once brought here in a lighter moment. As he stood in the waning light from outside, he noticed a blue ribbon draped over the sign and tied in several loose knots. Between the knots were three shiny objects. Moving closer, he saw that they were irregular in shape, reddish, metallic–copper pipe fittings! Hedges stood staring at the once-familiar objects, their proximity to the sign, and imagined Livia arranging this. Feeling nostalgic warmth, he lifted the ribbon off the sign and carefully stored it in his pocket, fittings still attached. This was all he'd take; Mona could have the rest. He'd mail her the key from the waterfront post office.

23.

Chloe sat at the bedroom window with her birdwatching binoculars. She was wearing her new swimsuit, a modest but stylish one-piece, and scanning the far side of the cove for signs of Hedges. She also ranged out to sea and back across the cove to the beach and properties. There was no sign of Hedges, but she sighted Wang inspecting some building materials that had been dumped on numbers 13 and 15. The new receiver had gained clearance for the house they wanted on number 14. Chloe was happy to be rid of Fauss, feeling close to Kurt again with the intruder gone, but also felt the insatiability that had claimed her at puberty. The peace here didn't calm it, just gave it free rein. She now considered Wang as he adjusted a tarp over cement sacks.

"Nice enough body," she murmured, "but that mind-set. Too much of a work thing."

She waited a while longer for Hedges to show, then got up and stretched, liking the swimsuit's feel on her body. She knew she was slightly ungainly, but why should that matter when she was slim, and feminine, and willing to relate warmly with a quality man? She got along well at Kurt's side with the various people they met, those that mattered at least, her occasional forays simply ornaments on their successful life. Kurt had his own idea of success, of course, always wanting more, needing to *affirm* himself as much as possible. And so here they were on this island, hiding and recuperating, establishing a resource for later. Well, it was part of being married to him, which wasn't all that bad.

She stepped into her sandals and clopped out to the stairway, descended to the ground floor of the model. Kurt was bent over his laptop at the dining table.

"Work or play?" she asked.

"Oh, let's see. Playing at work, I suppose. Sprucing up programs before I see Numerian."

"Hm," she intoned, glancing at a jumble on the screen. Kurt's work always bored her.

"Going for a swim?"

"Maybe." A hesitation. "Kurt, would this extend our stay here, your getting involved with Vasquibo?"

He stopped pecking keys.

"I don't know. Not necessarily. We'll have to see what works out, if anything."

She moved her hand from the chair to his shoulder.

"And what works for *me*? You said it was just a season here–get acquainted with the retreat, move on. Back to the flow, the real people."

He covered her hand with his own.

"Darling, I know what I said. And I know I want the best for us, you especially." He smiled. "But you know, we do have a new house going up here. That's something else we have to attend to, anyway."

Chloe wasn't moved.

"That hairball said they put these up fast, almost as fast as that box for Wang."

"Well, we know better now than to trust Mr. Fauss, don't we?"

She withdrew her hand.

"It's dull here, Kurt. We have to face that. Maybe not for you, with your number crunching or whatever, but I'm different. I have–"

She was struck suddenly by the earnestness in his face. She realized that, whatever her other needs, she needed him more than anyone. She returned her hand to him, caressing the side of his face.

"I think I'll swim now."

"Sure."

Instead of heading right to the water, however, Chloe walked down the beach to their home site. Wang would still be puttering around, she thought, and she could use his conversation, however vapid, to dilute the effect of Kurt's. Then she could lose herself in the cove, relax freed from guilt.

Wang was talking on his cell phone, however, sitting on some lumber with his back to Chloe as she approached. She waited a few moments, thinking the call might be brief.

"I'm very lucky to still have this job," Wang was saying. "If they hadn't removed Mr. Fauss, he'd have fired me instead. Your lawsuit would've been disastrous for all of us. Your uncle can't save the business by himself, and Tia would never have the money for university."

Wang listened, Chloe a short distance behind him.

"No, Bing. You must drop the lawsuit. It's not on my behalf, no matter what the lawyer says. There's no guarantee of ever getting anything and everyone can be hurt, as I've said. Don't you have other prospects, maybe for a better job?"

Another interval, Wang grunting a couple of times.

"RV components, I don't know. Gas prices the way they are, that's probably why they're selling cheap. Still, it sounds better than the other thing–loans of credit ratings, did you say? Sounds very shaky. So, how were you going to finance that RV move?"

Chloe stepped away toward the water.

The sun was not yet at zenith and there were more clouds than usual, though still white and scattered. The water would be rather cool but still looked inviting as Chloe approached it. She wanted to be refreshed. It occurred to her that this view of the cove, its opening to the sea, was ideal and would always be theirs from the new house. Kurt chose well. It separated him from men who floundered in life. Still, with all he gave her and allowed her, she constantly felt the need to be renewed. She waded into the water, eventually reaching a depth for swimming. The water invading her swimsuit provided its usual ephemeral thrill. She moved with her long, awkward strokes toward the mouth of the cove, not intending to exit but to hover there, at the gateway to riskier waters. That was her method, she realized; she was basically a flirt. She actually went farther than flirting but never really risked anything. She always pulled back before anyone could claim her from Kurt.

Treading water between the points, Chloe sighted Hedges on the beach, walking from the landing area toward Wang. He'd arrived on the water taxi, she supposed. Given the time of day, he must have been on the big island overnight, probably with that woman. Chloe recalled her binocular view of Livia, the other woman's graceful walk as she visited Hedges. Chloe again felt the rising envy but angrily dismissed it as being ridiculous. She watched the two men on the beach proceed to the prefab, perhaps seeking liquid refreshment. She began swimming toward the southern point, Hedges's cottage, but slowed and stopped before touching bottom. She was on track to what she'd done the other time, she realized, and she didn't want that. It wouldn't work and, however brief, there would be the humiliation. Maybe more this time, with him just back from that woman and drinking now with Wang, with her in the modest swimsuit she bought to appease his shyness.

Chloe reversed course, swimming across the cove's mouth to the narrowing beach before the model.

Kurt wasn't around, apparently on the errand he'd mentioned. Chloe shed her swimsuit and had a shower, using far more soap than was necessary. She needed to be cleansed of something deep, she thought–her whole self. She needed to start life anew, as the birds did with each short flight, each call or chirping. A purified present, affirmation–I exist! She sighed as the warm water rinsed her, felt innocent in its flow despite her desires. Later she took her time drying, then nestled in her lilac robe since Hedges's was returned. Wanting to clear her mind and drowsy from the shower, she stretched out on the bed and quickly dozed off.

The sound of a door slam awakened her. Still cozy on the bed, she heard Kurt at the fridge and liquor cabinet, preparing an early drink. Celebrating, perhaps? She warily raised herself, gained her slippers, and descended the stairs.

"Total washout," Kurt informed her. "They're somehow back on track with the initial strategy. No resources now for alternatives." He shrugged. "I don't know, I guess they found another smart ape."

Chloe had to turn away, hide her involuntary grin.

Thank you, ape, she thought.

* * *

The magnate and his doctor walked from the 18th green to the clubhouse, their well-tipped caddies retreating to store the clubs. The weather had been iffy when they started out, but the sky had cleared nicely and signaled a pleasant, cool evening. They took a table on the terrace.

"Bring us each another in fifteen minutes," the magnate told the server who brought their drinks. He was an exacting, pre-emptive man who left as little as possible to chance. He lit a cigar and looked out over the grounds, his face assuming its business expression. It was time for some news, good or bad.

"So, do we have a green light, then?"

The doctor, deferential as he'd been on the course, leaned forward.

"Almost, if you're sure you want to go ahead."

The magnate laughed.

"What other direction *is* there at my age, except down?"

"You're healthy enough for 71, and there are risks inherent in any operation."

"Surely the procedure is well vetted by now."

"Yes, they've done an exacting sequence of trials. Only a final test run remaining. Dr. Numerian has the highest reputation for skill and precautions."

"On balance, then, for a man of my means, it's a simple choice. Five or ten years of decline into senility, or centuries of life in better shape than now."

"Barring accidents, yes."

"Being rich gives you incentive to be careful."

The doctor hesitated, swirling his drink.

"There will be documents to sign, a lawyer or two to see, perhaps a financial person."

"Sooner the better. Do it before I die!"

"You're absolutely sure, then? I have responsibility as your physician."

The magnate sat back and smiled.

"Don't worry, doc. I'm still of sound mind."

The doctor considered telling him that he wouldn't be alone, that there would be two other paying clients at the project with him. He decided not to, just now. The magnate would find out soon enough anyway, and he might think the doctor was encouraging him. That would hardly be appropriate, the doctor thought, since he doubted he'd be seeking the procedure for himself later. For that matter, he doubted that Dr. Numerian would.

It wasn't just being rich that made you careful. So did being wise.

24.

Noelle led Hedges to the compound from the rough growth above the south shore boulders. A crescent moon hung in the sky, raising a lesser glow from Noelle's features. Hedges was now used to her gratuitous mutters, though he wondered what other odd qualities she had, what secrets. It was somehow part of her appeal, he thought, though it was what she'd revealed, promised, that was the ineluctable force in their relationship.

They approached the EAU, entered with Noelle's key.

"They like visitors," she assured him.

He followed her in, caught the odor of animals, sensed their stares from the shadows. The light was stronger toward the back, whence metallic noises could be heard. Noelle hastened ahead to have a look.

"Anna!"

"I'm just finishing up. We'd let the mice cages slide."

Hedges came up and Noelle introduced them. In their lab coats, Hedges thought, Noelle looked thin compared to Anna, though the assistant was normal build.

"He's here to meet Laffer," Noelle explained.

Anna nodded knowingly.

"Sort of a layman's appraisal," Noelle added.

"Yes. Well, I'll just be going."

As she left them, Hedges noticed, Anna glanced back with something beyond curiosity, beyond professionalism. A flicker of something he couldn't fathom. Was she remembering Talbot and his fate?

"Anyway," said Noelle, "this is Laffer over here."

The larger male chimp had been moved to Popper's old cage, its lock thoroughly cleaned and tested.

"He's kept separated from the others?"

"The other young male, Lipper, got the chromosome as a control. It shouldn't affect him much, but if it makes him feisty with Lilypad we don't want Laffer involved. We want him perfectly primed for transplants."

"Lilypad is a female chimp?"

Noelle nodded with a little smile.

"They came as a lot. There's no plans for her at present."

Hedges stood before the cage, rusty in his appraiser's role. The cottage had been ordered new, and he hadn't checked out a vehicle or shipment of pipe fittings for a long time. Now here he was, negotiating organs. He eyed Laffer warily, the chimp responding in kind. Did he somehow know what was on the table? His existence would end, of course, if the full procedure were performed. He couldn't know the specifics but sensed that a great brutality awaited him, Hedges thought. He viewed the ape's chest while touching his own, considering those specifics, the incredible operation this was leading to. He felt slightly sickened and Laffer shifted in his cage–relaxing? Hedges turned away.

"Talbot did this?"

"Viewed his donor? I'm not sure. But in his case, with his age, there wasn't much choice. And he only got individual genes."

Hedges nodded.

"Your husband and you, of course–no surgery."

Noelle looked startled, recovered.

"It was a much different situation. We weren't market-oriented."

She sat back against a table.

"Terence's first interest was immunology but more exposure to science led him to bio-technology. We met as research assistants, worked together through many long nights, meeting deadlines for a professor. Terence made a discovery that could facilitate chromosome construction. The professor claimed it as his own, but that's par for the course in universities. Terence wanted to take things further, get into therapeutical applications, but the professor was against it. He didn't like controversy, he was comfortable as he was. There was a national initiative at the time and Terence was able to get public funding, to extend the research on his own. Those were good days for us, for a while."

She hesitated, drifting in recollection.

"What happened?" Hedges probed.

"Well, news got out on what we were doing, the potential for life extension. Some people didn't like it–'tampering with nature,' ' playing God,' all that. Our old professor joined in, disowned us. In government they raised social and economic issues, always some kind of fear to weigh against us. The upshot was we lost our funding, had to move from a modern lab to a closed middle school, a disastrous lack of materials and controls."

"And yet, you kept going?"

"Terence did. He improvised, unwilling to see the work stopped. I found it difficult–not having the precision, the normal number of tests and trials, the confidence. I wound up in a supportive role, almost an observer. We were short on test animals, didn't even have a primate at the crucial juncture, so Terence had to experiment on himself."

Hedges winced.

"That must have been really hard for you."

"I guess I should have stopped him, but the work had come to be everything for us. Anyway, the chromosome created an imbalance in Terence, his nervous system unable to handle the alterations in metabolism. He had trouble sleeping and was often depressed. He was able to make an improved chromosome, but was hung up on a substitution process, so I asked him to give it to me with a carrier virus. I had to contribute something at that point, to make things better in some way. I guess I might also have sensed Terence going down, that his work might be lost with him forever. As it happened, he died the night after the procedure. Went out for a walk and perished in the park from stroke."

"I'm sorry."

"Thank you. His work has gone on, though. He lives for me through the work. It hasn't been easy reconstructing things–deciphering his notes, converting to well-equipped methodology. But this facility has been perfect for it, just about. There's the marketability thing, the combined strategy with the surgery, but I've accepted that. Rarefied science and general benefit to humanity don't sell. I certainly learned that with Terence. It takes people like Dr. Numerian and Jens to have a real chance for progress."

The mention of surgery reminded Hedges of himself and Laffer.

"This surgery, say I didn't have it. I just got the chromosome. I'd basically have the same results you did?"

"No, the benefits would be proportionate to your general condition, primarily your stage of life. However, um–" She thought a moment. "You'd avoid the minor flaws that existed in the version Terence gave me."

"That glow in the moonlight wouldn't be a flaw for a lot of people."

Noelle smiled.

"Indirect effect of increased immunity, masked in the current model. Not many people would want those baby monologues, though, would they? Neural configuration, corrected with our improved processes. And one more, one we decided not to change."

There was a note of eagerness in her voice. Hedges braced himself.

"Stay there," she said.

She moved down the aisle a little and undid her lab coat, glancing back over her shoulder at him. She was wearing a light sleeveless top and shorts underneath. When she turned to face Hedges, he saw why she'd appeared scrawny next to Anna. Though indeed slender, Noelle's body was perfectly proportioned with near-perfect muscle and skin tone, no excess fat or settling of frame. It was the body of a girl in her early teens.

"Reverse aging?" asked Hedges.

"Not exactly. Reversion in body form, distribution of tissues. Not in size, though, the skeletal dimensions."

"Are you still going back?"

Noelle laughed.

"No, I'm aging. But very, very slowly."

"Will this happen to me?"

Noelle glanced back at Laffer.

"Just with his help. Otherwise you'll look like you did at 50 to 55."

"Did that happen with Talbot?"

"No, he was past his potential for reversion, besides only getting transgenes. His benefit, what should have been his benefit, was the slow aging. He could have added decades to his natural life. Without Laffer, it'd be your main benefit, too. Though your pickup will be around a century." Noelle paused. "Of course, with the full procedure–with Laffer–you'd be like me!"

She held out her arms, smiling an invitation.

"What's your projected lifespan?" Hedges inquired.

"Accidents aside, more than half a millennium."

Hedges smiled and nodded, let it all sink in. He was amazed by the small woman before him, her gameness and dedication, her offer to him of a superior life with her. It raised their relationship to something more than human, he thought. At the same time, weighing 100 years against 500, he didn't feel compelled to look past that first century–not if it required having Laffer stuffed into him. The first 100 years would be the best anyway, he thought.

His appraisal skills were returning, he thought further.

25.

Wang sat at the airport bar, time on his hands before the flight home. Hedges had offered to see him off here, but Wang had said no. No sense his friend wasting a day. They shook hands on the pier, Hedges handing Wang's luggage into the water taxi. It occurred to Wang that he should have kept one of those trade magazines Hedges always gave him. They weren't of much interest on the island but–well, the pharmacy business was all he had now. Something that could showcase their products, glorify them like those pipe fittings, would have to be a help.

"Another drink, sir?" the bartender asked.

"No, I'm done."

He swung off the barstool, thinking he might call Hedges, ask him to send one of the magazines to his address back home. Like jewels they were, Wang mused about the fittings.

The airport seemed much different from the last time he was here. All that tension when it should have felt welcoming. Today it was relaxed and airy, a scattering of casual travelers wandering about. No one to harass him, no pressure–as long as he got the hell out. He strolled into a business services area near the arrival and departure gates. A plaque proclaimed it was courtesy of the Ministry of Commerce, with the name and ornate signature of the prince who headed it. Wang saw that one still had to pay to use the Internet connection.

"Cash only. Pay in tobacco shop."

Deciding he should email his daughter, he went to pay the fee.

Settled at the console and relaxed from alcohol, he slowly typed his message:

Greetings, Tia. How are you, I wonder? Fine I hope. You might be surprised by this message I'm sending you. No need, it's just I wanted to tell you something. I'm coming home. Not for a visit, to stay just briefly and then return to this place, but for good. You see, something happened with the company I was working for. They no longer own the property. The new owners do not require my services. So, I will be coming there and will work in our business. I think I can improve it so it is much more successful. Please do not worry about money for your education. I will be handling that, if not with the business then with something additional. Just pay attention to your studies so you qualify for university. I know you find chemistry boring but it can be important later, qualify you for things, so please study it for me. Well, I'll see you soon so we can talk some more then. My regards to Mother. Take care.

He sent it off and sat back in his chair, gazed into space above the wall of the cubicle. A part of his life was done, he realized, his residence in this country and his work on that strange island. Had there been some meaning to it beyond helping Tia? Those conversations with Hedges, talk of the unknown, the void, potential in all the emptiness. He wished he'd had more education. Perhaps he should do more reading once he settled in back home.

Elsewhere in the Kingdom, Mr. Ulib stood on his veranda with Senator Vua, father of the police captain. They held cocktails with tinkling ice and viewed the city and waterfront in the colors of sunset. The rooms behind them were quiet, the senator having stopped by unexpectedly. He was well-dressed like his host, but shorter and with less girth.

"From here it's just like always," he remarked, "yet so much has changed."

"Yes," agreed Ulib, "a different world from when we started out."

"Ah, the world. You'd know that better than me. Your contact with so many foreigners now, from all over, with their competing interests."

"Yes, it's an effort keeping them straight, styling our communication. They have their different values, cultures and such. All different ways of doing business."

"Quite a challenge. But, you've always been up to it. I know the minister holds you in high esteem, always has."

Ulib nodded, not wishing to discuss the do-nothing royal who was technically his superior. The senator no doubt sensed this, shifting his stance and sipping his drink, preparing to raise the reason for his visit.

"So," he said, "how do you think Scooter's doing on that situation?"

The childhood nickname of Captain Vua had followed him to adulthood.

"Progress Island?"

"Yes. He was hoping to do well on it, gain credit toward promotion. You know how young men are. They want their expensive toys."

"Well, he's doing fine, I suppose. As much as *can* be done, anyway. Nothing much has happened since that ape washed up."

Senator Vua studied his drink.

"I understand there were marks on it, scars from an operation, similar to those found on the Australian."

"Evidently, yes. Though we no longer had Talbot's body to compare."

"Nor those missing parts, the internal organs."

"No."

The senator appeared thoughtful. Mr. Ulib wondered where this was going.

"Scooter mentioned an alert from Interior, a change of title out there. You heard?"

"Yes, between the two companies. It seemed of little consequence. The project people bought most of the bankrupt development. The new receiver is apparently more competent than the one who shot the ape."

The senator nodded.

"The world is full of oafs. Too bad he saw fit to slander you, taint your reputation."

Ulib was inwardly disturbed.

"Do you think I'm tainted?"

"Of course not, not personally. In the public eye, though, there could be questions why he involved you that way. The mere flaunting of clout would seem crude, unnecessary. Though if a man is incompetent, well, I suppose there are no limits."

"So what is implied then, in the 'public eye?'"

Vua shrugged.

"Perhaps some knowledge of their operations, of something valuable. Something that tempts an honorable man to involve himself with a sleazy go-between."

"And how would I have gained such knowledge? *Insider* knowledge, after all?"

"Well, there are still those missing organs, nobody explaining–"

Vua gestured in the air, as if at a loss. Mr. Ulib now felt wronged.

"We've done everything we can to straighten that out. Your own son is witness to our efforts. I've worked closely with him. Anyone who makes such baseless accusations is as bad as the idiot who started them!"

The senator smiled and gripped Ulib's shoulder.

"Relax, my friend. No one doubts you, no one who knows you at least. These are idle rumors you should know about, that's all. So you can be ready, not be bothered if you happen to hear them somewhere."

Mr. Ulib allowed himself to be placated. He shouldn't become too upset, he knew, or it might suggest guilt. And there was much he honestly didn't know. If only that moron Fauss hadn't come by that day. Then he'd be fully honest in his protestations.

An ocean and a continent away, the focus of Ulib's ire was

phoning his old mentor. Fauss had been drinking, though the large stein on his night stand was now empty. He was sitting up in bed, his laptop before him, its screen the room's only illumination.

"It's rather late, Edgar," Frank informed him.

"Yeah, but I gotta know something."

"And what might that be?"

Fauss tried to collect his thoughts, remember some terminology.

"I been bringing up files, including Deville's, and I seen you made a sale on that Reverie Cove thing."

"Yes, that's true, Edgar. The Vasquibo Institute bought all remaining properties, 25 of an original 27, as I recall."

"Yeah, right. But what—I mean, how could you do that, Frank? You didn't sell short or nothing. They coulda had the whole island for less before Deville even got there."

"They've apparently had an influx of investment capital. Something sparked a strong interest in their work there. Having most of the island gives them better security, also more room if they need it later."

"Security, right. Nobody shooting their chimps now." Fauss's tone was sulky.

"Now, Edgar. We need to put things behind us. Remember?"

"Yeah. Yeah, I know. But say, Frank?"

"Yes?"

"You *sure* nobody got nothing back on it? This sale you did, Reverie Cove?"

Frank cleared his throat.

"I think we'd better get some sleep, Edgar. It really is very late."

"But what about it? Was there, you know—"

"Good night, Edgar."

The connection was broken, Fauss's hellos not bringing Frank back.

* * *

Senator and Captain Vua sat in conference in the older man's office. The father had lit a cigarette and paused in thought, smoke curling around him before a backdrop of framed photographs. Edgy in a guest chair, his son awaited his feedback.

"So you don't think your man just lost him. He just never appeared."

"He must have gone in the middle of the night. Killed time somewhere before his flight. There's that strip by the turnoff."

"You're sure that's him on the manifest?"

"Yes, diplomatic passport."

"And the wife was already gone."

"Traveling in California, the servants said. They were closing up the house. He left instructions, promised to send them their pay."

The senator sighed deeply.

"No doubt his resignation will also come." A hesitation. "I've known Ulib a long time, always a faithful ally. I didn't think you'd discover anything, really. I was just settling doubts."

Captain Vua looked down, giving his father free rein.

"I think we can assume it has to do with Progress Island," the senator resumed. "The events out there and his interest in them, that Fauss fellow's story, and–wasn't there an aide of his who also took off?"

"Yes, Livia Poe. She handled the E List before it was banned."

"Hm. So she would have connections on the island. And the list was stopped because of incidents connected to Vasquibo. She and Ulib were close, I believe, longtime associates. It would take money to make people disappear like that, big money, and a strong desire to conceal something."

"They're not a publicly traded company. We checked."

"No, of course not. They'd never want to be scrutinized. At least not until later, when they've succeeded here, when they have what they need to make *really* big money!"

"Then they pull out?"

"Maybe, maybe not. One thing's for sure: we'll never see any of that money."

"What about taxation?"

"Thanks to Mr. Ulib, the island is autonomous. They pay fees for defense and emergency services, and for the refuse barge. That's all we get from them."

They were silent a moment.

"They might just fail, anyway," the captain ventured.

"Unlikely. The investors seem to have full confidence."

But then the senator's face lit up, piquing his son's curiosity.

"Your investigation is still open, is it not? The missing organs, the ape with scars, the connections to Vasquibo?"

"Officially, yes. But–" The son gave a helpless gesture.

"Never mind. All that matters is you have access to them, to the project. Difficult, perhaps, but potentially a way to discover this resource they have, this source of extreme wealth. It's too bad for our country, unable to benefit from a discovery on its own soil. But we're also citizens of the world, Scooter, individuals like those foreigners out there, and we are family. There's no reason we shouldn't benefit even if our country cannot."

Captain Vua nodded. A loyal son, he'd accommodate his father. The vision of riches didn't make it any harder.

26.

The helicopter bringing the new team of guards arrived about midday. There were five of them, including a sergeant to relieve Jens of some supervisory duties. The helicopter remained on the pad to remove the outgoing guards from the project.

Aware of the transition, Anna came out of the synthesis lab and discreetly watched from a distance. She found herself put off by the voices and mannerisms of the new arrivals. Their brusque militarism stirred unpleasant memories of her own repressive culture. Lun and his colleagues had tempered their role with a relaxed Pacific mood. This new group would require adjustment by her, perhaps avoidance at first, however necessary they were.

Anna walked between the buildings to the area behind the compound, where she and Lun would sometimes meet and talk. The trees leading to the cove were in the distance. She moved parallel to them, toward the southern coast, regaining a view of the approach to the heliport. She didn't want to miss Lun's departure. As she came to the rough growth above the shore with the boulders, she saw a man picking his way through them, departing.

Mr. Hedges, she thought, our next test subject. He didn't see her. She considered calling out, decided not to. It didn't seem right, somehow.

A strange, empty feeling came over Anna. Here was

another unconnected person, suddenly here in this isolated spot, but unaware of her. As she'd been of him. They shared involvement in a tremendous project, which might be reason to not call out, thus maintaining their roles, protecting them. But did it justify their isolation as people? Was their sad lack of partners truly prerequisite to the roles that helped achieve so much?

She turned away from the retreating figure, thought of Lun.

"I can take you from here to my country," he'd said.

For a moment she pictured going over the sea by outrigger, sneaking into his village behind tall reeds. How utterly crazy, and yet she suddenly felt a pull toward the compound, more resolved than ever not to miss his departure.

She quickly walked back, taking a route to the front of the compound.

She lingered outside the EAU, spotting Lun and the others as they left the residential unit with their packs. Since they were encumbered, she easily intercepted them on the path to the heliport. She thanked them for their work but the others kept moving when Lun stopped. Jens and the new sergeant were watching from the compound.

"What can you do?" Lun shrugged.

She offered her hand. He gripped it gently.

"Until we meet again," he said.

"I admire you," Anna replied.

He smiled and turned to follow his comrades. Anna retreated to the compound, away from Jens and the sergeant, and waited in the shade of a tree for Lun to vanish.

* * *

The fence separating the western end of Progress Island from the original Vasquibo property had been removed. The Hoagles' new house at 14 Reverie Cove was near completion. The couple was expected to vacate the model, now Vasquibo property, as soon as possible. Wang's prefab was gone, as was Wang himself, his visa becoming void once his employer sold out. Hedges was free to cross through the trees to the project's compound, having become a key participant there. While he'd declined the Laffer option, disappointing Dr. Numerian, a great breakthrough was anticipated when Hedges received the chromosome.

"So you're satisfied with the stability?" asked Anna.

"Yes," Noelle replied, "it's constructed as well as it can be. Just keep its environment as steady as possible until the procedure. The subject's too, when he checks in."

"Dr. Numerian will want a final examination."

"There won't be any problem. He's exceeded standards for a subject his age."

"We had him on so few supplements, even less than the chimps."

"He didn't need much. He's had Terence's catalyst, so he's fine."

"Hm, okay."

Anna returned to her microscope. Noelle almost kidded her about worrying too much, but held back. Anna had been a bit down since the guards were changed, Jens bringing in a more aggressive group. She'd apparently been sweet on the one who'd helped exercise the animals. No doubt she felt the loss, here on this small island, despite the challenging work that kept them busy. It was something Noelle could relate to, of course, after Terence. On the other hand, she now had this bond with Hedges with its promise of love and common cause for their extended futures. Much of what she'd personally lost with Terence would be restored. Her shortcomings in the mistakes–the disaster–would be vindicated, more or less. This feeling might be cold, Noelle thought, but things were much more complicated for her than for someone like Anna, who could just track her lover down when they were through here.

"Are his forms all in?" Noelle asked.

"Mr. Hedges? Yes, but he was sketchy. For his emergency contact he only had an email address. Livia something."

"That's all right. After Talbot, Dr. Numerian's not looking to talk with relatives."

An ocean away, in a chilly city, the Livia in question was

meeting with her employer. She'd been working as a nanny and normally had evenings free, but the father had called from his office and asked her to stay. They were in his study now. The children and their mother were elsewhere in the house, a part-time cook preparing dinner.

"You've been wonderful with the children," the father said, "but there's been a development. Something that could improve your situation. Here in America, I mean."

He referred to the continent, Livia being north of her eventual goal. She didn't comment but listened attentively.

"I was contacted by the Institute today. There's been some real progress at the facility back in your homeland. It's apparently due to a new team member, someone they say you know, a Mr. Hedges."

"Irv?"

"Fellow with a cabin there, lives by himself."

"Yes, Irv Hedges. But how—he was in copper pipe fittings, retired—"

The man shrugged.

"All I know is he's with us now, though he likely won't remain on Progress Island. He'll probably be returning to his old haunts, south of our border here. Given your—well, acquaintance with him, everyone might be better off if you lived and worked in the same area. Two team members, mutually supportive. If you're willing, of course."

Deep within her, Livia felt wild excitement rising.

"You can arrange this?"

"Vasquibo can. As of now, I mean, with this outlook for success."

"I don't know what to say. But yes, I'm agreeable. This is so sudden—"

The man smiled.

"It just seems that way. All great accomplishments do. But they actually develop over time, with great effort, expense, patience, and risk. That's the Vasquibo view, anyway."

"Yes, and of course I agree with it."

As she had with Mr. Ulib, then Dr. Numerian, Livia listened to the details of her impending transfer. She'd been moving farther and farther from her past, the needs and aspirations of her youth, but she now felt she was returning to something. A man she cared for, empowerment, the ability to do things and travel as she wished, even visit the Kingdom. She thought she knew now why people were attracted to the Vasquibo Institute, became committed to it. It made the possible *happen*. It was bold.

* * *

Hedges lay in a narrow bed in a room of the Operations Unit. There was a larger bed against the opposite wall, heavy duty and equipped with restraints. The recovery spot for the chimps, he guessed. Talbot had likely lain where Hedges was now, surfacing from a sedative of some sort. Dr. Numerian's need for control, Hedges reflected. His own decision-making had stopped with declining the Laffer option. After that it was all following instructions, following orders. He supposed it was for the best, but felt a rising urge to return to his cottage, his own little corner of Reverie Cove.

Not that he hadn't been dreaming *here*, after the infusion. As he was coming up, he experienced a mélange of fragmentary scenes, himself at the center but getting no special notice. On city streets, in lobbies and hallways of large buildings, in train or subway cars, there were plenty of people but always a sense of something lost, missing, or undone. In a lecture room, a dingy restaurant, or waiting for something on hard chairs, he had companions yet none he could name now. There was an overwhelming sense of mediocrity. Finding himself in this plain, utilitarian room, recalling Noelle and the procedure, Hedges had been greatly relieved.

He had to chuckle, thinking how it had come to this. All those years with the business, the clumsy dates, his foggy understanding of life. Then he stumbles in here and gets lucky.

He wondered how Livia was, how she was getting along, and found he really cared.

* * *

Captain Vua and a junior officer, both in civilian clothes, had stopped at Tufa's before proceeding to the night's business. They had drinks at the bar and ordered a second round, but left before finishing as if called away on an emergency. They were actually just putting in an appearance in case alibis were later needed.

They drove a short distance to the apartment of a grocer's son who was also a reserve officer. There were two other men in the cramped residence, both perhaps still in their teens. Cigarette smoke filled the air as Vua's colleague pulled down the shades.

"You can vouch for these two?" Vua asked the reserve.

"Yes. And they're good on the water. From the resort coast."

The captain grunted and cleared space on the available table. He unrolled a hand-drawn map he'd carried in from the car. It was an enlargement of Progress Island as it appeared on the police map of the Kingdom, with added details reflecting development by the purchasers.

"We know the pier is here," Vua pointed out, "and we know the houses on these two points, but the rest is approximate. You will have to judge what is the main office, or the main laboratory, and be very silent getting in."

"Hombo is good at breaking locks," said the reserve. "He's at the casino now. We could perhaps fetch him."

Captain Vua considered for a moment.

"No, he's too awkward, not serious enough. I don't want someone blowing this." He looked back at the map. "Now, our plan is to get in and out without being seen. There are guards but they're just store cops, drinking and chasing lady workers. Just don't act like Hombo and they won't even notice you."

Nobody laughed, though Vua's colleague cut a smile.

"We want laptops or hard drives," Vua continued, "paper records if they look important. But only take what you can carry easily."

"We'll be operating from offshore," his colleague explained.

"Yes," said Vua. "The launch will have lights out as we land in the dinghy. Not at the pier, of course. Beneath this rise, the least visible point." He straightened and looked at each of the men. "We need to use extreme caution. Do not hurry but keep moving. And later, of course, absolute secrecy. You will all be amply rewarded."

By the time they left the night was well along. Music and drinking owned the streets, subsiding as they approached the dock and police launch. It would be quite late when they got to the island. They'd settle in a spot of maximum advantage, Vua thought, and go in to strike at the quietest time. Even the latest workers would be done for the day, busy with other things if not asleep. And not much was needed, after all, just a little information. It should be easy.

27.

Shots in the night.
Hedges, back in his cottage, raised himself on an elbow and listened. There was more than one gun this time. After the firing there were shouts in European accents. The new guards, one closer than the others.

As the voices subsided, Hedges got up in the dark and did his inspection. He saw nothing unusual from the windows and so returned to bed.

* * *

In the morning, as Hedges moved toward kitchen and coffee maker, the gentle light and lapping of surf brought to mind the other dawn after a shooting. Wang had knocked at about this time, with the remains of Popper in the cove behind him. Well, he wasn't around to knock today, poor guy, having been canned. But then, as he handled the coffee maker, Hedges was nagged by this thought, as if maybe he should take a look anyway out of respect for the caretaker. It's crazy, he told himself, but what the hell. He had more time than ever now.

As he discovered, there was in fact another form in the middle of the cove.

Dutifully wading out to the rumpled mass, Hedges was warmed by a sense of communion with the familiar. Though the water was chill and dark, the light indirect as it filtered over the eastern rise, he was sharing a ritual with Wang and his former, pre-chromosome, self. He felt confident and accepting, with none of the trepidation he'd felt on approaching the dead Popper. He could handle this creature, he was sure, whatever it was.

He found it was an inflatable dinghy, partially deflated from a couple of bullet holes. It was marked with a simplified crest of the Kingdom and "Nat. Police Marine Ops." Looking around, Hedges saw no bodies or other objects in the vicinity. The beach was peaceful, as was the land beyond it, the Hoagles not yet stirring from their new home, number 14. Seeing he was on his own, Hedges awkwardly dragged the dinghy toward the beach. He assumed the police would want to reclaim their property, not let it drift back out to sea.

Following earlier procedures, he called the police and reached Captain Vua.

"Mr. Hedges? Thank you but we know already about the intrusion. Mr. Jenssen and Mr. Hoagle called when it happened. We've been delayed slightly in responding."

The shots, Hedges thought, and those voices.

"This is something else, Captain."

"Oh?"

Hedges described his find in the cove, Vua not responding, waiting Hedges out until there was nothing more he could say.

"So, did you want to pick it up then, or what?"

"Yes, well, I'll tell you what we should do on this, Mr. Hedges. I greatly appreciate you notifying us and I'd like to ask for further assistance, if you don't mind. What I would like is, please compress the craft as best you can and please store it in a secure place on your property. We will retrieve it when we come to investigate the, ah, intrusion. That will be later today. Can you handle this for us as a citizen, Mr. Hedges?"

"Yeah, I think so."

"Good. And by the way, please do not tell anyone about this, okay? At least for now. We don't want to compromise our investigation. You know, about who stole it and such."

"Okay, sure. I understand."

"Thank you very much, sir. We'll be there in a little while."

About an hour and a quarter later, two men came walking along the beach to where Hedges stood waiting with the Hoagles, who had just gotten up. Neither of the men was Captain Vua, though one wore a stiffly starched uniform similar to the captain's. The other, larger man was in a short-sleeve rugby shirt with "Hombo" over a numeral 7 on the back. He also wore a crinkly-brimmed canvas hat, sandals, and denim shorts with a "Special Deputy" badge pinned to them. The regular officer explained that Captain Vua and an assistant were investigating in the project compound, that he and his partner would join them when they finished in the Cove. The Hoagles and Hedges must be interviewed separately, he said, so they should please return to their respective houses. He then entered number 14 with the Hoagles, leaving Hedges with the casual special deputy.

"That it?" asked Hombo, indicating Hedges's cottage.

"Yes," the owner replied, unsure how to address the other man.

Hombo strode off briskly on his own. Hedges noticed he was carrying a brown paper bag with items of some weight in it. Hedges hurried to catch up.

"You got the package for us, right?" Hombo called back.

"Right. It's on the patio."

The visitor quickly found the dinghy, removed the plastic furniture that partially concealed it, and dragged it off the patio toward the outer shore. He laid it out so the markings were clear, then retrieved his bag from the patio. He took out a small can of paint or primer and was soon brushing a generous coat over the markings. Only when he was well along did he look up at Hedges.

"We have to decommission it," he stated. "Prevent impersonation."

Hedges nodded dubiously. A bullet-riddled dinghy seemed a poor resource for impersonating police. It also appeared that the coating over the markings was corrosive, completely obliterating the dinghy's pedigree. As the special deputy stepped back to inspect his work, Hedges asked if he'd like something to drink.

"Beer if you got it," Hombo replied.

By the time Hedges brought back the bottles, his supposed interviewer was bundling the dinghy with a roll of wire from his paper bag. The wire was copper, Hedges noted, though of suspect quality. Hombo pulled and tied the wire with impressive strength.

"So," Hedges said as they drank on the shaded patio, "you have another job also?"

His guest grunted.

"Security at the casino. Cheap pay."

"It's nice you can get some extra work."

Hombo laughed.

"Dirty work. They want to keep their uniforms clean."

He drained his bottle and went to get the dinghy, hoisted it on his shoulder and carried it off down the beach. He slowed as he approached number 14, waited as the door opened and the regular officer came out, taking his leave from the Hoagles. The police walked off together and Hedges rejoined his neighbors.

"Not much of an interview," Kurt commented. "I just repeated my phone call, basically. Shots and shouts."

"He asked about the places we've been," Chloe added. "The famous cities."

"Seemed like he was killing time," said Kurt. "How did yours go?"

"Similar," Hedges replied. "Nothing much to it."

Elsewhere on the island, Captain Vua and another officer were interviewing the Vasquibo employees. Vua himself handled the professionals and their assistants, while the other officer debriefed the guards and met with kitchen and maintenance staff.

"They came from off the east end of the island," Jens explained, "below the hill for minimum visibility. Swimming or in small craft, main boat offshore, lights out. We think two got past the heliport, proceeded to the office or lab units. We don't think they got in."

"There was information of value there?" Vua inquired.

"It's *all* of value to *us*, of course. But others with good contacts could also profit from some of it."

"It's an area of much interest? There is great public demand?"

"You might say so, but right now we're only at the experimental stage."

Vua didn't press the point; it wasn't his purpose here. That effort had been made and botched. Now he was on damage control, acting in a way directly opposite to what his official role demanded. Rather than trying to identify the intruders, the planning behind the raid, his goal was to conceal any link to the department, himself, and of course his father. The irony didn't amuse him, given the disaster that more failure would bring, and his grave manner seemed to impress those he questioned. Here was true dedication, perhaps they thought.

"As with the others," he said to Anna, "I must ask if you have any knowledge, any suspicion even, about who these intruders were."

She hesitated, looking away to a corner of the room.

"You mean any possibility? Even remote?"

Vua felt his eyes open, quickly dropped the lids.

"Yes."

Anna gave a little smile.

"I'm sure there was nothing to it but–well, one of the guards, the ones who were here before, he and I would talk sometimes. You know, while working, and–"

She reddened a bit, searching for words.

"Yes, go on."

He listened professionally, a sphinx in khaki, as Anna related her chaste relationship with Lun. She was amused anew by Lun's vow to return for her, but Vua maintained his solemn demeanor. He'd been working to appear curious and astute, but now without effort he absorbed Anna's story, appropriated it. Success for the day was at hand, he saw.

With the arrival of the investigators from the cove, Vua commenced a search for physical clues. He told his men to scour the area by the work buildings, as well as the route to shore past the heliport. He asked the Vasquibo people to stay clear of where his men were searching. He himself circulated along the search area, ready to ensure that any discovery was handled right. One of the officers disappeared over the hill, descending toward the shore, while Vua kept an eye on Hombo, picking through weeds near the heliport. There suddenly came a call from the fourth officer, working near the synthesis lab.

"Captain, I've got it!"

Vua affected calm as he strode to where the officer beckoned, a clump of brush next to an isolated tree. The discovery was a large wrench usable for breaking door locks, government issue. Vua glanced back and saw Hombo approaching curiously.

"Bag this object and put weeds around it so its shape doesn't show," the special deputy was ordered. "Then take it to the boat and stay there. Guard everything until we arrive."

The finder of the wrench went to get the searcher on the shore, who'd found a cigarette lighter and a washed-up shoe. Deciding that the remaining shoe was in the water and wouldn't be of added value, Vua ended the search and said they were finished on the island. The three policemen were walking toward the compound's exit when Jens and Dr. Numerian came out of the office building. The policemen halted.

"We've completed our investigation," said Captain Vua. "We appreciate your cooperation and that of your staff. Please thank them for us."

"I will," said Dr. Numerian, "certainly. And we appreciate your thorough response. You clearly understand our concern. Were you able to determine anything, if I may ask?"

"We're taking some evidence back for analysis–articles left on the shore, some possible body fluids on weeds. But based on our interviews, I have a preliminary conclusion. I don't think your project is in danger, doctor. This seems to be an affair of the heart, a former guard from here coming to see the assistant lab lady."

"Anna?"

"Yes. She herself is not at fault, of course. I don't think she's in danger, but perhaps one of your guards can watch her for a while."

"We'll do that. Does everything end here, then?"

"For you, I think yes. We still have this evidence to process, and there's the matter of foreign nationals invading our territory. I will have to speak to our foreign minister."

"Well, we certainly appreciate your efforts. Thank you again, captain."

"You're most welcome."

* * *

Hedges sat with Kurt on the Hoagles' veranda, the sun dipping low as they had cocktails and viewed the cove, the sea beyond it. Behind them were the sounds of Chloe preparing a light dinner. Kurt had related his afternoon call to Jens, the apparent conclusion drawn from the day's investigation. Hedges had listened with tightly set lips.

"Seems a little far-fetched," said Kurt, "doesn't it?"

Hedges shrugged.

"People in love, they can do crazy things."

"Hm. I think it had to do with their project. They must really have something there. I offered them new approaches but they turned me down cold, at least Numerian."

"Well, I suppose time will tell."

"Yes. Too bad we won't see it through. We have to be leaving soon or Chloe will leave without me. You'll still be here though, I suppose. Do you still feel real attached–perhaps committed–to this place?" A sly smile began.

He knows about Noelle, Hedges thought. *But that's all right. Secrets are just a bother.*

"I don't know," he replied. "It's a big world out there. And I've been feeling bigger myself lately. More whole."

Kurt reflected on this, sipping his drink, while Hedges gazed over the water and Chloe tossed a salad indoors.

28.

In her room in the residential unit, in the haze of shallow sleep, Noelle would revisit her experiences with Terence. There were versions of the experiences, nuanced by factors beyond her control, but they all pointed to her inevitable widowhood. Her dreams were steps to Terence's doom and yet subconsciously she clung to them. They were her contact with him.

"You'd better sleep," she said, "don't you think?"

He was puzzling over his notes and reference books, his microscope at arm's length amid a scattering of slides. He didn't respond.

"Take it up tomorrow. A fresh look. I can stay with it awhile."

She leaned close to him and stroked his hair, tousled and needing a wash. His face was lined, especially around the eyes, his complexion sallow.

"Limited cell accommodation," he said, "the requirement for undersizing. If it could only be overcome. We could do so much more, still cover the risks."

"Darling, all you can do is prioritize."

She hugged him from behind, pressing her face to his, seeing what she loved in him. It was the briefest warmth, however, because the scene changed and it was she herself at the work bench, testing formulas for preparatory nutrients, seeking a catalyst to facilitate replication. Terence was standing nearby, intently examining a dog.

"It's looking good except for 20a," she said, "the mushroom. Can we do without it? You know the doctors won't like this many herbals, anyway."

"Won't like herbals?" he answered in mock surprise. "My, my. Since when do we care what the doctors like? Let them reread their Hippocratic oath."

He never looked up from the dog, but the scene again changed and he was noiselessly shouting, exasperated, the night dark through the windows behind him. She was trying to comfort him, her hands raised, but all that would work was to agree with him, to nod yes, yes, desperately agree that he knew what he was doing and she supported him.

Noelle half-woke, let the tension ease in existential mists. Did it really happen? Am I in that life now? Where is here? But there were good times too, came the saving thought, presenting at once herself and Terence on the lawns by a college stream, studying. So far they were from the realities of funding, conflicting ideologies, self-interest of health-care industries. Another season and they were in a pub by the fireplace, joking friends getting tipsy. But not she and Terence, walking now in town, by the sea, stealing moments of intimacy, expressions of their spontaneous love. And the visit to her parents, that first time, so clear now at the table, then her parents talking later as they would.

"He seems nice but quite shy," says her mother. "Not adjusted."

"Serious type," her father proffers.

The images evaporated and she saw her darkened room, faint cracks of light around door and window. The familiar sense of loss encroached, one that would work its way back to Terence, his essence, and beyond that to herself, her lost identity–her natural, pre-engineered self. She felt an impulse to resist, not give in this time. She was who she was, here and now, and Terence's work lived on. It was good and great. She'd never give it up. She'd go to it now, she decided, go to Hedges, purify her past in the glory of Terence's legacy.

Donning the spare lab coat she used as a robe, Noelle slipped out of her room and the unit. She deliberately passed the guard staying close to Anna. It was better than being discovered farther out, and her glow didn't show so much in the lights.

"Everything all right, doctor?"

"Yes, I couldn't sleep. Just taking a little walk."

"Be careful."

Noelle made her way westward, toward the stand of trees that preceded the old Reverie Cove development. She turned more to the south, toward Hedges's end, and was soon through the trees with the point before her. The night was clear, as usual, the sea the only sound, and a sudden memory loomed as she sighted her destination.

"You did it!" she saw herself saying, hunched over a sedated mouse. "Resistant to all pathogens!"

Terence reacted with an expression, one he hadn't shown since their schooldays: positively beaming, luminous, all traces of strain and bitterness gone.

She now looked at her hands, luminous also–Terence's gift–and ahead of her that expression, growing in this man who shared the gift with her. She'd seen it since the procedure, part of his innate understanding of their superiority, their post-banality lives. She took a deep breath, refreshed by the night air, the power of the sea, and with slow, deliberate steps approached the cottage.

* * *

They lay in each other's arms, the glow from her body lighting the contours of his face, the edges of each of his features. He was still a bit stunned, as he'd been when she appeared at the screen, and when she'd dropped her ersatz robe to reveal her full body. He was fully accepting, though, knowing at some deep level what she herself never questioned: they were lovers of a higher creation, refinements beyond all the world had known.

"I guess I can ask you now," he smiled. "That little *sotto voce*, the low talking that runs on. What exactly are you saying? Do you know?"

"Yes, I know," she teased. "It's been recorded."

"So, what is it?"

"Well, it's–" She hesitated. "It's Latin. Names of organisms I had to memorize in college. I'd be lying on the grass, or in a nook at the library."

"All still in there, huh?" He tapped her temple.

"The names, yes. But that's all it is, the little *sotto voce*." She laughed. "I hope you're not disappointed."

"I can live with it. I can live with anything now."

Noelle wasn't sure how long they slept then, but she woke with a sense the sky would soon be lightening. Hedges lay heavily beside her, seeming massive though of rangy build. His breathing was slow and deep. Noelle sat up, mentally preparing to leave. Hedges didn't stir. She spoke his name but there was still no response.

"Irv, I have to get back."

He mumbled something.

"What? I have to go, Irv. Can you hear me?"

"Cut copper pipe with hacksaw or copper tube cutter. Both make satisfactory cut but tube cutter ensures square cut. Use jig or miter box when cutting with hacksaw."

"What?"

"Helps ensure square cut. Make jig from wooden board or block with vee notch to hold pipe in place. Slot in jig will guide saw at right angles to vee notch–"

He became unintelligible. Noelle eased herself back and off the bed, stepped softly to where her lab coat lay, slipped it on. She peered for a time into the darkness containing Hedges, but no parting comment seemed appropriate.

As she made her way along Reverie Cove, back toward the trees and the compound, she couldn't avoid the contrast between Terence and Hedges. The intensity in her husband's life and efforts, his cause, was a stark backdrop to the casual confidence, almost insouciance, shown by her new lover. But it's an unfair comparison, she realized. Hedges is a beneficiary of Terence's work as I myself am, which is what Terence intended. In furthering his work, and now sharing the joy of its results, I'm promoting progress. I'm a catalyst for Terence's success, like the nutrient formula he found.

Sighting the Hoagles' house, she recalled a comment made by Jens.

The man in there called me a goddess, she thought. But goddess of what? Extended life? Romantic sleeps on tropical islands? Or maybe–yes! Copper pipe fittings!

Noelle smiled and proceeded through the trees.

29.

"Actually," said Dr. Numerian into the phone, "we now have good accommodations here on the island. There's a furnished three-bedroom on the property we annexed."

"Vacant?" the attorney inquired.

"Yes, and complete with beach. A warm, gentle cove."

"The associates will love that."

"I'm sure, and you might enjoy a dip yourself."

"I'll be doing most of the work, I'm afraid. I'm giving them a treat before things get busy. That and they should see the project, know what they're working with."

"Of course."

"There's not much more than a day's work, really, but we'll stay for two or three. Let them unwind, make sure we don't miss anything."

"We'll be at your disposal. Anything I can do, just let me know."

The attorney paused. Numerian heard papers rustling.

"Your last test subject, the partial procedure."

"Mr. Hedges?"

"Yes. He owns one of the lots not titled to Vasquibo. One of the two?"

"Yes, I believe that's the case."

"Hm, too bad. Better for us if he were renting."

"Oh? How's that?"

"Well, we won't really want him around when things

start opening up–the press, publicity and such. He's not a representative client. He only got the chromosome without the surgery."

"Yes, he's mostly Noelle's work."

"Plus he didn't pay. But there's also the human test-subject issue."

"You think that would be a problem? I mean practically?"

"The press might jump on it, draw parallels with things in the past. Unsavory things. I don't want to worry you. You're well insulated legally. But the financial effects, well–"

"What can we do?"

Papers rustled again on the attorney's end.

"I'll be looking into it. In the meantime, don't cite Hedges as a success unless you have to. The less attention he gets the better. Then, once you've done something with a paying client–the full procedure–make that your showcase work. Trumpet it."

"All right," Dr. Numerian agreed. "We'll do that."

"Good. We're moving ahead rapidly now, doctor. Vasquibo will grow on the same scale as your success. You and your colleagues should be very proud."

"Thank you. We have an excellent team."

* * *

There was activity around number 1 Reverie Cove, the former model that had been vacant awhile. Hedges learned from Kurt that a team of lawyers working for Vasquibo had moved in. They would deal with patents, marketing rights, and corporate development required by the project, and with protecting the Institute against litigation.

"I can well understand that part," Kurt asserted.

"How many of them are there?"

"I counted four, three men and a woman, all quite young except one of the men."

Later there were noises from the cove, childlike shouts, and Hedges saw three of the lawyers splashing about on the northern side. Another man, probably the fourth lawyer, came walking down the beach in tee shirt, trunks, and sandals. He was met by Kurt, who directed him to Hedges's cottage after a brief exchange. The man resumed his walk while Hedges waited by the door.

"Mr. Hedges?"

"Yes."

"Hugh Bernard, from Trotter, Baytes, and Wilke."

He was tall and rather husky, with red hair atop a high forehead, earnest eyes, very light skin and freckled. Pure country, Hedges thought, yet he's a lawyer. They shook hands.

"Something to drink?"

"Yes, thanks. Whatever's handy."

Hedges got them each a calimansi juice. He knew he should cooperate with whatever was going on. He was part of the family, more or less, as far as Vasquibo was concerned. He hadn't the faintest idea what he'd be doing, however.

"I guess you're pretty well settled," said Bernard. "It looks quite comfortable here."

"I like it."

They were in the living room, sunshine and shouts filtering through the screens.

"We won't disturb your paradise long. We're only here a few days on legal matters concerning the project. As you know, I believe, it's at an advanced stage now."

"Yes, of course."

"And you've been a big part of it."

Hedges sipped his juice.

"Are you all right with the follow-up?" asked Bernard. "The checkups and such?"

"Sure, no problem."

"Good. We want to be sure you're thriving, and also that the procedure was problem-free." He hesitated. "You should stay with our doctors for a while, Mr. Hedges, for anything that comes up. They're familiar with your new condition and, frankly, you can't trust outsiders. There are people out there, strongly motivated, who'd like nothing better than to steal this discovery. They can be very unscrupulous. I understand there was actually an attack on the island by such a group."

"I thought that was a love affair, a former guard trying to pick up a lab worker."

Bernard laughed sarcastically, looking toward the window.

"Pure cover-up, someone's bull running loose." Another hesitation. "They failed but we can't assume that's the end of it. There are others out there more sophisticated. Word will spread through the medical fields, with the potential for profit obvious to all. This island will remain a target, I'm afraid."

Hedges listened to the cavorting young lawyers, recalled shots in the night, then Noelle's luminescence. It's true, he thought, the island is special.

"If you wanted off for a while," said Bernard, "or for good, we could facilitate things for you. Say back to the West Coast, your home area. We have our associates there, you'd have continuity of service, medical and all."

"I wasn't planning to leave, actually."

"Sure," Bernard smiled. "We just want you to know that, in case your 'new self' starts feeling footloose, it's okay with us. You're not tied to this island. There's just that caveat for a while on the medical, and a need for caution with people approaching you."

The attorney left his card. He was Hedges's contact with Vasquibo, he said, from now on. The people on the island were there for technical work only. Hedges asked no questions, not wanting further complications. He watched Bernard walk off.

Hedges stood for a while letting his mind settle, absorbing the lawyer's visit. Slowly he walked through to the game room. He picked a cue off the rack, balanced it in his hands, put it back. He looked out over the patio. The noise from the young lawyers had stopped. It was very still, it seemed, the stillness inviting action, a reaction on his part to Bernard. He wasn't, after all, his old retired self. He was his "new self," as the lawyer had put it, with greater potential for action, and therefore choices to make. At the very least, he should reread Livia's email.

It had appeared a few days before. Hedges had opted to

A Truly Higher Life Form

not react and mentally shelved it. He'd felt he had enough to process with Noelle and his new self. Now, however, he felt different and brought the message up on his laptop:

> Hello Irv, I don't know what to say. Disappearing like that, to your eyes I mean, I'm sorry about the confusion. I wanted to tell you. I couldn't. I heard you were looking for me. It warmed my heart but made me feel bad for you too. The thing is, it all has to do with the company, there on the island. I've been told you're also in the group/network whatever now. So it's okay that you know they helped me get here, around where you used to live. I had to leave the Kingdom, for many reasons. We can talk about it in person some day, I hope. I mean soon. For now I want you to know that I'm okay, I have a nice job and place to live, and I love you and miss you.

Hedges set the laptop on the coffee table, sat back and viewed the message from afar. He'd come to this place, 27 Reverie Cove, Progress Island, to be isolated from complications and involvements in the world, things that had mostly never worked for him. Yet now here he was, at the center of a major world development, his two best relationships with women occurring at the same time. He reflected on the irony but saw no deeper meaning. Those were simply the facts of his situation, what he had to handle. And he *could* handle them, he thought, being the new person he was. It was inevitable. Challenges were less daunting when your resources increased, opportunities more accessible.

An extra hundred years, he thought. Amazing. Yet looking ahead to them all he saw was Noelle–a beautiful life with her, yes, but nothing more. What exactly would he *do?* Maybe it didn't matter. Just having the time might be enough, especially with her. When he finally died though, looking as old as people can, Noelle would still be fairly young, another 400 years to go. What would he be to her then, or after the next century? No one else would remember him so why should she? And of course she'd have other relationships, layers of experience over the dusty myth of himself. Time is a tricky thing to play with, Hedges thought.

He retrieved his laptop from the coffee table. He read Livia's email again and decided he should reply. It had been several days already. He typed:

Great to hear from you. Don't worry about the disappearing. I got a close-up look at the Kingdom out of it, the high and the low. Your sister is nice. She lent me a key to your place so I went and snooped around, looking for clues. I found the pipe fittings on the Home Sweet Home sign. I somehow guessed from it where you are, maybe just hoping. Anyway, it's true I'm involved with the project or company people. Details at another time. I have a lot to think about just now, what's happening here and you over there, the future etc. So I'll be in touch then, okay? I love you too.

He sent it off. Later, his laptop put away, Hedges thought about his talk with Hugh Bernard. What the lawyer had hinted at, suggested really, meshed nicely with what Livia seemed to want. Maybe it would be for the best, given those lifespan issues with Noelle. Of course, he was fixed to outlive Livia, but maybe she could get the chromosome too, even things out. Hedges smiled at his mental manipulations. He really was becoming a Vasquibo person. He'd better watch out. He wanted to keep some Irv Hedges in his great new self.

But as he thought this, rising to go outside, the image came to mind of Noelle in the night, her unearthly glow and power. Fantastic, he thought. Maybe irresistible.

30.

Noelle and Dr. Numerian were having coffee together in the lunchroom of the Vasquibo compound. There was no one else in sight, no sound except the air conditioning. He brought out his cigarettes and offered her one. She accepted and he lit them both up.

"It's do-it-yourself for lunch also, I'm afraid," said Numerian.

"They'll still be tied up? All day, you think?"

"I certainly hope not, but it's clearly more than a dusting."

Jens had detailed the kitchen and maintenance workers to number 1 Reverie Cove to prepare it for clients arriving that night. The visiting lawyers had left it in well-used condition, Jens explained, more like abused. No guards could be spared for the clean-up due to current security needs.

"What time are the subjects arriving?" Noelle asked.

"Nine-thirty, flight conditions allowing. We'll get them right to bed and leave a staff person, apprise them as a group about this time tomorrow."

"Three at once. Quite a change in our operations."

"We must keep them in successive stages. Any delay in the lead subject's treatment means corresponding delays for the other subjects. No leap-frogging."

"Safety first. And less strain on us, less chance of error. Optimal conditions."

Numerian smiled.

"I increasingly count myself fortunate to have you as a colleague."

Noelle returned the smile, raising her cigarette for a draw. She knew there could never be anything personal between them. However close they worked professionally, he and Jens regarded her as a freak, she believed. It might be different if the chromosome weren't flawed.

"Where in the sequence is our female subject?" she asked.

Numerian refocused, looking past her toward the kitchen.

"I have her second. I wasn't expecting a woman this early, but it will certainly help with marketing. So I see no reason to delay."

"Perhaps an 'Adam and Eve' motif when the story is leaked?"

Numerian almost laughed.

"Certainly not. Enough of that will follow by itself. Anyway, I've decided on an earlier leak after the first subject's transplants, to preempt any exposés out there."

Noelle looked at him in surprise.

"That'll put some pressure on."

"I'm sure you and Anna can handle it. Plus, success in the spotlight will maximize marketing potential. Of course, we'll tighten security as needed so we can work in peace."

Noelle nodded, tapped ash from her cigarette.

"Mr. Hedges won't continue as a credential," Numerian went on. "His infusion got results in our network, this trio of clients arriving, but we'll be playing to a much bigger audience now. Successes with these three–complete, age-specific procedures–will essentially establish the industry." He brightened. "Vasquibo's industry."

Noelle looked at him, tried to picture their work as an industry.

"Of course," she said, "the infusion by itself can be a secondary product."

"Of course," Numerian agreed. "But we know humanity, don't we? Its proclivity to deny mortality, to procrastinate, even in the most vital decisions and actions. Hence our primary focus: the full-service regimen, to be demonstrated on tonight's arrivals. There's a real beauty, I think, in the way things are turning out. A sort of scientific destiny."

The helicopter bringing the clients arrived on time, spoiling the starry sky over Progress Island. It's approach was seen by Hedges and the Hoagles from the couple's veranda. This was Kurt and Chloe's last full day on the island, maybe for a long time, so they were savoring its reality with their only neighbor. Kurt had invited Jens but the Vasquibo man was too busy. Hedges would return in the morning to see the couple off.

"They must be working late at the project," Kurt said as the chopper passed.

"I haven't seen it around for a while," Hedges observed.

"Well, they had those disruptions, the dead ape and those rascals invading. But I guess it's back to business as usual now."

"Yes." A hesitation. "Usual."

Hedges gazed over the darkened cove toward the opening to the sea, searching for what exactly was usual, what the concept meant to him now.

"Care for a nightcap?"

"I don't want to keep you up, you must still have packing–"

"No, we're fine," Chloe spoke up. "Please stay for one more."

Kurt went to mix the drinks. Chloe, who was sitting between the men, leaned toward Hedges and spoke quietly.

"I've been meaning to apologize for that first day. I had to say something before we left. I'm ashamed of the way I acted, how I bothered you that day."

"You don't have to–"

"No, let me finish. I'd like to be able to say there's something in my past, some experience, that makes me that way. But there isn't. I've always been that way, at least after childhood. Something in my nature, deep inside. Something in the genes."

"Genes," Hedges repeated. "I can understand genes." But she meant in the usual sense, he reflected. She's back in the world of the usual. "Well, for sure you don't have to apologize then," he said. "We can't control our genes. Everybody knows that."

Chloe smiled.

"Kurt has accepted it. That's part of the love between us. I'm happy if you accept it, too. I want to feel we're the best of friends after I leave here."

"Sure, no doubt about it."

She quickly kissed his cheek.

"I think the drinks are coming," he added.

Chloe laughed and sat back. Kurt rejoined them and the evening wound to a close, the departing helicopter foreshadowing the Hoagles' own exit. As they were finishing their drinks, they saw the lights go on throughout number 1, figures moving in and out, an occasional raised voice piercing the night. Hedges took his leave and returned to his cottage. When he looked out before getting into bed, he saw that all the lights were off at numbers 1 and 14.

He was up early the next day to help the Hoagles move out. The golf cart used by Wang had devolved to them, so Hedges used it to move their things to the pier. There was no activity at number 1 as he passed it, though he sensed its occupation. And something else. He wouldn't have noticed it in the past, or he'd dismiss it as silly, but now he felt a danger of some sort, something ominous. He knew he wanted nothing to do with the people in there.

After the Hoagles had left on the water taxi, Hedges checked the locks at number 14. He'd offered to keep an eye on things to supplement Captain Vua's services. Finding all was secure, he decided he could use a swim after his morning labors. He returned to his cottage and was soon stroking through waves off the southern coast. As he was gaining the familiar sense of isolation and peace for which he'd come to the island, another helicopter bore down in the project's approach pattern, its noise dancing off the waves around him. A flicker of irritation passed through Hedges. He watched the craft pass around the hill and then settled into a more vigorous swim. He felt a sense of purpose, though with unclear focus. Perhaps he simply wanted or needed some purpose for his new strength.

As Hedges was getting his lunch later, feeling relaxed after his swim, he heard a ruckus of some sort in the direction of the Hoagles' house. Peering out through the screens, he was startled to see several apes running about between the trees and the beach. Noelle's assistant and one of the guards were chasing after them, trying to grab the apes' leads. Hedges glanced at some fruit on his table, thinking it might calm the apes, but then remembered these were experimental animals, no doubt on special diets. Thinking he should help, he stepped out from the cottage. This distracted the apes and slowed them down. Anna and the guard each gained a lead, with another guard coming through the trees to assist. Order was restored.

"We just had a couple come in," Anna explained, "so we tried walking them with Lipper. It got out of hand, of course. We'll have to go back to two at a time."

"These are for patients, these new chimps?"

"Clients, yes. They're staying down the beach. But there are three, actually."

"Oh." He hesitated. "How's Laffer doing?"

Anna gave a coy smile.

"Well, I can't say he misses you."

"Same here." He looked down the beach toward number 1. "Guess he'll be getting involved with someone else now."

"Could be. We haven't matched them up yet. There's a lady client, so she might get Lilypad instead."

Hedges nodded.

"They'll be having that meeting, like I had with Laffer?"

Anna hesitated, perhaps remembering the look she gave him that night, a sort of warning it had seemed.

"Maybe. We'll see. Whatever seems best for each client, his or her procedure."

Later, in the synthesis lab, Anna raised the question with Noelle.

"Mr. Hedges brought it up," she added.

"Hm. Well, they can't take a lesser alternative, like he did. Any backing down and it's a wasted trip, not to mention the big deposit they paid. We'd be doing them a service not to let that happen. Let's avoid the eye-to-eye, just drop it. I'm sure Dr. Numerian will agree."

Anna resumed her work without responding. Noelle

wondered if she'd sounded brusque. She admired Anna's compassion, but thought herself compassionate also. She simply saw things in terms of accomplishing the project, achieving the greater good. Anna should understand this with her loyalty to Vasquibo. But then there was that basic difference between them, that inevitably different outlook when one's life is extended by half a millennium.

* * *

The magnate rose from his chair and excused himself, saying he was going out for a smoke. He and his fellow clients had just heard the order in which they'd have surgery. He would be the first, which didn't surprise him, given that he was aggressive and had likely conveyed more enthusiasm. The others were a bubbly heiress, easily awed and talkative, and a South American rancher, suavely fatalistic.

Lighting his cigar, the magnate squinted at the numeral 1 on the door of the former model. His number, all right, but why was it on there? Another house well down the beach, he saw, then a small one far off. 2 and 3, perhaps? He shrugged and walked off toward the dock. An armed guard was standing on the pier scanning the water.

"Good evening," said the magnate.
"Good evening, sir."
"Lovely evening."
"Yes, sir. Excuse me."

The guard turned on his heel and strode away, taking a course along the line of trees above the cove. The magnate had a puff in isolation, considered going on toward the project, decided instead to explore down the beach path.

He came to number 14, puzzled over the number on the door.

"Well, I'll be," he muttered. "What does it mean?"

He saw a man lurking by the small house on the far end, the point. As the magnate began walking toward him, however, the man made his way inside and shut the door.

"What the hell," said the magnate. "Same to you, fella!"

As he turned away, his gaze swept the cove, its opening to the sea directly across. It looked inviting after the rebuff from the point. Smiling at the notion, the magnate decided to wade in a bit. He shed his sandals and felt the fine sand caress his feet. The water, still warm, lapped about his ankles with a faraway sound. Faraway because it had been so long, he suddenly realized, since he'd done anything like this–simple, spontaneous, with real heartfelt interest. For many years he might as well have been dead. But that would all be over soon, he thought. The emptiness would be filled. How he ached to have this treatment done with!

Some seabirds flew over. The magnate turned and tried to follow their flight over the trees. His toes snagged something in the sand beneath the water. He bent and raised the object in the meager light. It was a swimmer's watch, waterproof. Flicking on his lighter, he saw that the watch was still running, its dials enclosed by a horseshoe inscribed *GOOD LUCK*. Turning the watch around, he saw the name inscribed on the back: *D. Talbot*.

"Well, Mr. or Ms. Talbot," said the magnate, "I don't mind having some luck with this surgery. Now I'm readier than ever!"

He pocketed the watch and headed back to shore. It had been a good walk after all, he decided. He looked forward to success in this place, feeling as usual that he deserved it.

31.

The sky above Progress Island was overcast, occasional drizzle sweeping in from the sea. Jens stood unperturbed atop the hill overlooking the heliport. Despite the weather, he thought, this day is beautiful. It was one of his rare stints as the man in charge, Dr. Numerian and others needing to rest from a marathon transplant operation. From all indications it'd gone well, but the assistants were taking turns sitting with the client, Jens checking on them with each rotation. The guards had been redeployed, guarding the dock against intrusive media and watching the cove as well. Jens didn't put it past the *paparazzi* to come in by outrigger or even as frogmen. He'd called a company contact to request doubling the guards, citing the operation, and was told it would happen tomorrow. Soon he'd make another call that would make guards even more necessary. In fact, checking his watch, he saw that it was time now.

Jens descended the hill, briefly considering how rain might affect the new guards' landing. It'll pass by then, he decided, and turned his thoughts to the more important matter. His part was rather simple, actually, but what followed would shake the world. Just a few facts, most of them mundane, recited to another contact. But one feature of the story would stun people, strike an innermost chord in everyone who heard it, the thought of which gave Jens a thrill, a sense of mastery over the world, over history. What more could any scientist–any man–want? Granted, he wasn't central to the achievement, but he was party to it and the one who was announcing people's salvation. He would deliver hope to mankind against its greatest fear.

After checking once more on the client, Jens hastened to his office to phone.

* * *

The article first appeared in the Internet edition of a European retirement magazine, in the medical news column. It was quickly picked up by the news services for worldwide dispersal. The original article read:

ZURICH—Researchers from the Vasquibo Institute have reportedly developed a process for extending the human lifespan by centuries. (!) According to a source within the Institute, a team of experts has been working on the project on a remote island in the Pacific Ocean. They have been led by Dr. Conrad Numerian, an accomplished transplant surgeon, and Dr. Noelle Kenilwerth, a controversial molecular biologist. The source emphasized that, while initial skepticism is expected, the Institute will soon release irrefutable evidence of their success. Further, the law firm of Trotter, Baytes, and Wilke has been retained to protect Vasquibo's rights surrounding this discovery.

The report was embellished as the day wore on, reporters digging for background and citing supposed experts on life extension. Ethical issues and social implications were expounded. Skeptics delighted in scoffing, religious types in ranting. Behind the excitement, of course, was the overarching question: "What's in it for me?" People were cautioned by the sager commentators, however, to await the evidence and consider it carefully before making changes in their lives or beliefs.

"A tall order, that," said Frank in the commission chair's

office. He'd come to see Don at once on hearing the news. A small TV emanated follow-up.

"Yeah," Don acknowledged. "It doesn't take much when people want to believe. And this isn't just flying saucers."

"What gets me is how close we were, Edgar anyway, without even knowing. The power, the immense potential for profit, and we're next door trying to cut our losses."

"Deville's, yeah, and their creditors'."

"Think we'll catch flak for dumping it? Reverie Cove?"

Don considered a moment, Frank twisting in his chair, frowning.

"Possibly. Value would've skyrocketed if we'd waited. But how could we have known? We weren't in the loop."

"Edgar got involved in that deal to buy in with them, with Vasquibo."

"Damn, that's right." A hesitation. "Well, don't worry about it. We're protected from personal liability. You, me, Judge Nichols. Just public officials performing in good faith. Untouchable."

"What about Edgar?"

Don made a steeple of his hands, stared at it.

"I know you go way back with him, but he's a case where we need to cut our losses. He'll have to be on his own on this. Around here, *persona non grata*. Sorry, Frank."

"No, Don, that's all right. I understand."

Across the country, Mr. Ulib sat with a glass of wine on the balcony of his condo. His wife had gone out alone when he said he didn't feel like shopping. Mr. Ulib had considered a stronger drink but, feeling it was too early, decided a glass of wine would go nicely while reflecting on his folly. He should never have allied himself with that blowhard Fauss, he thought. He should have had sufficient confidence in his commercial instincts, well-honed after all, to approach the Vasquibo man directly with his proposal. He'd shrunk from the bold course in favor of neurotic caution, conditioned by the insecurity of his tiny country. And for what? A position and ersatz status that he later abandoned anyway. Now, with the scale of Vasquibo's prospects almost beyond comprehension, his retirement

A Truly Higher Life Form

would proceed in the towering shadow of his failure. It was all so different from what he'd foreseen in emigrating.

The phone rang inside. He got up to answer it.

"Hello, old friend," came a familiar voice.

"Senator Vua?"

"We've missed you. People have come to appreciate you in your absence. We have need of your skills and wish you to return."

"Well, ah, I've retired. There was the letter I sent, the resignation."

"All that is immaterial now. With the big news, the fountain-of-youth story, our country stands to reap a bonanza. Progress Island is within our border, so the Kingdom will be known as the country that nourished the miracle. We need you to help us capitalize."

Mr. Ulib tried to compose himself, follow Vua's logic, evaluate it.

"I see what you mean," he said, "and I appreciate your offer, but of course we're all settled here and—"

"There's been a conference with the prince," Vua interrupted, "your former superior. He will vacate the post of trade minister once you accept it. A special promotion giving you full latitude to exploit our new identity, our windfall."

Mr. Ulib was silent, confirming to himself that he'd heard right.

"So, what do you say?"

Across the ocean, much closer to the Kingdom and Progress Island, another sort of opportunity was seen. In a small warehouse off a narrow crowded street, Wang listened skeptically to his son's latest proposal. Cartons of pharmacy goods surrounded them and there was a shipping setup in one corner. As Bing spoke in his enthusiastic way, Wang's brother and business partner came in and sat down.

"With the new name your business will take off," Bing was saying. "Think of it: 'Immortality Brand' on the packaging and labels, all your advertising, 'Developed on Progress Island' right underneath it."

"That's all bogus," Wang objected. "Nobody will believe that."

"It's *not* bogus. You were working there the same time they were, thinking how to improve this business. So you developed the products there. And we can back it up with your personal story on a company website, with a link to order your products. And another even stronger slogan, something like 'Live for Centuries!' inside a starburst."

"Now, Bing," Wang began, but found he liked what he was hearing.

"You can add new products with a 'Reverie Cove' angle, show there's more to the island than just Vasquibo. Call it the 'Island of Health.' You can give interviews, be on TV health segments, maybe regular talk shows. Everywhere you go the company and the products get mentioned. Business will be booming."

Wang looked over at his brother, who nodded sagely.

"After a while," said Bing, "others will want your endorsement for *their* stuff!"

* * *

As the overcast day grew darker, evening settling in, Hedges made his way down the beach to check on the Hoagles' property. He'd thought of it earlier in the day, but the people from number 1 were out strolling and he wanted to avoid them. He'd seen the stories on the Internet and assumed these second and third clients would cause further waves of sensation. Very soon, of course, the waves would surge back, an unwelcome tide of scrutiny washing over his retirement retreat. He was increasingly bothered by the thought.

The locks on the Hoagle house were secure, the golf cart parked in its accustomed spot. Standing by the house, Hedges found that he missed the owners' company, and somehow Chloe more than Kurt. Whatever her flaws, he felt, she exuded a certain humanity, an endearing vulnerability, that distinguishes human beings in nature. The delicate intricacy of human life is what makes us respect it. The couple in number 1, as well as the client recovering from surgery, sought to overcome their vulnerability. He himself had also, to a lesser extent. Vasquibo sought huge profits from this, its employees places in history. Hedges didn't blame anyone for wanting these things but felt hollow in the midst of it. He'd live an extra hundred years, right, but was it really such a big deal? Was it human? Maybe the human lifespan was its given length because it was all you truly needed. Plenty of time, plenty of life stages, for every worthwhile experience. Immortality might just be excess, repetition, stagnation.

 It started to drizzle and Hedges walked back to his cottage. It was time to dig out that business card, he thought, call Hugh Bernard and see what he had to offer. Time to move on.

32.

Noelle sat before the mirror in her small bedroom, brushing her abundant black hair. She stopped suddenly when she caught a certain look in her eyes, a look of disillusion, almost cynicism. She ran two fingers over her pale face, assuring herself she was the same as always, growing older with abnormal slowness. Standing, she ran her hands down the sides of her body, tracing the adolescent figure clad in underwear. Countless men would desire her, she knew, and yet the one she'd chosen to succeed Terence was taking his leave. Granted, she'd had her own doubts about their future, his casualness wedded to her intensity, but it was still rather hurtful. A personal comedown, not quite humiliating but less than what she deserved.

He'd dropped into the lab that day and asked to speak with her alone. Anna overheard and said she was about to leave anyway, something about the animals. Hedges had been to see Jens, discussing his departure by helicopter, something he'd arranged himself with Vasquibo. He said he was leaving for good the next day, and waited for Noelle to react. But she was in her professional mode.

"We'll be sorry to see you go, I'm sure. All of us."

"I want you to know–about us, I mean–I'd like for things to go on, but–"

"No, I understand. With all that publicity, it won't be the

same here. Maybe very hectic. I know that's not what you—well, not *for* you."

Hedges was still contrite, visibly bothered. Noelle felt rising sympathy for him, hoped she wouldn't cry.

"If you'd like to come by tonight," he said, "a farewell time together—"

She'd agreed with no real thought about it, a purely emotional reaction. It was to end the scene in the lab, a personal awkwardness she hadn't felt in years. It was the only response within reach. Now, with the coming of night, his final one on the island, it was time to make good on her promise.

* * *

She wore a dark blue dress, midnight blue, instead of her usual lab coat. He seemed surprised by this but pleased, ushering her into the living room with some ceremony. He set out wine glasses and opened a fresh bottle. He asked if she'd like some music but she said no, the sound of the waves was fine. They were sitting apart, a certain formality having encroached on their relationship.

"Nice," she said, looking around and listening. "Sure you want to leave all this?"

"Right now, no. Not with you here and all."

"Mm, the world at peace. The far end of the earth, anyway."

"Yeah, the farthest end." He looked down reflectively. "That was my plan."

Noelle studied him as she sipped. Had she interfered with this man?

"You know," she said, "I'm all right with what you're doing now, your moving. We had—well, we had our own plan more or less, but of course things change, things become more clear. We've both been through enough to know that."

Hedges looked up and smiled.

"It's generous of you to say that. I appreciate it."

They sipped in silence a few moments. Once their eyes met, Noelle gave a head tilt toward the bedroom.

"Want to go in there?"

He gave a look of pleasure but then peered into his wine. She made no move to get up, just sat back and observed him.

"It has to be 100 per cent between you and a woman, doesn't it? Otherwise, nothing much happens. True?"

"I'm sorry."

"No, it's okay. Because actually I'm that way, too. Ever since Terence–well, except with you awhile–I just haven't been that interested. My passion has been the work."

Hedges nodded but made no comment.

"How about a walk on the beach?" he asked instead. "We can bring the wine."

They carried their glasses, and Hedges the bottle, as they left the cottage and trod the fine white sands of the cove. The night was partly clear, the moon half-full, with sporadic breezes rippling the water. Noelle's hair lifted in the wind and she could feel her companion's glances, his admiration, perhaps regret. But neither of them said much until they reached number 14, turned up toward it, settled themselves on the porch with their wine. They were facing across the cove toward its outlet to the sea, to what lay beyond.

"Reverie Cove," Noelle mused. "Does that mean it's like a dream here, or just that you dream more than usual?"

"Intended as the former, no doubt," Hedges replied. "In reality, the latter."

"I guess some people see value in that, just dreams by themselves."

"Yeah, I guess they do."

They were quiet awhile. Hedges refilled their glasses.

"It's really nice sitting with you here," he said. "Having those plans, the feelings behind them, seems wild now, but I'm grateful for it, grateful to you for the experience. You lifted me out of my old crummy self. A little too high, maybe, but now we're fine, settled. We can see things as they are, be sane. Just demigods, not god and goddess."

"There's still the future, Irv. A long one for us."

"Yeah, that's right. I guess our paths could cross."

A Truly Higher Life Form

"Especially since we're both with Vasquibo. 'Colleagues,' shall we say?"

Hedges smiled and raised his glass.

"That's right. Here's to business!"

* * *

In the end, Noelle thought, there's never much to say. It's just action that brings finality. Hedges had walked her through the trees, watched as she returned to the compound. She'd promised to be at the heliport next day when he departed. Now, as she returned to the residential unit, her small bedroom, she was aware of the need for one more action tonight, something to correct an imbalance she felt in her universe. It wasn't the relationship with Hedges but something more fundamental, a basic assumption that ran through all she was doing here on Progress Island. She'd never doubted Terence or his work, was willing to allow commercial interests to use it, but perhaps she'd misjudged the value of success. Maybe more thought should be given to what to *do* with added centuries of life. What, eventually, would be the true *worth* of immortality?

She slipped out of the blue dress but didn't prepare for bed. Instead, she put on the spare lab coat she kept and went out again. It was late and no one was about; the guards were watching the coastlines.

Noelle walked calmly yet purposefully to the synthesis lab. She used her key to enter and locked the door behind her. The dim security lights were on, creating a specter of secret activity appropriate for the hour. Terence's notes were locked in their usual drawer; she'd decide later what to do with them. The computer was turned off for the night, Anna still following their original thrifty protocol. Noelle turned it on and sat at the console, brought up the heavily secured file on the chromosome. She wouldn't change much, just two or three minor details in the painstaking process of construction, maintenance, application. She'd have liked to change Terence's catalyst too, but Anna might know the formula by heart. Noelle herself could remember the changes she was making now, if she wished.

She turned the computer back off when she'd finished, then braced herself for the hard part. It was as if Terence were there with her–watching curiously, not comprehending.

"I have to do it," she said softly.

She went to the storage and containment area at the back of the lab, past the climate-control chambers to the rarely touched vials and arcane equipment. She spotted a container of EMS, ethyl methane sulphonate, and considered how she could use it. It would take very little to induce mutation, defeat the purpose of the chromosome, perhaps imbue negative effects. A small enough amount could be consumed in reaction, though what about a by-product or residue? There should be no sign of sabotage; the chromosome had to be seen as failing on its own, and responsible for any damage. But she needn't use a chemical mutagen, she knew. With a little more trouble, she could foil any analysis.

Noelle walked back to the climate-control chambers and opened one that was locked, using the key pad beside the door. Inside there were seven vials, chromosomes in solution, two each for the new clients and Hedges's left-over backup. They'd been constructed by exacting standards, resulting in the virtually perfect entities envisioned by Terence. Immortality, even just from aging and disease, requires perfection. A most delicate balance determines one's fate, both what you are and what happens to you.

She removed the vials and packed them in an insulated carrier. Without stopping for further thought, she left the synthesis lab with the carrier and proceeded to the EAU. She avoided any show of haste in case a guard spotted her. The animals were curious when she entered their night but she ignored them. She went back to the examining station opposite the mice cages and set down the carrier, keeping it clear of equipment she had to move. She swung down an X-ray apparatus and adjusted it, using a raised stage as if for a mouse. She turned the mechanism on. Unpacking the carrier, she moved the seven vials onto the stage in close rank. She then took cover, counted to three, and gave the vials a jolt. Some seconds passed, Noelle not moving, then she hit the switch again. It was over.

Cautiously, lovingly, she returned the chromosomes to the synthesis lab, their climate-controlled chamber for ensuring stability. Tomorrow, after Hedges left in his helicopter, the client with transplants would be infused from one of the vials. The second client on the island was scheduled for surgery that evening. Her donor would be Lilypad, the female chimp, finally being allowed a role in the project.

Despite the late hour, Noelle felt the need for a walk.

* * *

She stood on the hill above the heliport, watching the shifting clouds in the night sky, behind them the stars. Another 500 years, she thought, but of what? Perhaps she could do research on individual diseases. But what about her personal relationships? The others would be true mortals, 120 years at most, dying off through the centuries while she hardly aged. Would she have children, grandchildren, et cetera and watch them pass away while she herself lived on, regretting more and more what she was?

The tragedy of Terence wasn't that he died or was wrong, but that humanity wasn't ready for his gift. People shouldn't have added life because it only brings pain unless something exists to balance it, a world friendly and fulfilling to them. We're not yet living in such a world. Terence in his fervor didn't consider this, and one shouldn't try to save humanity unless he clearly sees what he's doing.

Some day things would be different, Noelle thought. Civilization moves sluggishly on, irrational forces falling away in their rages. But for now, for her anyway, the manipulation of life and death was over. Except, it suddenly struck her, for herself. As she scanned the dark waves through which Talbot had his last swim, losing himself in the currents, she saw herself following him. She would just walk, though, and if she couldn't walk on water there would be one less goddess to confound humanity.

But no, she loved life too much. Life was what she'd always been about.

She turned her back on the waves and descended to the compound, her waiting bed. The night breeze lifted her hair over her preternatural glow. Death was behind her.

One more irrational force had fallen away.

33.

Three Years Later

During an all-Mozart program at the Sydney Opera House, a phone vibrated in the suit coat of a man seated near an exit. The man, Ian Newcombe, observed the caller's number and knew he should leave to call back. Reluctant to leave his party, he considered waiting for intermission. His respect for urgency intervened, however, so he whispered regrets to his wife and discreetly exited.

Entering the hall, Newcombe was highly visible to any who might be there. He was six-foot-five and 260 pounds, with broad shoulders and steel-gray hair worn longish. He was thus spotted by a man who was ambling unsteadily from the direction of the bar. Newcombe vaguely recalled the man from business luncheons, but wasn't sure of his name. Was it Reynolds? Raymond? Mediocre people were just globs after a time.

"Late from intermission," the man explained. "Wife'll be ticked." His face had a cherubic look, his wispy moustache not lessening it.

"Another's coming soon," Newcombe advised. "You can slip back in."

"Eh? Oh, yes." He seemed sloppily thoughtful.

"Well, if you'll excuse me—"

"Say, I wanted to ask you something."

"Yes?"

The man smiled conspiratorially, Newcombe returning a pokerface.

"I hear your stock's shot up since you landed Kenilwerth."

The man was referring to the Progress Island venture, which Newcombe had launched when another firm collapsed there. They'd been into life extension, while Newcombe's success was in derivatives, but he was a dilettante of the first order.

"We're not selling stock yet."

"Good. Glad of that, actually." The man suddenly seemed sober. "Let me in the group, Ian. I can stake as much as any of them."

Newcombe hesitated, judging the man, then: "Group's closed for now. The others would have to agree. I'll bring it up with them and let you know."

With that he briskly moved on. The familiar feeling of being a stallion running with geldings returned to him. But he knew that no man was an island, not if he wanted any real success. There were networks and systems to work through, resources to be negotiated, meeting and dealing and wining and dining. He'd seen this starkly one bleak afternoon as he perched atop a Himalayan peak, watching as frigid gales swept over the immense, timeless crust. He was nothing, he realized, and neither was any man on earth, past or present, no matter how strong or brilliant. It was only by working with others, or using others, as well as human institutions, that he would be of any significance. And so he resisted his loner impulse, continually alert to the environment in business, seeking engagement, and indulged this outlook in other areas as well. He willingly patronized the arts, though he didn't understand them, and the sciences which he appreciated more. He saw science as the key to progress, with which he naturally identified, and thus had been drawn to the legacy of Progress Island.

He came to an empty alcove and ducked in, reconnected with his recent caller.

"They're sending a researcher from WHO," the voice said.

"Investigator, you mean."

"If you will. New fellow there, bit of a break maybe."
"Name?"
"David Pons. Know him at all?"
"Hm, no. When can we expect Mr. Pons?"
"Better think tomorrow. Is your manager good for this?"
Newcombe frowned in thought, people passing his alcove.
"Andrew's fine with pressure, got through that other project. But I think more precision is needed on this. Diplomacy. A productive handling of the visitor."
"Want us to fly someone in?"
"No, I think I'll go myself. I'd like to turn this to our advantage. Get us off the defensive in the larger picture."
"I'm with you, Ian."

* * *

Livia was listening to a radio broadcast of the concert from Sydney. She was in her apartment in the capital of the kingdom of which Progress Island was a part. As the orchestra's efforts filled her living room, Livia paged through some work she'd brought home from her office at the Ministry of Culture. It concerned a proposal to form a touring company of musicians from the Kingdom. Being deputy minister, Livia would be expected to provide meaningful and perhaps decisive input.

Though she was nearing fifty, Livia appeared to be only in her mid-thirties. This was due to her receiving an artificial chromosome from an earlier effort on Progress Island. She had long black hair, naturally wavy, and a light golden complexion. Her American husband had received the chromosome earlier, but he'd returned to his homeland, not wanting to live indefinitely in the Kingdom. They had only been visiting, actually, but Livia found she was still as popular as when she'd emigrated. In addition, there had been a government purge and the new regime had offered a big promotion from her previous work. The country was a constitutional monarchy, with the royals' authority now much diminished.

The phone rang on the table next to Livia. It was her sister Mona, who lived in another part of the main island. Their other relatives lived on the outlying smaller islands.

"I'm worried about Cora," Mona said. She was referring to her daughter, the youngest of her three children.

"It's getting worse?"

"No, the same. But she's getting older, fourteen now. So compared with other girls, their activities and all, it shows up more. That lack of stamina. It holds her back so."

"And you see it more than anyone, being her mother. Yes, of course I sympathize. But you've done all you can, Mona. The doctors, all those tests. They didn't find *anything*?"

"No, everything normal, supposedly. But you know, Livia, one of them hinted there was maybe something hereditary. So I told him about aunt Cow-Eyes, but then he said that it wasn't his field."

"He didn't want to deal with Cow-Eyes, just as no one wanted to before. She was a puzzle, it's true, and quite a burden for people."

The sisters were referring to their great-aunt Xixxia, who would spend most of the day in bed with no apparent malady. She never married or performed any useful work.

"Oh, Livia! To think Cora might end up like *that*!"

"Now, Mona. Cora's not anywhere close to what Xixxia was. There was probably something psychological, and at that time—"

"But what if there wasn't? What if it's in our genes—gender-linked and skipping generations?"

Livia hesitated, Mona having pressed into a delicate area. Her concern must have grown intense to so override her discretion.

"Well, I'm not really an expert on it just because—well, that was different, Mona."

"You have the contacts though, Liv. You know the people out there."

"What, you mean Progress Island?"

"Yes."

"But it's much different now, Mona. Most of the *people* are different, and there's those clones. They're not really seeking immortality any more, just trying to guarantee health through genetic manipulation, with life extension secondary."

"Yes. Yes, I know."

Livia saw that she'd strengthened her sister's position, clarifying what Mona was hoping to get for Cora with Livia's assistance.

"I don't know," she said. "I don't see how I'd approach them, or how Cora would fit in with what they're doing now. It's all experimental, Mona."

"But you could find out–right, Liv? You're a deputy minister and they're foreigners here, even though they're autonomous. You have some *authority*."

"I can't use it for personal gain though, including for family. Remember the purge?"

"There must be some way, though. At least to get information, to see what's possible. Can't you go through someone else?"

Livia saw that she'd have to make the effort.

"I love Cora too, Mona. I'll check around."

* * *

Returning from the hotel's VIP dining room, David Pons lingered over a view of Manila. A sea of lights, as in other cities, but seemingly less intense here. Perhaps the humidity, he mused, or actually less power. He was a bit below average height, slender, with sallow complexion and dark blond hair, floppy though it was trimmed short. He was 26 years old and held a master's degree in anthropology.

David was stopping over on his way to Progress Island, his assignment from WHO. He'd checked in at the Manila office but received a cool reception. It was understandable, he decided. His study was within their district and rather close to them, so why was he–an apparent lightweight–being sent all the way from Geneva? But David little cared what they thought. He'd serve the higher authority.

He proceeded along the corridor to his room, recalling the sunlit window behind Dr. Shashamene at his desk.

"I want *you* on this, David," he'd said, "because I want the wider scope. Not too much focus on medical technicalities. A more general view of the situation is needed–the history of the island, the cultures involved, the politics of the Kingdom, and–well, the moral direction."

"Moral direction, sir?"

"Not in the religious sense, of course. There's already oversight on that from fanatics the world over. But we must ascertain the purpose, the central values, of the people driving this effort, this project and its ramifications. Where do they honestly place the welfare of humanity among their priorities?"

"I see, sir. I'll make that my central inquiry."

"It should help that you have a contact there. The manager of the island facility, in fact. Remember Andrew? From the conference when you started with us."

"Yes, I believe I do. Yes, that should definitely help. I can apply myself more closely. Assiduously."

Dr. Shashemene had smiled.

"Good! That's another reason I'm assigning you, David: your seriousness. I'm impressed with your dedication."

David well knew that, in his values, he was an idealist. Since this often put him at odds with others of his generation, he could sometimes feel anachronistic. In his assessments of situations, however, and his approach to solutions, he was coldly realistic. The idealism rested in his desired end results. This had impressed the recruiter from WHO and, together with David's references, had sealed the position for him. His personal history hadn't hurt, either. He'd lost his father in childhood and lived with his mother and younger sister, yet excelled as a student as far as he'd wished to go. He was apolitical and non-religious, had no "significant other" and few friends. He was thereby free to work assiduously at his job.

He unlocked his room with the plastic card, entered and switched on a light, enjoyed the sensation of entering a private place, which was always relaxing for him.

"Perhaps a little more wine?" he spoke aloud, and crossed to the mini-fridge.

He poured the Cabernet into a clear plastic tumbler, regretting he hadn't brought his glass from the dining room. He took a sip and reflected on whether he was happiest in hotel rooms. No, he decided, the little apartment in Geneva was better, despite his vulnerability there, the lack of anonymity. One had some need for familiarity, a settled haven, no matter how flexible one was. Yet he could easily step away from it and function fully on the road, he thought, and he meant to demonstrate it on this assignment.

He carried his wine to the small balcony outside his room, through sliding glass doors. Another view of the city lay below him.

"Behold," he said, "all this I will give to thee," and briefly smiled.

No, he answered within himself, I have no need of your seedy delights. They're of no interest to me. They're separate from my existence, my functioning and affirmation. My empowerment. And his thoughts turned to Progress Island, its people, its clones. An energy gathered within him, facilitated by wine, narrowing his focus to the coming strategy: intense scrutiny, dissection, mastery of any and all involved. His report would be comprehensive, incisive, flawless.

"I'll ride through the valley of darkness," he proclaimed, "and it will be mine."

34.

Nameless and unused through most of history, Progress Island gained fame as a venue for experiments in life extension. First through altered and artificial chromosomes, then through cloning with mind implantation, the ultimate goal was always immortality. Now, in its third incarnation as scientific utopia, life extension was downplayed in favor of high *quality* in living. This gave Newcombe Ventures a more positive aura than its predecessors. Over time, of course, goals could be adjusted in response to commercial factors.

The island retained its autonomous status under a nearby island kingdom. The government of the Kingdom, a constitutional monarchy, still smarted from the purge triggered by the scandal of the first life extension project. To forestall more upheaval after the second failure, the government accepted a proposal offered by Newcombe Ventures. The island and its resident clones were purchased, with the provision that the Kingdom be privy to operations. An official liaison was named and the country was to share in the project's benefits.

A number of new structures had been erected on the island for the latest project. Beyond the ribbon of forest behind the cove cottages, a dining and recreation building had risen above the rocky shallows of the southern coast. There were tennis courts adjoining this building to the north, then open meadow extending to the dock on the northern coast. East of the meadow, in the scientific compound, a large new lab had been added to the south of the existing buildings. This was needed to serve the medical needs of the clones and included special equipment to test their development in various areas. Further to the south, not far from the dining and recreation building, an education center had been built. Finally, on the fin-like northeast corner of the island, a guard building now stood. The hill on the southeast corner would have seemed more practical, but the psychological impact on clones and visitors had to be considered.

Andrew, the project manager, chose to reside in the old staff residence within the compound. It was close to the office on the northern end, where his presence was expected. Others, including Dr. Shah, chose to live in some cove cottages not used for clones. Andrew and Dr. Shah had worked together in the preceding life extension project, though they'd had little control and were not at fault for its failure. Their experience was thus of value to Newcombe Ventures. They also worked congenially as a team, frankly discussing any issues requiring leadership.

"Well," Andrew was saying, "I guess this was bound to happen sooner or later. It's certainly sooner than I expected, though." He was nearing forty, trim, clean-shaven with light brown hair.

"Yes," Dr. Shah responded, "our monitors and instruction on prophylaxis should have precluded it." He was short with a round face, dark hair combed flat to the side.

"For a scientific project, it might indicate a lack of controls, a chance occurrence that will influence our findings. Should we terminate like the others?"

"Well," the doctor smiled, "no one need know it's unintended. And the child could be very useful to us, give us a quick start on our research of offspring."

Andrew thought a moment.

"It's not like those others, I suppose–from that out-of-control situation."

"Wandering like animals," Shah nodded.

They were referring to the scene they'd inherited on the island, untended clones making their own erratic way, following their basest instincts. Two abortions had been performed.

"Do we know the father?" asked Andrew.

"I'll be taking saliva samples from the males. We'll compare their DNA to foreign DNA fragments in the mother's bloodstream–that is, fragments from the fetus." Shah grinned. "The smart money's on Kittridge."

Andrew returned a smile. The clone in question was a frisky male who'd been carrying the name of his donor, a successful but elderly businessman.

"We'll have to rename him soon. Legal precautions. But, on the DNA matching, you've talked to Noelle about it?"

"She's my next stop. Actually, I think she'll be able to map a complete genome."

"For the fetus?"

"Yes."

"And from there–pre-natal enhancement?"

Dr. Shah raised a cautionary hand.

"I'd wait on that for a pairing of our selection. And supervision. We can then have full controls. This case can give us a run-through on procedures, though. Some practice."

"And, if there are genetic defects?"

"We should just observe, I think, save ourselves–save Noelle–for the real work ahead. She does have her limits, after all, despite her enhanced nature."

"Yes, I suppose so. And we know she's the key to things now, at least for the company."

Dr. Noelle Kenilwerth had just recently come to work for Newcombe Ventures. She'd also been a key figure in the original work on the island, which focused exclusively on life extension. While she'd left that work with the project's collapse, she continued to benefit from it through an artificial chromosome designed and infused in her by her late husband. She thus could not escape the concept of genetic enhancement and was open to the supporting views of others. Despite some reservations, she was inclined to join the current project so that her expertise would fashion a greater good. It was a natural move for her, she thought, and no great sacrifice since she was to live for centuries.

As Andrew spoke with Dr. Shah, Noelle sat in one of the older labs, her original work station on the island. She had the appearance of a very young woman, petite with wavy black hair and pale skin. She was studying the genomes of the island's clones, mostly developed under her predecessor in the second project. A few clones had still been gestating and so were unfinished products. Noelle saw a great deal of work ahead, especially since the project's goals went far beyond physical matters to mental and social development. The behaviors of all the clones would have to be closely monitored with constant reference to their genetic make-ups and alterations. Enhancements had to be timely, compatible, and maximally effective.

Noelle opened a desk drawer, took out a stack of notebooks, opened the top one to a random page. She studied the hasty writing, the diagrams, imagined the writer's motions and smiled.

"Terence," she whispered, "it should be you sitting here."

She proceeded to page through the notebooks as she often did, seeking inspiration for her work. She was aware that, officially, life extension was secondary in the work here. But it must be a rather close "second" for them to seek her out, there being many others working in genetic improvement. The corollary goal of a 140-year lifespan had been mentioned. They would eventually want more, she knew, since the market would and this was a commercial enterprise. Still, with other enhancements improving the *quality* of life, eventually for whole societies, this use of Terence's work was more justified than the first time around.

"Yes," she nodded to the notes, "this will be your legacy, your redemption."

* * *

The water taxi bringing David Pons arrived in late afternoon. He was met by Andrew and Dr. Shah, along with a helpful clone who wanted to carry David's bag.

"Thank you, no."

"It's all right," said Andrew. "He enjoys it."

"I'd rather take it myself."

"Sure thing. Back to the beach, Robert."

David watched curiously as the Adonis disappeared down the path to the cove.

"Our compound is this way," Andrew gestured.

They departed in the direction opposite to Robert's. A tropic buzz accompanied their steps on the dusty path, the ground rising as they neared the entrance to the compound, where an armed guard was posted. Little was said on the way.

"We'll get you settled," Andrew said, "then have some refreshments."

David was shown to a room in the old staff residence, where Andrew himself lived. Also staying in the residence was Ursula, a financial consultant from Newcombe Ventures, who'd arranged a light dinner to welcome David. She was in her thirties with golden hair cut fashionably short. She sat in with the men as eating gave way to discussion. They were in the lunchroom adjoining the project offices.

"We're flattered by your organization's interest," Dr. Shah was saying. "Our work here is still in an early experimental stage. Practical application is quite far off, if ever."

"And yet you conduct your procedures on human, or humanoid, subjects."

"Humanoid, yes. Evolving, as it were, to the human."

David looked at him blankly. Ursula broke in with an office smile.

"They were roaming all over when police from the Kingdom came. They were ready to treat them like animals. Our company stepped in just in time."

"With our enhancements to their natures," Dr. Shah explained, "they can be educated, socialized, truly live as human beings. That's all I meant to say."

"You have professionals from those areas on your staff?"

"We currently bring teachers over from the Kingdom," Andrew spoke up. "As for social skills, Ursula is doubling as advisor to the caregivers."

David Pons looked skeptical.

"The Kingdom is a partner of sorts in our work," Ursula pursued. "There's an understanding they'll be among the first to benefit from our success. Our subjects here might be integrated into their society, become solid and productive citizens."

"The clones?"

"Yes!"

"Ah, along the way," injected Dr. Shah, "some genetic refinements will be made available to certain citizens over there. This will benefit their society and make them more receptive to the, ah, relocations from here."

"And for the world beyond The Kingdom?"

"I will submit to the medical journals, personally, all findings of use in combating major diseases and disorders."

David softened a bit, resembling more a guest.

"Well, that would certainly be welcome."

"We do admire your organization," said Ursula. "We'd like you to see us as partners for world health."

David didn't respond.

"Anything we can do to help," Andrew added, "in your study or later, feel free to ask. We have tight security, of course, but you have full access to our facilities and staff."

"Thank you."

The dinner at an end, Ursula returned to her office and Dr. Shah left for his residence on the cove. Andrew led David on a walk to the hill on the island's southeast corner, from which he could view the compound and more. Evening was settling in, a clear orange sky gradually fading to a tapestry of very bright stars.

"Is that a helipad?" David asked, looking toward the eastern shore.

"Yes. Little used now, but we keep it for medical emergencies."

David was thoughtful, then: "Dr. Shah, talking about findings, said you'd release any discoveries on major pathologies. Am I to understand, then, that it's only in minor areas, what you *consider* minor, that you'll be claiming trade secrets?"

Andrew hesitated, tried to imagine Ian Newcombe's response, couldn't do so.

"Well, I'm not a legal professional, but I expect that, being a business after all, we'd want to have proprietary rights for some processes we end up marketing. They could be important, be marketable, without involving major health issues. They might involve cosmetic changes, perhaps development of talents–"

"And maybe longevity? Life extension?"

Andrew picked up the pace.

"Hopefully people will live longer–and better–from *all* the work we do here. But I know what you're getting at, David. We're fortunate enough to have Dr. Kenilwerth on our staff. Actually, though, she has a *range* of experience in her field. She's spent the last few years on research of those major pathologies. I'm sure she'll be happy to tell you directly about her work, both past and present."

They ascended the hill under the dimming sky, Andrew feeling pleased with how he was handling the situation.

35.

Because of Livia's acquaintance with the past of Progress Island, the Ministry of Culture considered it natural for her to monitor the current project. Their role wasn't on the level of medicine or commerce, but the project would eventually impact the Kingdom's society, so they needed to be prepared. Livia was content with music programs and the like, but she had no good reason to refuse the task. It also provided an approach to the island on behalf of her niece with the strange malady. As Mona had suggested, she could go through someone else to avoid any ethical questions, and Livia had duly sifted through her contacts. By far the most effective would be the police liaison to the project, Lt. Col. Troy Duillu.

Like Livia, Troy was from an outlying smaller island of the Kingdom. This had at first hampered his career with the national police, but the government purge had extended to their department and opened doors for him. He was almost a decade younger than Livia but, because of her genetic change, Troy appeared a little older. He was strikingly handsome and retained a sunny disposition he'd found useful during his struggling years. He had a natural attraction that made Livia reluctant to work with him, she valuing her marriage and professional standards. But now there was Cora's illness to handle and, as she found when she met Troy for lunch, other imperatives as well.

"So," he said after small talk, "Progress Island?"

"Yes. We've never really discussed it except in the committee."

"Well, we have different priorities. Though it's always nice to talk to you, of course."

Livia smiled but quickly went on.

"Have you had much contact with them recently? Do you go out there?"

"Actually landing? No, they have their own security, high quality it seems. I do have something coming up, though. The Commerce Ministry wants an escort for the CEO, Mr. Newcombe, when he visits out there. I'll be with him from the airport to the island, perhaps also on his return."

"Is something special happening?"

"Not really. It's just because someone from the World Health Organization is out there, doing some kind of inspection. I guess the CEO wants to talk to him."

"So you'll be out there awhile, then."

Troy shrugged.

"As long as I'm needed."

"And all the important staff will be around."

"Well, he *is* the CEO."

Livia hesitated a moment, then yielded to inspiration.

"Any chance I could go along?"

She'd asked with her old hostess smile. A look of pleasant surprise crossed Troy's face. He reached for his cigarettes, offered her one. She accepted though she was cutting down.

"Of course," Troy answered. "I know you have an interest in the place, along with your ministry. Come to think of it, you did this sort of work with the Commerce Ministry."

It had actually been more complicated, but Livia had put those days behind her.

"It'll make my current job much easier," she said. "I won't have to look like another WHO inspector keeping tabs on them. Plus, we'd sort of get to work together."

"Always a pleasure," Troy smiled through the smoke.

It was much better this way, Livia felt. She didn't have to review Cora's problem with Troy, getting him to understand and be motivated. She could work her way into the Progress

Island circle more smoothly. Best of all, maybe, she needn't be indebted to Troy beyond the escort task. They'd remain just professional friends.

She could cover all her bases after all, Livia thought.

* * *

David Pons had had a full day on the island. Now, as night gathered after dinner, he descended the path to the docking area, reflecting. They'd given him a tour of the compound and outer buildings, explaining the functions of the facilities. Much of the equipment in the labs, especially the new one, was too arcane for his understanding. He didn't let on, of course. He'd been impressed with the education center, well equipped with computers and media, and the dining/recreation center as well. The clones themselves continued to mystify him, distracting him from his hosts as they showed him around the cove. He'd decided to have another look once night had fallen, when the clones were confined to their quarters.

Passing the dock, he continued on the path to Reverie Cove.

Andrew and Ursula had stressed the holistic treatment their project would offer both the individual and society. They were not simply producing beautiful people, they insisted. That was already possible, had been done. They were also concerned with the subject's internal development and interaction with society, and with societies themselves by improving the inherent capacities of their citizens. A given population would increase in really quality people, especially as they had offspring. Granted, this would be through genetic enhancement, a process that was seen as artificial. But the end result would be a better natural world, as ideal as possible, and achieved using the intellect that is natural to humans. Their paradigm, therefore, was a natural solution to most of what troubled the world. David had nodded thoughtfully to all this, refraining from skepticism. It seemed they were on to him as an idealist.

He passed the northern point of the cove, the lower-numbered houses extending out toward the sea. At the end was number 1, larger and better built than most of the others, the residence of Dr. Shah. He and some others felt free to use the clones as servants, "for their own good," as David was told. He questioned the doctor as to whether clones were being deliberately bred for such specific roles, servile or otherwise.

"Of course not," Shah had answered. "We're in a research phase here, not applications, and certainly not making-to-order."

"Nevertheless," David countered, "by implanting certain characteristics, such as reduced aggression, you render them manipulable in a given direction."

"But we don't *seek* specific directions. The qualities with which they're enhanced give them access to a generally better life, and a better ability to live with others. Your example, reduced aggression, obviously helps with interpersonal relations and being a good citizen."

"You have no doubts about where your research may lead?"

"When doubts arise, we resolve them. It's all science."

Reaching the beach, David removed his shoes and walked southward in the sand. There was a path that fronted the houses, a ridge of firmer footing, but he wanted to avoid encounters and observe from a distance. The fine white sand was cool and oozed pleasantly between his toes. Above, the moon was full and already bright, stars in full abundance. He could see why this place had once been sought for retirement homes. Besides number 1, number 14 was also superior to the others, and a small house on the far point looked good too. That would be number 27, David figured. The tackier houses were either fully lit or totally dark, meaning they were either used or available for clones, while the nicer homes had normal, partial lighting.

He continued down the beach, coming to where it narrowed toward the southern point. He stopped before number 26, which was dark, and put on his shoes. He wanted to take a different route back, above the southern shore. As he left the beach and looked for passage through the houses, however, he saw Noelle reclining on the patio of number 27. She was holding a wine glass and looking southward over the sea. The light from the cottage fell behind her, leaving her mostly in just moonlight, yet her face and limbs were distinct and softly glowing. It was a strange luminescence David hadn't seen before, at least from a human being.

She noticed him and looked over, her eyes seeming to flash.

"Hi," she said, and lifted her glass. "Care for some wine?"

He'd talked with her briefly on his tour, but her replies to his questions had been stilted like those of the lesser staff members. He'd had the feeling she was holding back. Now, however, away from the others, she seemed entirely relaxed. It was he himself who had to deal with discomfort, steel himself against her strangeness.

"Thank you," he said, "I will."

He took a seat at the patio table as she went to fetch the wine. She returned with a glass for him and the bottle, then sat in a different spot than before, where light from the cottage reduced her strange glow.

"Long story," she said, touching her face.

Despite his role, David felt compelled to be gentle with her, a reaction that surprised him. As usual, however, he'd keep his personal feelings to himself.

"There were hazards in your work, I suppose."

"Yes."

Her eyes searched his features, her thoughts apparently elsewhere. David sipped his wine, an excellent Pinot Noir that itself would have justified the stop.

"I suppose," he said, "it was mostly your work in life extension that attracted Newcombe Ventures."

Noelle smiled serenely, totally different from her laboratory persona.

"Could be," she said.

"It's important to them, then, as part of the package they'll be marketing? Perhaps the most important part?"

"I don't know about *most*. I can understand–"

Her eyes dropped to her wine, which she swirled a bit.

"I mean, I can see why people think that, why people want it. They always have."

She looked up and their eyes met directly, David again noting a sparkle in hers.

"Don't get me wrong," he said. "I admire your work, the good that you've done, and of course your courage."

Noelle shrugged.

"I wasn't alone."

She couldn't help searching his features again, his expressions. The edge in his voice and his persistence added to their effect on her, their evocation of Terence. He was saying something now about the future, about after their research, about societies, the world community.

"Would it be good then, that is, ethical, to provide a sort of immortality to countries based on their wealth? In striving for a perfect human strain, in selling the process to highest bidders, doesn't it encourage the notion of a nation–a race–of supermen?"

Beneath his manners was his intensity, Noelle saw, and felt a familiar warmth rising. She couldn't begin to deal with his question.

"Well–" she faked, frowning as if thoughtful. And after a hesitation: "Why don't we move inside, take some more comfortable chairs?"

She was moving while yet speaking; David had little choice but to follow. They passed through a room with a pool table to a drably furnished living room. David was attracted to a stack of arcane magazines on the coffee table. He picked one up.

"Copper pipe fittings?"

"Previous resident," Noelle smiled. Another long story, she could have added. But it wasn't the one she wanted to tell tonight, not to this man who might already be picking up her feelings. She wanted him to know about Terence, understand him maybe, as well as why she was the way she was, and why she cared about him.

"I have some background on all this," she told him, and returned to her graduate research days–hers and Terence's. There were his early findings, the stolen credit, discouragement from going further. There was the censure, loss of funding, the compulsive persistence that led to self-experimentation. She'd been unable to help him in the end, was herself changed to something a creation apart from her original self. Yet his spirit was stamped on her own and she was dedicated to the fruition of his work, his vision. It was a gift to humanity that he'd died for.

"I think you're one who can understand," she said. "Aren't you?"

While her glow had receded in the artificial light, Noelle still exerted an allure on David. Her account of the other man had struck an unfamiliar chord in him. A remote part of his nature, unknown or ignored, had sensed kinship with her late husband, and its complement in the deep mystery of Noelle.

"Yes," he answered, then caught himself. Things were getting out of control. "But I really should be getting back now. Your CEO, Mr. Newcombe, is coming tomorrow and I should be rested for our meeting."

Noelle smiled and glanced toward a darkened adjoining room.

"Stay here. You'll rest like you never did before. I guarantee it."

David's resistance, any that existed, collapsed and melted away. Incredibly to his conscious self, he heard himself complying. His mind saw Dr. Shashamene, his superior, at his desk with the sunlit window behind. But soon that melted away as well.

36.

Having decided to meet personally with the WHO researcher, Ian Newcombe hired a free-lance journalist to report on his visit. The journalist wrote for business and consumer publications, as well as their Internet outlets, and was sometimes interviewed by broadcast media. Newcombe was uneasy about the researcher's presence and wanted to pre-empt any negative effects. At the same time, he thought he could prime the market for the project's eventual services.

"Now, Harry," he said on the plane, "you understand the story is contingent. You'll get your fee, of course, but if you can't put a positive spin it's no-go. The WHO can do their own disseminating."

The journalist, a neatly ordinary man, was nonplussed.

"Sure, Ian. I *have* been at this awhile."

Newcombe gave him a glance. But you haven't been with me, he thought.

"We'll be met by local officials. They don't know much about the project. They're just window dressing for your story."

"Got it. And the clones–will I be talking with them?"

"No. And try not to call them that in the story."

Harry was silent, mentally rummaging for a synonym.

They landed at the Kingdom's airport, soon being met by Troy and other police, along with Livia. The visitors were whisked past security checks and into a pair of police cars that sped off toward the capital and harbor. The occasional cyclist or peasant with farm animal was honked aside. Newcombe scowled at the clouds of dust and stench from huge mounds of garbage they passed. At a crossroads they passed a cluster of tacky businesses including the Big Gong restaurant, the gong on its sign flashing in the sun. This had better be worth it, Newcombe thought, but then he smiled. Window dressing, indeed. Harry would be taking his notes in the other car.

A police launch took the party to Progress Island, Newcombe's imposing size making him conspicuous to his welcomers. They were the same people who'd met David Pons, with the addition of the sergeant of the guards and an additional clone Robert had brought. There were no bags for them to carry, however, since this was a day trip. Ursula had brought a camera and duly recorded some handshakes and smiles to accompany Harry's story.

"But where's our guest of honor?" Newcombe asked Andrew.

"Mr. Pons? Seems he slept in today. But I'm sure he'll soon be about. He's a driven sort of person."

"Driven, hah? Well, let's get him driving in our direction."

As the group advanced to the compound, Livia walked with Troy and his junior officer. Carefully watching the people ahead of her, she tried to identify a helper for Cora's illness. Dr. Kenilwerth wasn't present and might be reluctant anyway. Livia needed someone with authority but not too long with the company. Dr. Shah seemed to defer to Andrew so, if she could just get Andrew alone, maybe . . .

But, on reaching the compound, they found David Pons having a late breakfast in the lunchroom. Unusually relaxed, he was content to bask in the convivial atmosphere afforded by Newcombe and his group. David could only convey positive impressions of the project, emotionally disinclined to argue or mount challenges. Ursula trained her camera again on the handshakes and smiles, Harry took easy notes, and the great meeting was quickly done with.

"Time to get the hell out," Newcombe muttered to Harry.

"We won't go around the island?"

"You can use some stock footage. We quit while we're ahead."

With some bemusement and trailing Newcombe's long strides, the group retraced its steps from compound back to police launch. As the other visitors were boarding, Livia laid a hand on Andrew's arm.

"I'd like to come back and see your new facilities, the education and rec centers, and see how they help the residents."

"Of course," said Andrew distractedly. "We're always available to you." Then, as if to be more friendly: "Maybe you can try the tennis courts!"

"Oh, do you play?"

"Well, I fool around a little with, ah, the residents."

"Okay. I'll be looking forward to it."

The launch pulled out and headed for the capital, a mood of accomplishment prevailing on board. Newcombe's impressive figure stood iconically above the waves.

* * *

Harry's report on the meeting, with supporting photographs by Ursula, spread quickly through the international media, chiefly in the business news. It was received with some surprise, since the very involvement of WHO had suggested some obstacles for the project. With the harmonious outcome, however, there appeared to be clear sailing for what could be a very profitable venture. This was especially appreciated by a group that had previously failed on Progress Island, causing them to meet in a special session.

A profound gloom filled the conference room, blinds fully closed against the bright sun outside. There was serious business at hand. This was a meeting of the Rumpers, a name assumed by the remaining investors–the "rump"–from the Vasquibo Institute, original underwriter of research on Progress Island. Most had quit the group, of course, following failure and liquidation, but these were the more stubborn of the colleagues. They'd believed there could be residual benefit, perhaps substantial, from their original bold commitment, and so they'd stayed together, pledging support for whatever opportunity might arise. The *de facto* head Rumper, seated at the head of the table, fully looked his part. Very broad and expensively suited, he sucked on a cigar that added to the room's opacity.

"So, Mr. Bernard," he said, "where do we stand on fulfilling our interests?"

The man he addressed, seated halfway down the table, was not a Rumper. He was Hugh Bernard, partner in the law firm of Trotter, Baytes, and Wilke. The firm had been retained by Vasquibo during the promising first project, Bernard serving as lead counsel, and stayed with the Rumpers on an advisory basis. Bernard was tall and husky, with a high forehead, reddish hair, and faded freckles. His expression conveyed loyalty tempered by frankness.

"In terms of material gain," he said, "I don't see a successful action."

"Nothing on proprietary rights? Kenilwerth *was* our employee."

"Before you abandoned the project and later dumped the physical plant. No marketable process existed, that we know of anyway, and of course none is legally recorded."

"What about partial credit?" piped a Rumper down the table. "Can't we get a piece of the action based on it starting on our watch?"

"It *wasn't* started on your watch," Bernard responded. "The basic, flawed discovery was by Kenilwerth's husband, long deceased. It would be hard to show any progress at all while Vasquibo was running things."

There was silence, a billow of smoke from the head of the table.

"Surely," said the head Rumper, "we must have *some* option. We're alive, after all."

"I'm afraid I don't see a course."

Again the silence descended.

"What about–" began the man across from Bernard. "You

have contacts, don't you? The firm, I mean. Special teams and that?"

"We use our own consultants occasionally," Bernard answered cautiously.

"No, I mean something more like action. Going outside the box."

Bernard eyed the man, perhaps the youngest member and normally a quiet listener.

"I don't know what you mean."

The head Rumper guffawed and slapped his palm on the table.

"Come on, Quentin! You started strong, let's hear what you've got. We need some movement on this!"

"Well, we've been talking about grabbing scraps, crumbs. Panhandling off Newcombe Ventures' success. But what if we were to make it *our* success, or at least threaten to? That might bring Newcombe to its knees."

"*His* knees, you mean?"

"No, the group. The big man's not in it alone. He can't stiff us without their consent."

"So where's this success we threaten them with? They're the ones with the operation, the data, and soon the marketable process."

"But not yet. That's my point. Like Mr. Bernard says, nothing's been patented and such. The whole golden fleece is still up for grabs."

"You didn't answer the question, Quentin. Where's our leverage on this? We simply don't have any as far as I can see."

The young Rumper spread his hands, palms upward.

"We take it."

Hugh Bernard closed his portfolio, stared down at it with a grimace.

"You mean, *physically*?" someone asked.

"Yes."

"So the talk of special teams was–"

Sabotage, Bernard thought to himself. Theft. He waited for objections, but none came. Instead there were neutral murmurs, a hint of interest.

"I don't like the way this is going," he said.

"Now wait a minute, Hugh," rejoined the head Rumper. "We have to get all options on the table here."

"Not with me around," and he rose and left the meeting.

A few seconds of silence followed the door closing. The head Rumper took a puff on his cigar as he surveyed his colleagues.

"Well," he said, "I guess we need a new lawyer."

* * *

It had been cloudier than usual when they took the court, and soon grew completely overcast. Livia was paired with Ursula for a friendly doubles match against Andrew and the clone known as Kittridge. Livia had improved her rudimentary skills while living in California, but the clone's aggressive game and matching demeanor distracted her. When the contest was reduced to Andrew trying to keep Kittridge friendly, the manager led the clone away and the two women played against each other. The air became less charged despite the overcast.

"Sorry about Kittridge," said Ursula. "He was the raw kind of clone, directly from a single genetic donor."

"You're working to, uh, socialize him?"

"Yes, and he's a candidate for aggression reduction. With gene therapy."

Livia paused, holding the ball.

"Can you go the other way on that? Someone's not aggressive enough, say a woman?"

Ursula stared at her, taken aback. Not her area, Livia thought.

"Kind of a finer point," Ursula smiled. "Might be down the road a bit." Then over her shoulder, taking up her position: "Andrew would know about it!"

Strange she didn't say the doctor, Livia mused, or the molecular biologist. But it was just as well. Andrew was the one she needed to reach.

When a light rain began they decided to call it a day.

Andrew had returned and was standing by the entrance to the dining/recreation building. He suggested they have refreshments in the cafeteria, but Ursula said she had work to do so they should go ahead without her.

"But you'll get wet," said Andrew.

"I'll grab a shower at home," she said, edging away, then broke into a trot toward the compound, the old staff residence.

"She's very dedicated," Andrew informed Livia. "I couldn't ask for more in a financial consultant."

Livia could see they worked together closely and, given the situation–their being on the island and living in the same small building, were probably personally close as well. There was an edge of fondness to Andrew's professional praise, and warm deference toward him by a woman otherwise rather cool. Livia saw a need for discretion in exerting her personal charm, perhaps relying more on her official role, her authority.

They had coffee by a large window overlooking the southern shore. Large boulders could be seen dotting the water for some distance out. The continuing rain subdued the panorama.

"They had to clear a lot of brush here for the building," Andrew commented, "but it was worth it for the view. There's a salmon-colored sky after sunset, usually."

"Yes, it must be very nice," and Livia gazed into the rain. "I wanted to ask you about something though, Andrew. I mentioned it to Ursula but she said I should ask you."

Their eyes met and she waited a second, gaining his full attention, then described Cora's condition in as much detail as she could. Andrew listened patiently.

"She happens to be my niece," Livia concluded, "but also a citizen of the Kingdom, so I'm wondering on that basis if the project here can help her."

"Because of the agreement with your government?"

"Yes."

Andrew nodded thoughtfully, took a sip from his coffee.

"I hope I don't sound indiscreet," Livia continued. "I just thought it might be worked out. My sister, you see, the girl's mother, has been after me continually–"

"No, I understand," said Andrew, instinctively diplomatic. "As I understand it, though, the genetic basis of personality becomes very complicated when you're concerned with multiple traits. It's a lot bigger job than, say, curing Kittridge's aggression. It would likely have to be dealt with on a chromosomal level, a process Noelle–Dr. Kenilwerth–is working to perfect. I don't know how close she is exactly, I'll have to talk with her. But, even when she succeeds, the early applications will be considered experimental. I don't know if the parents, you know–"

"They're desperate, at least my sister. It's been going on so long."

Andrew paused, tried to see a larger picture.

"Whatever might be possible," he said, "there should probably be a non-relative involved in the request. We'd want it to be clear that it's all within the agreement, not something secretive that can get people in trouble. Or our company."

Livia nodded, averting her eyes to the rocky coastline in the rain outside. The handsome features of Troy Duillu appeared to her, suggesting him once again as the most promising contact for this.

37.

Several cars and a van from the Sydney police force were parked before a downtown office building. Everyone wanting to go in or out was subjected to search and questioning. Some of the elevators were not in service, still being examined for evidence of the overnight break-in and vandalism. The seventh floor was closed to all except authorized personnel. Here the headquarters of Newcombe Ventures, its outer offices defaced with spray paint, computers and other equipment tossed about, was presenting a challenge to local law enforcement. In the well appointed but also trashed office of the CEO, Ian Newcombe stood conversing with the officer in charge.

"You'd no recent contact with the sort who are into this kind of thing?" the officer asked. "You know, rougher types?"

"Certainly not. We run a highly sophisticated business here."

"Well, it's clear you were singled out from the other firms in the building. There was nothing of much value, you say, among the items you noticed missing?"

"The wall decor was all prints, the vases and statues out of a kitsch catalog. There was no sane reason to break in and steal them."

"Which brings us back to the damage, sir, as if intimidation, perhaps revenge–but wait! What about information? Have you checked your records, files–paper *and* computer?"

"That would take some time, especially with the office in this state. Of course, most of what we do is public knowledge anyway. We're not a cloak-and-dagger operation."

"No, of course not. But it seems someone else is."

As the police work continued, a call came in on Newcombe's cell phone. Observing the caller's number, he knew that he should take the call. It was the same man who'd called him at the opera house to warn about David Pons. Sidling out of the room, Newcombe talked with his caller amid the hostile graffiti in the outer offices.

"Heard about your incident," the other man said. "Much damage?"

"Mostly just messy. We'll be back running in a day or two."

"Tap into the backup systems?"

"As needed, yes."

"They get anything I should know about?"

"Unknown. If so, it's in deep encryption."

"I'll be ready on the legal end. But you should know, if you don't already suspect, they might go after Progress Island next."

Newcombe hesitated, then: "So the game's afoot?"

"Afraid so. I was witness, actually, to the preliminaries."

"Aha!"

"You'll need to protect your interests, Ian. Physically. Sorry I can't help on that, but of course I'd risk exposure."

"I understand. But thanks for your other help, Hugh."

"Anything for an old schoolmate. Just about."

* * *

Livia road in a tricycle to her lunch with Troy. The motorized three-wheelers were still the Kingdom's main taxi service. She could have called a government car, but they were meeting at Poseidon's restaurant, where she used to meet her husband before they were married. The tricycle was the best she could do then, so she took it today out of sentimentality. There was also a personal note, a hint of romance, that she planned to employ at this meeting, so arriving as she had before would prime her psychologically.

She put a hand to her hat as the tricycle whisked along. She was in the double seat behind the driver, a canopy above her. They left the city center and entered the commercial ring where it coincided with the waterfront, eventually stopping before Poseidon's. Troy was sitting at a shaded table on the terrace, only having a soft drink since he was on duty. Livia alighted, regretful that she again had to barter her charms, yet committed to her purpose.

"You look beautiful today," he said, but he always complimented her.

"Did you have trouble getting away?" she asked.

"No, a quiet day. A cooler one, so quiet. Emotions simmer down, get mellow."

"Anything mellow on the menu?"

"Well, let's have a look."

She shouldn't have a drink, Livia decided, since Troy couldn't. This would hinder the kind of discussion she wanted to have, but it couldn't be helped. She therefore went right to the food menu to seek enrichment for their meeting. She selected an offering of prawns in glassy rice noodles with tiny blue eggs, while Troy ordered the local whitefish in sweet banyan sauce. Like Troy, Livia sipped calimansi juice as they waited for their food.

"So," Troy said, "you were back out at the project?"

"Yes, a little tennis playing. And some business, of course."

"Mm. A nice place to work, it seems. I get out there too, of course, but on the water. Not the same."

"It was nice going along with you that once. I enjoyed it."

Troy shrugged.

"Official business. We were both in our capacities."

Livia hesitated, tried to refocus.

"I talked with them awhile this time, the people in charge. Basically on how their work will affect our society, our country. There's the agreement that we're to benefit."

"Yes," Troy nodded.

"It seems they're pretty far along in their research, including an area Dr. Kenilwerth specializes in. You know about her background?"

"Well, a little." He looked embarrassed. "I didn't have much science, you know."

"I didn't, either," Livia said quickly. "But they're discovering ways to help people with certain kinds of problems. In ways that weren't known or thought possible before. They can maybe help people with deep, ingrained personality problems."

Troy sat back, folded his arms.

"So, this might affect police work, then?"

"Oh, well, I don't know. I was thinking more of people, of someone, who's suffering personally, missing out on life because–"

She broke off. Neutral and unassuming, Troy waited for her to finish.

"For a citizen to be treated, of course, at least at first, the request would have to come from a government official."

Troy smiled.

"That would seem to be you or the Ministry of Health. Personally, I'd vote for you."

Livia smiled and indulged the thought, but of course it wasn't enough here. She'd have to describe the girl, not mentioning her relation at first, then gradually bring Troy in.

"Thank you," she said, "but I think it might depend on the type of case, and the circumstances. For instance–"

Troy's cell phone rang on his belt. He immediately answered it.

"Yes, Mr. Newcombe."

Troy quickly appeared concerned, then uncharacteristically severe.

"The nature of the threat, yes. If only we had a better time frame. But if your source is that solid, yes, a response is necessary now. You can count on our commitment."

When the call concluded, Troy stood up from his chair and whistled loudly toward the inside of the restaurant. A second officer came running out, flicking aside a cigarette. Donning his cap, Troy gave Livia a hasty look of regret.

"Something's come up. Sorry."

And the two men were gone, jogging to their car parked down the street. Livia was alone in the pleasant shade, two unfinished drinks before her, thoughts and words involuntarily suspended. As the reality of the situation settled, the knowledge of having been thwarted, she also realized that she was relieved. She was still intact as a wife and professional, had not compromised herself. Somehow the wife identity seemed more important and she felt a flicker of yearning for California. Her loyalty to her niece and other family were still there, but how was she—one woman with one woman's life—supposed to gain what others wanted without losing too much herself? Cora could seek the treatment on her own later, or Mona on her behalf, when it was more proven and available. Or she could adjust to who she was in other ways. Aunt Xixxia, after all, had never seemed all that unhappy.

"Will the gentleman be returning?"

It was the waiter, placing Livia's food before her, keeping Troy's on the tray.

"No, not today."

"I will package this for you?"

"Yes, thank you." And, smiling: "My dinner for tonight."

The waiter, who'd served her for many years, bowed and moved away.

* * *

On Progress Island, Noelle sat on a high stool in her lab, peering through a microscope at her successfully constructed chromosome. It appeared stable and was within size constraints imposed by a cell nucleus with full complement of natural chromosomes. She'd had to give up some life extension potential to allow for genetic material to help humanize the clones. This was consistent with research for human therapy, however, since some more complicated conditions might also require genetic space in the extra chromosome. There was the one Andrew had described to her, that sadly unmotivated girl in the Kingdom. And, closer to her own heart, there were people like Terence, so talented overall but destined for ruin by a tragic flaw.

David Pons came to mind, her surrogate Terence. But no, Noelle thought, she mustn't think that way. He was a man in his own right. His control on his obsessions was proof of that, set him apart from Terence.

"I'll be doing a follow-up report," David had spoken into the phone. "That's why I'm staying on here. I know I might have seemed, well, effusive early on, but my end product will be totally objective. It really is going well here, Dr. Shashemene."

He was over there now in the cottage, number 27, or perhaps strolling among the clones, curiously attempting conversation. Would he like to receive the chromosome some day, the version fully for life extension? Noelle couldn't foresee, but it didn't matter just now. She was happy with what had happened: they had met, it was going to last, it meant so much to them. True, he had to go back to Geneva. But her work here wasn't of indefinite duration. She'd reached a watershed, a basic goal of her involvement in the project. It was simply a matter of transition now, a well-charted course of briefing other personnel, turning her work over to them. Then she could follow David to Geneva, or they'd go somewhere else.

Outside, the day that passed on the island was typical. A wider, panoramic view, however, might have detected forces that could disrupt the progress of the Newcombe Ventures project. Defensive forces might also be sensed, creating an overarching tension to which most on the island were oblivious.

38.

Shots in the night.

David Pons sat up in bed, alert, trying to judge the distance. They were coming from various places, single shots at random intervals. Then some voices and rushing about.

"Do you hear that?" he asked, assuming Noelle was awake.

She raised herself on an elbow.

"It's happened before. Just stay in bed."

But David followed his instincts. Crouching in the dark, he moved to a window looking out on the cove. No sign of shooters, but people–more likely clones–were running hither-thither in a panic. A tall fellow came down the point, stopped when he neared the end, then crossed between cottages to the south coast. David went to another window to check on him, but the clone had disappeared. There was nothing visible on the sea from this point.

"David!" Noelle called. "Do come back!"

Turning away from the window, David did. The clone he'd been seeking, Kittridge, was in fact well along the south coast already. He'd shared in the panic of the others at first, but with running and getting away he was feeling much better. The beach was quite rocky here so he moved inland a bit. Not too much since he feared the sharp sounds. He came to the stretch of boulders that extended into the sea like an archipelago. The dining/recreation building was off to his left. He'd just noticed a dim light on the sea, ahead to the east, when a man came running past the far end of the building, headed for the water. Kittridge instinctively headed for the boulders, seeking cover in their deep shadows. There was a sound of splashing as the man hastened into the water. There was the sound of a shot, then another that pinged off one of the boulders. Kittridge crouched in fear, a tight fetal position. The man's pursuers were running up to the shore. They stopped short of where the clone was hiding, talked in a language he didn't understand, first harshly and then calmly. Maybe about the light on the sea.

The men moved on, Kittridge sneaking a peek as they strode toward the cove. They were two of the guards who lived on the island's northeast corner. They'd see he'd run away, Kittridge thought. He sensed he'd better stay put, wait for the noise to stop, maybe for daylight.

"Be calm," Andrew always told him. "Just be calm." So that's what he'd do.

Andrew himself was huddled over his phone in the old staff residence, Ursula crouching beside him. He'd started for his office when the chaos started, but retreated when he saw an intruder. Now he was talking with David Pons, trouble having spread to the cove, and he felt as pressured and powerless as he had once before in a leadership role.

"You're all right, then? You and Noelle are all right?"

"Yes, but what's this about? What's going on?"

"Just sit tight, David. The island's been–we have some intruders. The guards are engaged with them. We have to lock ourselves in, just hide. Help is on the way."

"Help from whom?"

"A police launch on patrol between here and the capital. They might be close by now. I was in touch with Lt. Col. Duillu. We had an alert during the day."

"One police boat? That's it?"

"He also has their naval and air wings standing by, but–well, I don't know how soon they can get here."

"How strong are they?"

"Three patrol boats and two light transport planes, I suppose with guns."

"What does our–what does the enemy have?"

"We know of two or three crafts and these operatives who came ashore."

"They just swam in from the sea?"

"On the eastern shore, yes. Least visibility. They might have been here awhile before the alarm went up. I saw one leaving our offices. We might not have seen them at all without the alert. Extra guards were out tonight."

"I see a couple of men now. Out there with the clones. They have their guns out. There's light from some of the houses, but I can't tell if they're guards."

"Keep your own lights off, David. And doors locked. We have to protect you and Noelle." He hesitated. "It could be Noelle they're *after*. Can you keep her hidden for us?"

"Yes, of course."

"Thank you. And good luck, David."

The police launch of which Andrew spoke had slowed on its approach to Progress Island. The officer in charge, Troy Duillu, had sighted lights on the sea to the east. He had the launch turn and cruise past the docking area. Gaining a better view, he counted two boats close to the eastern coast and another farther out to the southeast. There was also something small, a motorized dinghy perhaps, making its way to one of the boats. It was too far along to intercept without risk. Troy had no doubt there were weapons on the stationary craft. He decided to make a sweep past the island, giving notice of police presence, and hopefully dissuade any further aggression. After he'd completed the maneuver, however, Troy saw that the boats weren't moving, and there even came a sound of gunfire from one of them.

"Move back to the docks," he ordered.

"Will we be landing, sir?"

"After I make contact ashore."

But before calling Andrew he checked on the activity of the naval wing. Two of the patrol boats were en route, he was told, having been delayed by a problem with the third, which was apparently inoperable. Irritated and a bit worried, Troy contacted the air wing.

A Truly Higher Life Form

"Get those planes in the air immediately!"

A tense period followed, Troy electing to stay on the water and observe, judging this more productive than adding four officers to the land conflict. After about twenty minutes, the two patrol boats arrived, one making an aggressive sweep between Troy and the nearest enemy craft. The other shot around the island, taking position on the far side of the two threatening vessels. They were left a wide path to the open sea, an invitation to leave.

Time passed. The boats did not move.

Finally, on the police launch, Troy heard the hum of light transport planes. They approached from the west at high altitude, passed the island and circled back. One descended and flew over the island east to west, leveling off above the two hostile craft. Almost at once, perhaps before the plane came down, the craft were moving out. The two planes stayed in their patterns, the patrol boats stayed close to shore. Troy watched as the enemies slowly retreated, reached a distance equivalent to the third boat's off to the southeast, then stopped. Troy grimaced. It seemed he might have to attack, risk most of the Kingdom's defenses against unknown weaponry and skill. He forwarded a command to the lead transport plane.

"Try another low pass, gradual descent. No firing yet."

The maneuver was completed and the defenders watched expectantly. For a minute it appeared the boats were moving out, but they were simply separating themselves more. Troy was nonplussed at their recalcitrance, tried to gauge the risk of attack, imagine a strategy. The unknown factors and his limited forces again presented their conundrum.

"Sir," said an officer with binoculars, "off to the southeast. Third ship."

Troy took the binoculars from him and sighted as advised. The distant vessel had been joined by another form, moving irregularly around it. The new craft was in the air, a helicopter of military design, apparently harassing the boat below it. Flashes of gunfire were visible. The chopper withdrew and hovered some distance away, as if awaiting a response.

"The hostiles are withdrawing!" another officer called.

Troy turned to the two closer vessels. Sure enough, they were moving out to sea, accelerating strongly. So that was it, he thought, a command ship that held them here. The chopper: someone knew and went straight to command. But who? Who do we have to thank? He raised the binoculars again. The third ship was disappearing while the chopper moved closer to shore. Troy strained to examine it in the light of the quarter moon.

"Australian markings," he said to the officer nearest him.

The transport planes withdrew as the threat subsided, the patrol boats staying to guard the island. The helicopter made a studied approach and eventually came to rest on the little-used helipad. Troy called for another police boat to assist with any prisoners, then notified Andrew as the launch docked on the island. The police were met by several grateful guards, as well as a number of stunned clones. The land conflict had apparently dissipated.

Andrew had seen the helicopter approach and so, having heard from Troy, decided to emerge from hiding and survey the situation. Ursula was still at his side, as she'd been throughout the ordeal. Together they looked out toward the helipad.

"Shouldn't we check the offices?" she asked. "See what's missing?"

"You can if you want. I have to meet whoever's in the chopper. I'm still the manager here, supposedly in charge."

Ursula glanced back at the buildings, but took Andrew's arm.

"We'll meet them together."

They walked through the field toward the chopper, on which the blades were slowing for lack of power. A door opened as the couple approached and a very tall, strong-looking man jumped out. He was followed by another, not as big but toting an automatic rifle. As the first man came into close view, Andrew and Ursula stared incredulously.

"Mr. Newcombe!" Andrew managed, as if to verify the sight.

"Yes," the CEO acknowledged. "Along with supporting cast."

Two more crew members had emerged and hung back with the rifleman.

"But how—" Andrew began, then simply spread his hands.

"Nothing unnatural about it, really. I'm still a reserve officer in our country. That and some personal pull, well—" He shrugged off further explanation.

"Well, thanks very much, Ian," said Ursula. "You saved the day."

Newcombe looked out levelly over the island.

"Group effort, Ursula. You held the fort till we arrived, along with our friends from the Kingdom. And that's what it's always going to take: people with intelligence and courage standing up against ignorance and evil. Against parasites like these tonight, itching to destroy or steal. Together we can stand against them, grind them into dust. Progress must go forward."

Newcombe's helicopter had been seen on its approach by Kittridge, who still lurked among the boulders on the southern shore. He'd also noticed its encounter with the third enemy craft, and the latter's subsequent departure. Now, with an air of calm descending on the island, the clone looked about and wondered what to do. He was without direction and, in his rudimentary mind, not without blame in this thing. He had run away, added to the problem, so he couldn't just go back and blend in. He had to do something else, something good, something that restored him to what he was before. But what had that been, exactly?

Kittridge rose from the boulders and saw the dining/recreation building. No one was about, the windows were dark. He cautiously circled the building to the entrance closest to the tennis courts. He knew this place and liked it, it gave him a good feeling. With a racket and some tennis balls he could play by himself till dawn, be like he was before, blend in. He stepped up and tried the doors but they were locked. They were heavy duty, just a foot-square window in each of them. Kittridge stared at them awhile, looked back at the empty courts, then slumped down against the doors, curling to one side. He'd wait here for Andrew, he decided.

He could try some force but he'd get in more trouble, and he feared the force he'd witnessed this night.

I don't want that, he thought, and he slept.

To the west, on the southern point of Reverie Cove, David Pons had taken a call from Ursula and learned of the situation. Andrew and Mr. Newcombe were talking with Lt. Col. Duillu, establishing security now that the threat had been repulsed. The guards apparently had a prisoner and there were photos of the intruders' boats. There would no doubt be follow-up, but David should rest assured that the work on Progress Island would continue for the welfare of humanity.

"Well, it's over," he said to Noelle.

"Good," she replied calmly.

They were in the kitchen of number 27. They'd been sitting in the dark but Noelle switched on the light over the stove.

"Shall we have some wine?" she asked.

"Why not?" David shrugged.

As they were sipping, Noelle glanced toward the door, each of the windows, the passage to the bedroom they were sharing, the bed.

"No matter how long you live," she said, "there are moments that live forever. In the aether, the upper reaches of all existence. Moments like tonight, the times of special significance. The trick is to avoid destruction, survive, and in good health. Then you can stay connected to the immortal moments and have their energy. You have it all to share with someone, one who's attuned to you. We reinforce each other then. It's something even greater than immortality: a state of being that's beyond description, beyond imagination."

Though the small light was on, David thought he saw a glow in her features. The quarter moon was visible through a window. He nodded in response to her and sipped, the wine a decent Beaujolais.

From where she sat, Noelle now saw that he wasn't at all like Terence. And this was good, perfect in fact, because her life had run a purifying cycle. Her youth now was sublimely better than it had been the first time. The nascent tragedy in her love for Terence was absent here, she and the world

A Truly Higher Life Form

gaining harmony with each other. A barrier of unreason had been passed to allow the rapid progress of humanity. A standard of perfection was at hand, the means to achieve it fast emerging, so that a truly higher life form might dominate the earth.

CPSIA information can be obtained
at www.ICGtesting.com
Printed in the USA
FFOW04n1547080514
5286FF